THE SILENCED ONES

A Ghost Mystery

THE FINGER LAKES MYSTERIES

ELIZABETH MEYETTE

BORIS PUBLISHING

We realize the importance of our voices only when we are silenced.

Malala Yousafzai

Published by Boris Publishing

BORIS PUBLISHING

ISBN: 978-1-7365864-2-6

Cover Design by Meyette Photography.

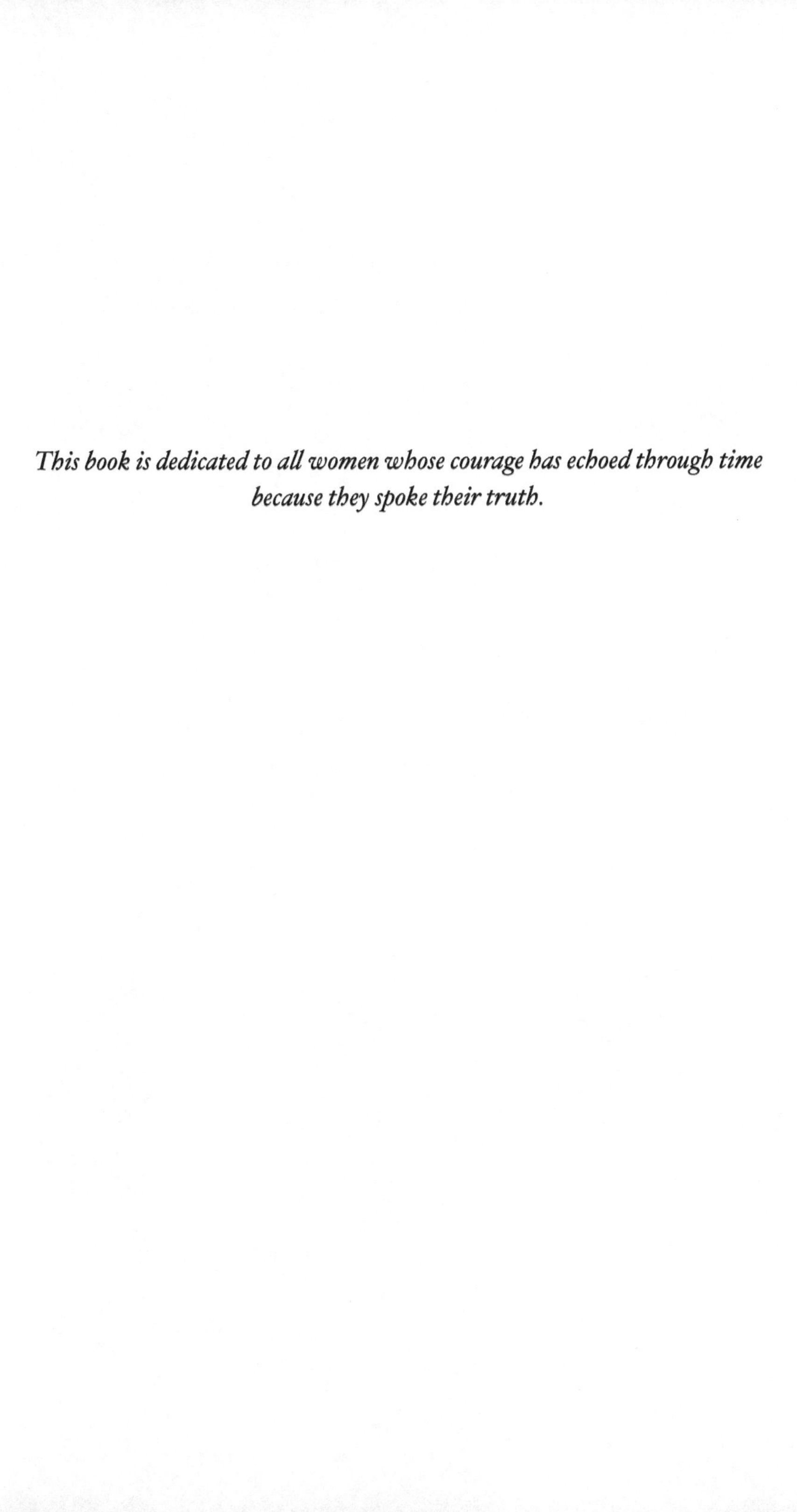

This book is dedicated to all women whose courage has echoed through time because they spoke their truth.

Chapter One

T hursday, *August 28, 1969*

Jesse Graham lay on her back in the narrow bed, prone like a corpse. Normally, she slept curled on her side, but not tonight. Instead, she listened for sounds she didn't want to hear in a room she didn't want to inhabit.

Light from the bright moon seeped through the curtains, glinting off the silver corpus on the crucifix above her head. The crisply ironed and starched sheets imbued with the fresh August air contrasted sharply with the reason she was here. Where she didn't want to be. In the convent at St. Bartholomew Academy for Girls.

A breeze billowed the curtain, its shadow shifting the moonlight on her blanket. Her ears strained for any noise. Nothing. No footsteps, no movement, not even snoring from an adjacent room. Even the crickets were silent tonight.

Rolling over, she pulled back the curtain and peered at the night sky.

An almost-full moon.

Surely if something were going to happen, it would be on a night like this.

And she was certain where it would happen.

Throwing back the covers, she slipped out of bed, welcoming the cool hardwood floor beneath her feet. Without having to look, she knew the wood gleamed in the moonlight, as would all the furniture in the room, what little furniture there was. The sisters led an austere life with only the essentials. A bed, a nightstand, a dresser.

Someone had freshened the room since Maggie left.

As she passed the dresser, Jesse caught her reflection in the small mirror.

I look like something out of a Hitchcock movie.

Her thick, auburn hair was a halo of tousled curls, and her green eyes shone eerily in her moonlit reflection. She pondered her resemblance to Helen Cavanaugh which had caused a stir when she first arrived in Seneca Corners. A stir that almost cost her life.

I sure don't need to think about that right now.

Grabbing her sandals, she eased open the six-panel oak door, slowly turning the brass doorknob to avoid a loud click. On one side of the hallway, all the identical doors along the wall were closed; on the other side, the moon cast crosses on the marble floor as it glowed through the muntin panes.

The eerie silence gave Jesse the sense she was the only one in the enormous convent. Until she passed the door of Sister Alphonse's room where a reassuring snore slipped out from beneath the door.

Jesse smiled and continued to the staircase. Her descent to the first floor slowed as she neared the bottom. Slipping on her sandals, she glanced at the front door with its heavy deadbolt. She wondered, not for the first time, if it was meant to keep people out or keep people in. Hurrying over, she released the lock and eased the door open to the humid night air.

She peered to the left at the dark, stately school building where she was sure she'd find her answer. Like it or not.

As she walked the path from the convent to the school, the waves of nearby Seneca Lake serenaded her. A stone edged into her sandal, digging into her flesh. She bit her lip to keep from crying out. Stopping to remove the stone, a rustling echoed in the shrubs by the front door of the school building.

Do I really want to do this? She brushed the chill bumps along her arms. *Do I really have a choice?*

The lock on the front door of St. Bartholomew's Academy for Girls was hefty but Jesse's key easily unlocked it. Slowly, she swung the massive door in. The familiar scent of floor polish, books, and a century of tradition mingled in the hall. The spit-polish cleaning had ramped up this week as students arrived on campus.

As she passed the shaded windows of the office, she paused and caught her breath. The memory of being trapped in there, her life threatened, pumped adrenaline through her body. She crept past the office door, stopping at the sight of the staircase to the left. If she were going to hear anything, she suspected she'd hear it in this spot.

This was where Sister Catherine had lain, her eyes gazing at nothing, her heart no longer beating. No sound from her lips.

And no sound now.

Only silence.

Chapter Two

Tony's Diner had emptied out after the lunch rush, busier than usual with tourists and cottage owners here to enjoy the Finger Lakes region of central New York State. Tony's nestled in downtown Seneca Corners not far from the shore of Seneca Lake with its brisk, underground-spring-fed waters.

Jesse claimed an empty booth near the back of the restaurant. The lingering smells of French fries and hamburgers made her stomach growl, and the Beatles sang about wanting to know a secret as she waited. Facing the door, she would be able to see Maggie arrive. When she did, Jesse snickered.

Maggie looked like Audrey Hepburn in *Charade*—a woman on a secret mission. Her huge black sunglasses covered half her face, and, except for some feathery dark brown bangs across her forehead, her short pixie cut was hidden under a light beige kerchief tied beneath her chin. She hurried to the booth.

"So, 007, what case are you on today?" Jesse teased.

Maggie didn't remove her scarf or her glasses. "Stop, Jess. I'm trying not to be recognized."

"Too many autograph hounds, Miss Hepburn?"

Maggie looked around at the near-empty diner. Slowly, she removed her sunglasses.

Jesse raised her eyebrows in encouragement.

Maggie slid her scarf down and untied it, tossing both accessories into her purse.

"When I run into people, they still call me Sister Angelina. It's awkward. Honestly, it gets old." She bit her bottom lip. "Plus, I'm still trying to figure all of this out. I don't want to be rude. Sometimes I don't say anything, but somehow, I feel like I owe them an explanation."

"You don't owe anybody anything, Mags."

"I know, but still..."

A waitress dressed in bell bottoms and a tie dye shirt came over. "Oh, hi, Sister Angelina! I almost didn't recognize you without your habit. Ready for school to begin?" She handed them each a menu. "Your hair looks great."

Maggie shot Jesse a quick "I told you so" look, then smiled up at the young woman. "Thanks, Ellen. Good to see you. Good luck at SUNY Oswego this year."

"Thanks! I leave after work today. Can't wait! I'll be right back for your orders."

Maggie cocked her head and widened her eyes at Jesse. "See what I mean? Do I tell my former student that I'm no longer Sister Angelina, or do I let her learn it on the street?"

Jesse laughed. "Well, first of all as I said before, you don't owe her an explanation at all. As far as learning it on the street, it's not like learning about sex, Maggie. And so what if she does learn it that way? That would be easier for you, right?"

They looked across at the lunch counter where Ellen was huddled with two other St. Bartholomew Academy for Girls alumnae.

Ellen looked up at them, her eyes wide. She quickly looked away.

Maggie sat back against the booth and sighed.

"See now?" Jesse beamed at her. "Wasn't that easy?"

Maggie sat forward. "So, tell me about Sister Therese's visit."

Jesse put coins in the jukebox at their booth, selecting more

Beatles songs. Then she leaned her arms on the table and lowered her voice.

"It was bizarre, Mags. Yesterday afternoon after Joe, Marty, and Jim left for their traditional Labor Day weekend fishing trip, Sister Therese showed up at my door. Maybe her timing was good since Joe's not so keen on me connecting with ghosts." She paused. "Gosh, Mags, I miss him already."

Though she'd met Joe Riley only a little over a year before, his Irish good looks and laid-back attitude had won her heart. It had taken him a while to understand Jesse's gift, but he supported her in her ghost investigations. His main worry was her safety.

"Of course you miss him! You've only been married a couple of weeks." Maggie whispered, "I miss Marty, too."

Jesse smiled. Officer Marty D'Amato had been smitten by Maggie when she was still Sister Angelina. They'd both struggled with how to navigate their love for each other, and now Maggie faced a journey into a whole new life.

Jesse sipped her drink. "I must admit, I'm a bit reluctant to pursue a ghost without Marty around. He's helped me so many times in the past, especially as a cop, but also as a friend. Since this ghost is in the convent though, I'm probably pretty safe. And Sister Therese would probably not let him in to help me investigate anyway."

Maggie leaned toward her. "I want every detail. The fact that she visited you at home is weird." Maggie pursed her lips to one side and scrunched her dark brown eyes.

"Sister Therese told me she's been hearing sounds at night. She looked like she hadn't slept well for a while with dark circles under her eyes. Of course, part of that is preparing for a new academic year. But she was fidgety, and she kept rubbing her arms."

"Did she say what she thought the sounds were?"

"She had a hard time saying the words. You know how she disapproved when I dealt with the ghost of the ancient Seneca woman."

"Not only the Seneca woman, but Helen Cavanaugh and my brother Timmy." Maggie's voice dropped.

"Right. Well, she hemmed and hawed and finally came out with it. She thinks the convent is haunted."

Maggie's already large brown eyes grew larger. "Holy Mother."

"Yes. She's being awakened at night by someone whispering 'Rosary. Rosary.'"

Maggie gaped at her. "Rosary? Really?"

"She asked me to come and stay at the convent for a few nights to see if I could discover what was going on. She asked me not to say anything to the other sisters. I guess she doesn't want to upset them. The story is I'm on a private silent retreat."

Maggie spit out the root beer she'd just sipped. "You? On a silent retreat? Miracle of miracles!" As she spoke, she grabbed napkins from the metal holder below the juke box and wiped up the table.

"It hasn't been easy, that's for sure." Jesse gritted her teeth.

"I'm sure it hasn't! Only the nuns could make you stop talking."

They laughed.

Jesse stirred the straw in her cola. "I stayed last night, Mags. In your old room."

Maggie stared past her. Then she smiled. "You're welcome to it, Jess."

"Actually, that makes me feel better. Thanks." She clasped Maggie's hand. "And I think I know who it is."

"Who?"

"Ready to order, Sis...I'm mean..." Ellen's face flushed, the order pad she grasped, shaking.

"I see you've heard my news."

Her voice quavered. "I don't know what to call you."

"You're an alumna. Please call me Maggie."

Ellen held up her hands as if staving off an attack. "Oh, no, Sister. I couldn't do that."

"Well, I'm still sorting through all this myself. So how about Miss Keegan then?"

"I'll try...M...Miss Keegan."

Ellen's hands trembled as she took their order, then she scurried away from their booth.

Maggie watched her hurry back to the kitchen. "People seem to take my decision to leave the convent as a personal affront."

"It's because you've impacted so many lives. They just need time to adjust how you fit into their experience. In a couple years, this will all be very natural."

They glanced at the girls sitting at the counter, sneaking peeks at Maggie, then putting their heads together.

"A couple years, huh?" She turned to Jesse, smiling. "Marty's worth it." She sat forward. "So, who do you think the ghost is? Did you hear anything?"

"Only Sister Alphonse snoring."

Maggie laughed. "We always assigned new postulants to the rooms on either side of hers. Her snoring is legendary."

"You were lucky your room was at the end of the hall. I never heard her until I got close to her door." Jesse took another sip of cola. "I think the ghost is Sister Catherine. It makes sense, Mags. She was murdered in the school. Why wouldn't she come back to haunt it?"

Maggie considered that for a minute. "Hmmm. Yes...it does make sense."

"I did sneak over to the school last night while the moon was still almost full. That seemed the perfect time for a ghost."

"Have any of your other ghosts specifically shown up at the full moon?"

Jesse thought about that. "No. But I went anyway and sat on the steps where Sister Catherine died."

"Oooh, Jess, that must have been really creepy."

"It was, until I fell asleep on the bottom step, and then it was just plain uncomfortable." She rubbed her shoulder and stretched the kink out of her back.

"But she didn't show up for you last night?"

"No. Or for Sister Therese. She told me that at breakfast. She also said she wants it 'taken care of' before Bishop Harris comes to say the inaugural Mass."

She studied Maggie. Her friend gazed into the distance, a slight furrow between her brows. "I know that look, Mags. What is it? You're the math teacher. What doesn't add up?"

Maggie tilted her head in thought. "I'm just wondering why Sister Catherine, who wasn't a sister at all, just working undercover, why would she say 'Rosary, rosary' to Sister Therese?

Jesse slumped back against the booth. Maggie might as well have lobbed an ice-cold water balloon at her.

Jesse rolled to her side, flinging her arm across her ear. The blanket was crumpled at the end of the bed where she'd pushed it in her sleep. Crickets serenaded her through the screen of her open window, which offered no breeze on this sultry late summer night. She could hear the insects despite her attempt to block out the noise that roused her.

The noise wasn't crickets.

A whisper echoed softly.

Rosary. Rosary.

Jesse had learned that ignoring that kind of whisper would only delay the inevitable, yet she was reluctant to succumb to what awaited her. She flopped to her back and stared at the ceiling, listening until she thought her ears were growing larger in the darkness.

Silence.

She rolled to her side again, punching the pillow as much to fluff it as to relieve the anxiety building within her. Even though she closed her eyes, even though she covered her ear with her arm, she was aware this night was just beginning.

The voice floated to her. *Rosary. Rosary.*

Tossing the sheet back, she climbed out of bed, grabbed her

robe, and eased into her slippers. Luckily, tonight she'd grabbed the flashlight from her car for just such an event.

She crept along the second-story corridor, the halo of her flashlight bouncing along the marble floor. At least that afforded some relief from the humid air.

She passed Sister Therese's door. If her principal heard the whispers, she wasn't coming out to investigate. She had abdicated that to Jesse. Just as well.

What would this ghost be like? Loving, like Helen? Desperate, like the Seneca woman? Innocent, like Timmy? Well, if this ghost was a nun who kept saying, "Rosary," perhaps she would be quite gentle.

As she approached Sister Alphonse's room, she was surprised the window-rattling resonance of her snoring hadn't blocked out the sound of the whisper. She tiptoed past the next bedroom wondering how anyone in there could be sleeping. Except for Sister Alphonse's snoring, no whispered sounds came from any of these rooms.

Only one more door stood at the end of the hall. She ran her flashlight's glow along it and up to the ceiling. During her tour, Sister Therese had dismissed it as only leading to the third floor. No sisters slept on the third floor in this wing of the convent. So, what was up there?

The handle of the door to the stairway stuck. She put down the flashlight and took the doorknob in both hands. The door was locked. She wiggled the knob again.

"What are you doing?"

The caustic question exploded in the silent darkness.

Jesse jumped, pressing her hands against her chest, her heart pounding like a jackhammer. Somewhere in the back of her mind, she'd noted that Sister Alphonse's snoring had ceased. She'd paid no attention, relieved to be free of the sound.

Now the woman stood behind her.

She turned to face a picture that could have been an illustration in an edition of *The Crucible*. Sister Alphonse wore a long, black nightgown with a white crocheted nightcap whose lace fringes trembled with her anger. Her gray hair stuck out from beneath the cap in angry tufts, and dark, almost black eyes glared beneath her fierce brows.

"What are you doing?" she repeated, spitting out the question. Sister Alphonse's harsh words were nothing new to Jesse. The woman had disliked her from their first meeting. Add to that the fact that Sister Alphonse's brother had almost murdered Jesse, and their every encounter was hostile.

"I'm sleep-walking."

The nun scowled. "How convenient that you remembered to bring a torch along."

"Is something wrong?" Sister Therese approached them. She was tall and slender, striding with the confidence of a woman in charge who brooked no opposition. The sisters had, after all, taken a vow of obedience. She expected no less despite the hour.

In the shadows, her face didn't show the lines that came with leadership. She looked younger than her fifty-five years, her light blue eyes gleaming in the moonlight as she passed a window. Her simple white cotton robe swished around her feet. She also wore a nightcap, though unlike Sister Alphonse's, hers had no lace trim.

Sister Therese disapproved of Jesse's ghostly encounters, yet she was the reason Jesse was here.

"I would say so!" snapped Sister Alphonse. "Miss Graham here is prowling around our convent." She glared at her superior. "Frankly, I don't understand why you're allowing her to sleep in our quarters."

Sister Therese smiled benevolently at the woman. "Jesse will be staying a few nights, Alphonse. You are to make her feel most welcome." Though her words were soft, the underlying warning was clear. "She has joined us for a time of prayer and reflection as she begins her new life with her husband." Her gaze fell on Jesse. "I see your sleepwalking issue has occurred again. How fortunate you remembered to bring your flashlight, just in case."

Sister Therese did a half-turn and gestured back down the hall. "Now I suggest we all retire so we're well-rested in the morning."

Jesse could almost hear the sizzle of anger as Sister Alphonse pushed past her.

Sister Therese arched an eyebrow, nodded, and led the way to their rooms.

Sister Alphonse glared at Jesse as she closed her bedroom door.

"Keeping this from the other sisters might be more difficult than you thought," Jesse whispered when they reached Sister Therese's door.

"It's imperative that we do so. Let me be clear, Jesse. This occurrence does not mean I have a favorable view of your occult involvements. I am concerned for the safety and well-being of my sisters, both physically and spiritually."

"Whether or not you like it, you have a ghost here. And from my experience these are just people with unfinished business. So, you may call it occult, and you may call it unspiritual, but these are spirits, Sister, and they need help."

"Paint this in any color of virtue you like, Jesse. It is still forbidden."

"Well, you called me." Gripping her fists at her sides, Jesse fought the rising anger. "And I'll need a key to the third floor." Sister Therese might find this distasteful at best and sinful at worst, but she had a ghost to deal with.

"We only use the third floor for storage now. We don't have as many sisters as we used to, so as I told you yesterday, no one resides on the top floor."

"I beg to differ. Someone is up there."

Even in the dim light of the hallway, Jesse saw Sister Therese's face blanch at her words.

And she took some satisfaction at that.

Chapter Three

Jesse rubbed her eyes. After two nights of being awakened to search for a ghost, she wanted nothing more than to sleep until noon, but she had been awakened before dawn for morning prayer and Mass. She hoped no one noticed her nod off during Father Steve's homily.

Sister Therese had insisted she pretend to be a on a silent retreat to conceal the true reason for her presence in the convent. That meant no socializing with the sisters during breakfast or any other meals.

How am I supposed to find out who is in the attic whispering 'Rosary'?

Since she couldn't speak with the sisters, Jesse eavesdropped.

She studied the nuns at other tables as they conversed. Most of them wore the new, modified habit of mid-calf length skirts and smaller veils that revealed their hair. But the more conservative sisters still wore the traditional habit with floor-length skirts, their faces peeking out from the white wimple attached to the long, black veil.

At the next table one sister grumbled about the recent changes resulting from the Second Vatican Council. She wore the traditional habit as did her three table companions. They were among those who for four years had resisted changes brought about by Vatican II.

"I miss the Latin Mass," she complained. "And all this talk of ecumenical dialogue! We're losing our traditions." She looked at a table of younger sisters in modern dress. "Pretty soon we'll be wearing GoGo Boots and mini-skirts."

The others commiserated with her until she rose and raised an eyebrow at Jesse.

Uh oh. Busted. Jesse's face flushed. *I shouldn't have been eavesdropping.*

But Sister Vincent, a large woman, smiled and held out her hand. Jesse's petite hand disappeared into her calloused one. "I think it's wonderful that you are starting your married life with a silent retreat with us," she whispered. "Such a sacred beginning to your sacrament."

When not working in the garden or teaching chemistry, Sister Vincent was the nurse on campus. Students found her gruff, but she'd always been nice to Jesse.

"Hssst," came an angry voice from the table behind her. Jesse didn't need to turn around to identify the hisser. She'd recognize that disapproval from a mile away. Sister Alphonse.

Jesse smiled her thanks at Sister Vincent.

Sister Therese approached. "Jesse, meet me in my office in ten minutes please."

"Tsk." Sister Alphonse softened her disapproval for her superior.

Finishing her coffee alone at the table, Jesse pondered her situation. Sister Therese wanted her to clean up this "evil spirit" but blocked her from gaining any information about the convent from the other sisters. She was silenced from telling them what was occurring a floor above their beds every night.

Maybe she should say no. Tell Sister Therese there is no way for her to discover the truth if these are the conditions. She sipped the now-tepid coffee as she thought about the other ghosts she'd encountered. They had one thing in common that made it impossible for her to turn her back on them.

They needed her help.

Stifling a yawn, she abandoned her coffee, heading for her meeting with Sister Therese.

She trudged along the walk between the convent and the St. Bartholomew Academy school building. The tops of the maple trees surrounding the lacrosse fields were tipped with hints of coming autumn, though the warmth of the late August sun competed with July's. Already, perspiration dampened her blouse.

She scanned the three structures of the convent, the school, and the girls' dormitory. Situated in the middle, the school was anchored by the other two buildings. The sturdy bluestone walls of each building rose three stories high. With arched leaded windows that complemented the blue and brown hues of the architecture, they were stately and imposing.

Though the school building was shrouded in silence when she entered, the sun slanted across the marble floor making the front hall more inviting than it had been in the middle of the night. But even in the daylight, memories of being captive in the main office with "Sister" Catherine's murderer covered her like a pall. A chill ran across her arms as she entered the office.

Pushing through the swinging half-door that separated the students from the office staff, she reached the open door of the principal's office. Sister Therese stood looking out the window at the grounds, her arms folded. "Come in, Jesse,"

Jesse waited in front of the desk.

The nun turned and nodded for her to be seated, then sat in her own chair behind the desk. She wore the modified habit, so Sister Therese's brown hair with strands of gray showed beneath her veil.

Jesse didn't wait to hear the reason for this summons. "This silent retreat idea isn't working. I need to talk to the sisters."

Sister Therese sighed. "I thought it would be easier for you to keep this quiet if you couldn't talk to them."

"Hiding your ghost isn't going to make it go away."

The woman started to speak, then pressed her lips together.

Jesse spread her hands in supplication. "If I can speak to the others about it, I might be able to solve this problem."

"What can they tell you?"

"That's just it. I don't know. I don't know anything about who this could be. Why is this ghost making its presence known now? All of a sudden? Who is it? A sister? A student? From what time period? We have no idea. Some of the other sisters might."

Sister Therese folded her hands on her desk. "I'll take all your points under consideration. For now, however, I wish you to remain silent while with the other sisters."

Jesse took a deep breath to stem her rising frustration. She ran her hands through her unruly curls.

"I need to access the third floor. May I have the key to the door?"

Sister Therese gazed out the window, tapping her fingers as she considered Jesse's request. Finally, she stopped, opened a drawer, and took out a key ring.

"I ask you to do your ... exploring ... when other sisters aren't around." She handed Jesse an ancient skeleton key.

"I will try to be as discreet as possible. But, Sister Therese, I don't determine when the ghost appears. That is that person's decision."

"Ghost. Person." She waved her hands in the air. "I just want this taken care of before Bishop Harris visits."

Jesse gripped the key and bit back her initial response.

"I'm sure the ghost does, too."

JESSE WOKE to a spray of water from the open window. The skies had burst, and rain pelted through the screen. A rumble of thunder above Seneca Lake signaled the beginning of a late summer storm.

Though she hated to do it, she closed the window against the downpour, immediately causing the room to close in with cloying humidity. A flash of lightning sparked in the sky illuminating ominous shapes of trees. She shivered despite the warmth of the room.

"Well, ghost, this would be a convenient time to make your appearance. The stage is set."

She lay back against the pillow, listening for the whispers, but none came. Thunder grew louder reminding her of Sister Alphonse's snoring.

She chuckled. "I don't blame you. I wouldn't want to compete with all this racket." Between the noise and flashing of the storm and the unbearable heat of the room, she could not fall back to sleep.

Slipping out of bed, she tiptoed down the hall grasping her flashlight and the key Sister Therese had given her. She welcomed the coolness of the marble floor against her feet. As she passed Sister Alphonse's room, she paused. The nun's snores were tough competition for the booming thunder.

Obviously, the door to the third floor hadn't been used in a while. The key stuck and she had to wiggle it to get it to fully engage. Finally, it turned with a click, and the doorknob rotated clockwise.

She gently tugged the door. With a groan, it swung open.

She tested the first step. A bit of a squeak in the middle. Treading lightly, she climbed the stairs, keeping to the outer edges to avoid more squeaks. When she got to the third floor, she flipped a switch. Only one lonely light above her lit up.

"Ah, the sisters removed all the other light bulbs," Jesse murmured.

Except for the dimness, she could have been standing at the end of the hall below. Cool marble against her feet, a series of ten oak bedroom doors along the interior, lightning flashing through the windows on the exterior walls.

She tried the first door on her right. It swung open easily and was a duplicate of the room she slept in. A single bed, a nightstand,

and a dresser. And, of course, the requisite crucifix on the wall above the headboard.

As she walked the length of the corridor, she checked each room and found them identical. At the end, where the dim light barely filtered down, was the room directly above Sister Therese's.

She halted.

Rosary. Rosary.

But no. That was not what she heard. She pressed her ear against the door. Grasping the doorknob, she hesitated. She anticipated how it would feel.

Cold.

Icy tendrils from beneath the door were already licking her toes. Sensations so familiar and yet so surreal.

Slowly, she turned the knob. Cold air slapped her face. She entered the room, freezing on this sultry summer night.

Instead of the spartan furnishings, this room was lined with crammed bookshelves. A long table stood where the bed should have been.

And when lightning flashed, alongside the window stood a figure dressed in black.

"*Rosary,*" she whispered.

But Jesse realized that "*Rosary*" was not what she said.

Jesse waited to sense the emotion of this ghost as she had in the past. With Timmy, it had been more than sensed. She'd taken on his emotions and almost lost herself in the experience. That had been scarier than the vicious attack by the Seneca woman. Now as she faced this apparition, Jesse tried to discern how she felt.

Aside from the usual fear and dread of facing a ghost.

I'll never get used to this.

Her legs trembled and sweat matted her hair to the nape of her neck. But she felt no emotions save her own. As she stared at the wraith, the image faded away. Another bolt of lightning illuminated only the window.

With shaking hands, Jesse closed the door and pressed her

back against it. Her legs were too wobbly to walk down the hall. She took three deep breaths to still her quivering. It didn't work.

This spirit was not Sister Catherine, as she'd expected. This spirit had just introduced herself.

Now to unravel who she was. And how could she do that if she couldn't speak to the other sisters? Sister Therese seemed to be sending two separate messages: get rid of the ghost but keep it a secret. What is she trying to hide? Or did she simply want to deny a ghost could inhabit a holy place like a convent? More likely she just found it distasteful given her opinion of Jesse's psychic abilities.

Oooh. She had never used that word for herself before. Psychic. Yet she was able to connect with those who had passed over. Marty, a cop who was usually skeptical of anything illogical or inexplicable, understood her perfectly. His grandmother had what he called "the sight." And he said once a ghost finds a channel like Jesse, others would follow.

And follow they had. This was her fourth ghostly encounter.

She'd finally calmed down enough to return to her room. The stillness of the convent contrasted with her still thumping heart. She relocked the attic door and turned, bumping right into Sister Alphonse.

"Oh, my God!"

"Thou shalt not take the name of the Lord, thy God in vain." Sister Alphonse glared at her, the beam from Jesse's flashlight casting a maniacal gleam in her eyes.

"Well, then, don't creep up on me like that." Jesse tried to brush past her, but the sister grabbed her arm. Her grip was claw-like and the image of a bird of prey passed through Jesse's mind. A hawk. No, a vulture. Jesse wrestled her arm away.

"I thought you were on a silent retreat." Sister Alphonse leaned toward her.

"I am, so you'd best stop talking to me." Jesse pressed her fore-finger against her lips.

"I don't know what you're doing here, but it has nothing to do with silence or prayer. Are you up to your ungodly ways again? Digging around for Satan's work?"

Jesse leaned into her. "Whatever I am here for is none of your concern."

Sister Alphonse glowered at her, opened her mouth to speak, then snapped it shut. A glint shone in her eyes. One corner of her mouth curled up. "As you wish."

She stalked to her room.

Jesse stared at the woman's closed door. Her sudden change in demeanor was odd, and her comment disturbing. Just what did Sister Alphonse know about this ghostly presence?

Chapter Four

The sisters had left the convent for an all-day outing to St Michael's Church parish picnic. Jesse used her "silent retreat" as an excuse to stay behind. With the sisters gone, she had free rein of the convent. Her first stop was the basement storage room.

Jesse wiped the sweat from the palms of her hands as she paused at the top of the stairs. She'd rather be in the attic with a ghost at midnight than in a basement on a sunny Sunday afternoon. Basements meant spiders and mice, her two biggest fears. She'd always disliked cellars, but since the time she'd almost been murdered in her own at the Cavanaugh House, dislike had morphed to dread.

C'mon, Graham, just get what you need and get out.

She hurried down the stairs and halted, gaping at the enormous space before her. The convent had been built in the 1800s, so the uneven stone walls and the high wooden ceiling increased the illusion of the size of the basement. Neatly stored provisions and household goods were tucked into the sturdy wooden shelves.

Labels written in perfect Palmer method cursive identified the contents of boxes and bins. Jesse walked along the household goods area until she found a box labeled "lighting." As she opened the box, a spider dropped from the shelf above onto her hand.

She let out a squeal and shook her hand until the spider was either dizzy or dead. She wiped the back of her hand on her jean shorts until it turned red.

"Oooh, oooh, oooh! This is why I didn't want to come down here!"

Summoning up her courage, she opened the box and found various sized lightbulbs neatly packed inside. She searched for a 100-watt bulb, but the closest she could find was 60 watts. She grabbed one and hurried to the stairs.

The silence in the convent was eerie with all the sisters gone. No rattling of dishes in the kitchen, no easy chatter in the common room, no soft music from the chapel. A formidable sense of foreboding crept over her, leading her to reconsider her plan. Perhaps a visit to the ghost's hangout when the convent was empty wasn't a wise decision after all.

She glanced at the sun pouring in the picture window in the common room.

"'Screw your courage to the sticking place,' Graham," she muttered as she climbed the stairway to the second floor. When she reached the door to the third-floor staircase, she fumbled with the skeleton key, not quite fitting it into the lock. She wiggled it.

"Success."

Pulling the door open, the now familiar musty smell of abandoned rooms tickled her nose and she sneezed. When she flipped the light switch, the dim bulb above her flickered on.

"Hang in there until I get this big ol' 60-watter in the room upstairs." Somehow, speaking aloud to herself settled her nerves. A bit.

While the whole convent seemed disconcertingly quiet today, the silence as she walked along the third-floor corridor was tomb-like. Maybe that was a good thing. That meant the ghost wasn't here. No one whispering, "Rosary."

Except now Jesse understood the ghost wasn't saying, "Rosary."

She stopped at the door of the room she had visited, the one furnished like a study or library rather than a bedroom. Her hand reached for the doorknob and stopped. This would be the test. If this brass doorknob was icy cold, the ghost was present.

She touched it.

Warm.

She let out a breath she hadn't realized she was holding. In the absence of the ghost, she could examine the room better.

To her left, bookcases lined the wall all the way to the window. To her right an oak table hugged the wall with a wooden office chair on casters pushed up to it. Directly opposite her, a table stood beneath the window, an open atlas on its slanted top, others nestled into the shelves below.

Jesse approached the atlas. The page was covered with dust. Brushing it off with the edge of her t-shirt, she squinted to see the map.

She tucked the lightbulb down the front of her blouse securing its base in her bra, then she rolled the chair to the middle of the room. As she balanced on it, she stretched to reach the ceiling fixture. The chair wobbled, and she lost her balance, catching herself in time, but jamming the back of the chair into her ribs.

"Oooof!" The impact was like getting hit with the bat that made the home run.

For a moment, everything went black save the starbursts. She caught her breath and steadied the chair as she clambered out of it. Rolling it to the bookshelves, she dragged one end of the heavy oak table to the middle of the room.

She scaled the table and screwed the lightbulb into the ceiling fixture. Jumping down, she flipped the switch next to the door and a mellow glow lit the room.

As she pushed the table back against the wall, she noticed a small book on the floor that must have slipped from between the table and the wall. Retrieving the book, she dusted it off, closed it, and placed it on the tabletop.

Intrigued by the atlas, she returned to it.

With the glow of the lightbulb, and a little more dusting, she made out an ancient map of the Middle East. It reminded her of maps she'd seen in Bibles. She found Jerusalem, the Dead Sea, and other familiar locales, but many of the towns were unfamiliar.

A rustling sound interrupted her study of the atlas, and she quickly glanced around the floor. The problem with dusty, musty attics is that mice liked them. She brushed away the goosebumps on her arms and returned to the map. Perhaps whoever used this room had been studying ancient history, probably Scripture.

She turned her attention to the bookshelves. Scanning them confirmed her hypothesis. Most of the titles were scholarly texts on Scripture study, ancient Israel, and the lives of the saints.

She sat in the chair and scanned the room. Someone went to great lengths to create a haven of scholarly study centered on ancient times. Somebody who was visiting the room again.

The air changed, getting colder. Jesse rubbed her arms, her gaze darting around the room. She didn't see the ghost, but the book she'd found under the table now rested on it.

Open.

THE SISTERS RETURNED in high spirits from St. Michael's parish picnic. A group of them had challenged the sisters who taught at St. Mike's to a game of softball. St. Bart's soundly defeated them.

Jesse sat at a table in the dining room eating a ham sandwich, and though the sisters smiled and waved, no one joined her. They had eaten at the picnic, and they respected a person's silence during retreat. She returned their smiles and nods, but inside her stomach roiled with frustration.

Grrrr. I need to talk to them and find out who used that study. I can ask Sister Therese, but she hasn't been very forthcoming.

When Sister Therese entered, she nodded, spun on her heel, and left the room.

And she's avoiding me. That will not be easy, my dear Sister.

Jesse left her half-eaten sandwich and followed the nun. Catching up, she tapped her shoulder. Sister Therese frowned at her.

Now what do I do? Pantomime that we need to talk? Forget it.

"I need to speak with you, Sister Therese."

Three nuns nearby stopped their conversation, the one facing Jesse raised her eyebrows.

Sister Therese nodded and indicated a small visitor's room off the front hall.

"What is it, Jesse?" She sounded tired, but then she had pitched for the home team and won the game.

"Your ghost—"

"Please stop referring to it as "our" ghost. It is ungodly and we are not about ungodly things."

Jesse's face heated as her blood pressure rose. Sister Therese may be her principal, but she would risk her teaching position before she would let this criticism continue.

Struggling to keep her voice calm, she took a deep breath and began, raising her fingers to count off her points.

"First of all, this is a person, not an 'it'. Secondly, this person is in distress and needs help. Thirdly, this person is yours because she must have lived here and died here. Fourthly, she is not saying "rosary."

Sister Therese's eyes widened. Jesse was sure it wasn't just from her impudence, but from her revelation.

Sister Therese whispered, "What do you mean, it...she wasn't saying 'rosary.'"

"She was saying, 'Rose Marie.'"

Sister Therese's face turned ashen. "But that's impossible."

"That's the truth. Was there ever a Sister Rose Marie here at the convent?"

Her mouth agape, the nun stared out the window.

Jesse waited a few minutes then repeated her question. "Sister, was there ever a Rose Marie here at the convent?"

She nodded. "Sister Rose Marie. She was Sister Alphonse's best friend."

Chapter Five

Since Maggie was a bit skittish about being seen in town, Jesse had suggested a picnic lunch by Seneca Lake. Gentle waves lapped the rocks that lined the shore, and the summer breeze held a slight September coolness. Cumulus clouds played hide-and-seek with the warm sun, and gulls called as they swooped over the water.

Families were making the most of the last couple days before school started, so the picnic area was busy. Maggie studied them, her shoulders finally dropping to a relaxed position.

"I don't see any St. Bart's families here." She flapped a red and white checkered tablecloth and let it float onto the wooden picnic table. Jesse hefted the cooler onto one end and plopped a beach bag on the other to keep the tablecloth in place.

She held her hand above her eyes to block the sunshine and scanned the area.

"Check the parking lot, Mags. No Mercedes or Lincolns. I think we're safe."

Maggie sank to the bench. "It's going to be so strange not returning to St. Bart's this year." Her eyes got misty. "Life has become so different, Jess."

Jesse sat across from her. "Are you having regrets?"

"About leaving the convent? About leaving St. Bart's?" She stared out at the lake. Finally, she sighed. "Not regrets, just sadness. I became a novitiate right after high school and attended Nazareth College with the sisters. This is what I've known my whole adult life. And I've loved that life."

"I'm sure Sister Alphonse would welcome you back with open arms." Jesse tried to keep a straight face.

Maggie laughed. "You goof, Graham!"

Jesse sobered. "What about Marty? Any regrets there?"

"No!" Maggie smiled and waved her hand. "Being with Marty is one decision I'm absolutely certain of."

"So why your decision to go on retreat?"

"I still have things to discern. This is a complete lifestyle change for me. I need to go into it grounded and with my eyes wide open. Besides, Father Kevin Murphy is at Holy Spirit Monastery and agreed to direct my retreat. He's an old family friend."

Jesse opened the cooler and took out two Genny Cream Ales and a churchkey. Popping the caps off, she handed one to Maggie. They clinked bottles.

"Cheers," they said in unison.

"Rituals."

Jesse stopped unpacking the sandwiches, holding them in midair. "Excuse me?"

"Rituals," Maggie repeated. "Like clinking our bottles and saying cheers when we open our first beer. Rituals are important, Jess. I've lived a life of daily rituals. Matins, evening prayer, confession on Saturday, Mass on Sunday. How do I transition to a day of no more rituals?" Her hand trembled as she brought the bottle to her lips.

Jesse's heart sank. How wonderful that Maggie and Marty had found each other and fallen in love. But at quite a cost for her best friend. She hadn't thought about all that Maggie was giving up. For herself, being stuck in a convent, having to rise before dawn for matins, attend every prayer service, follow all the rules sounded like what would have been Dante's tenth circle of Hell. Of course, she just committed heresy, so she'd also be in the sixth.

But for Maggie, that was a fulfilling, spiritual, secure life that she had lived and loved for years. Her new life with Marty would be totally different.

Maggie stared at the lake, and when she spoke, it was as if to herself. "I've never written a check."

Jesse reached across the table and took her hand. "Lots of changes in store for you, Mags. I'll be with you all the way. So will Marty."

"I know you will." Maggie smiled and squeezed Jesse's hand. "Now, tell me about this ghost at the convent."

Jesse took a sip of beer as Maggie bit into her tuna sandwich.

"Geez, I haven't been able to talk to you in so long, I haven't caught you up. Sister Therese thought she heard the ghost saying, 'Rosary, rosary,' but when I encountered her, she was saying 'Rose Marie.'"

Maggie stopped chewing and frowned. "Rose Marie?" Her brown eyes widened. "*Sister* Rose Marie? Holy Mary, she was a good friend of Father Kevin's. They came to our cottage a few times. She was a great water skier." Her face darkened. "Oh no. And she's the ghost?"

Jesse nodded.

Maggie took another bite of her sandwich and chewed slowly.

"I know that look, Mags. What?"

"She disappeared. Ugly rumors circulated about her and Father Murphy." Her gaze traveled back to the lake. "Some said they were having an affair and ran off together." She was silent. Her eyes met Jesse's. "Just like I'm doing with Marty."

Jesse took her hand again. "It's not the same—"

"Of course it is, except Marty's a cop, not a priest. But I've been a Sister of St. Joseph for more than a decade, and now I've run away."

"Mags, you're not running away from something. You're running to something. Something wonderful and loving and true."

"Everyone judged her," she shrugged. "But now I understand. Except..."

Jesse waited.

"Except she didn't run away with Father Kevin. He's still a priest." She closed her eyes, concentrating. "I'm trying to remember the timeline. I think he left the Diocese and entered Holy Spirit Monastery around the time Sister Rose Marie disappeared. People who didn't know him well wouldn't know where he went."

Jesse tilted the bottle to her lips, but she paused, setting it back down. To some, Maggie's leaving the convent would be scandalous, just like Sister Rose Marie running off with Father Kevin. Which she didn't do. So, what happened to her?

"This ghost is why Sister Therese has me at the convent under the pretense that I'm on a silent retreat as I begin my married life."

They stared at each other, then broke out laughing.

Tears streamed down Maggie's face, and she held her sides, almost doubled over. Jesse's ribs hurt she laughed so hard. She took deep breaths, trying to get the words out, but every syllable she tried brought about a new round of guffaws.

"You? On a 'good wife' silent retreat. Oh my God!" This time Maggie did double over. "I'm going to lose my lunch I'm laughing so hard." She wiped at her eyes. "So how did you get away this afternoon?"

Jesse took some deep breaths until she could finally speak again. "I told Sr. Therese I had to get a few things from my house."

"You lied? To a sister? You don't need a retreat—you need holy Confession."

"I didn't lie. I had to pick up the beer and make our sandwiches."

"Whew!" Maggie wiped her brow.

"The bad news is, I can't talk to any of the sisters to find out more about Sister Rose Marie. Sister Therese told me she was

Sister Alphonse's best friend. No wonder people thought she ran away."

"Now, Jess," Maggie used her teacher voice, "Sister Alphonse has some redeeming qualities."

"You should see her in her nightclothes, Mags. She looks like something out of Edgar Allan Poe. Quoth the harpy, 'Nevermore.'"

"I'm a math teacher and even I know that was a raven, not a harpy. When did you see her in her nightclothes?"

"When I heard the ghost above me on the third floor. I was trying to open the door to the stairway."

"In any event, she does have redeeming qualities. She's an excellent Latin teacher."

"Yeah, that's in high demand. Regardless, I can't even talk to her. And she must know something about what happened if she was Sister Rose Marie's best friend. Which kind of makes me wonder what this Sister Rose Marie was like if she hung out with Alphonse."

"You could talk to Jam—Sister John Mary. If you're not supposed to be talking, connect with her. She loves to break rules."

"Great idea, Mags. Tonight is my last night at the convent, so it's my last chance to also connect with Sister Rose Marie. Ugh! I can't believe I'm trying to contact a ghost."

"You seldom have a choice, Jess. They seek you out, wherever you are. Remember how Timmy showed up at the shack that killer took you to? Maybe you won't have to be at the convent to communicate with her."

"Good point. I'll see if Jam will talk to me. If I could talk with Sister Alphonse, I wonder what she would say?"

Maggie cocked her head. "I wonder."

"Unless of course she has something to hide." Jesse finished her beer.

Chapter Six

Jesse listened to the lively chatter surrounding her. She ate her dinner in silence, while the sisters conversed about the opening day of school. It wouldn't be the same without Maggie here, teaching math just down the hall.

She scanned the room, her eyes resting on Sister John Mary at the far table. She was the only Black sister in this convent and had often said the Sisters of St. Joseph had saved her life. With her ready smile and infectious laugh, no one would know the hardship she'd grown up in, living in the projects in Rochester, two hours north.

Jam made no secret of her delinquent past, regaling Jesse and Maggie with tales of her less than legal activities, most of them to put food on the table for her mother and little brothers. It was through the Juvenile Justice Program that she met the Sisters of Saint Joseph, and her life was changed forever.

As if sensing Jesse's scrutiny of her, Jam met her gaze.

Jesse scrambled to think of a way to signal she wanted to talk to her. She tucked her hand next to her mouth and flapped her thumb and fingers up and down like she was imitating a duck.

Jam raised one eyebrow. The sister beside her tapped her arm, diverting her attention. Jam responded to the sister, then looked back at Jesse.

Jesse again tucked her hand beside her mouth and repeated the gesture.

Jam's eyes twinkled and she fought a smile. She blinked her eyes shut twice, and the sister beside her asked another question. Jam nodded and rubbed her eye as if she had something in it. The sister patted her arm reassuringly.

Jam returned her gaze to Jesse and nodded slightly. She fanned herself and rose. In a louder voice than necessary, she announced, "I'm in need of fresh air and quiet meditation. Excuse me sisters." She cleared her place and left.

Jesse waited two minutes before she rose, cleared her place, and headed for the door.

The sun cast long shadows from the trees that lined the driveway. Birds chittered their nighttime rituals, knowing that sunset was less than an hour away. Walking into the breeze, Jesse brushed a strand of hair from across her face and scanned the grounds for Jam.

Not seeing her in the front of the building, she circled around to the back. If Jam really intended to meditate, it would make sense for her to go to the St. Joseph garden, Mother Mary's garden, or the grotto.

As she walked along the path in the St. Joseph garden, fragrant small purple flowers hugged the stones and scented the evening air. She didn't know the name of them, but they were pretty with their blue-green feathery greens. Not seeing Jam, she continued to Mary's garden where white roses clustered along the paths that wound through sculpted shrubs. Now roses she could identify.

At the far end, she spotted Sister Vincent on her hands and knees, busy in an area of freshly turned earth. Beside her a row of new rose bushes marched along awaiting their turn to be planted.

Jesse inhaled the perfumed air. She still hadn't spotted Jam, so she hurried toward the grotto.

Glancing across the grounds, she caught a glimpse of black

ducking behind the rocks that made up the grotto. Since the property didn't include any natural caves, the grotto was composed of large rocks built to create an arched cavern.

In the middle stood a statue of Mary Magdalene with streaming hair, folded hands, and her eyes raised to heaven. Here deep red roses flourished, a heady scent on the evening air. They created a sweeping invitation from the main walk to the grotto.

Jesse hurried to the site and peeked behind the rocky structure. No Jam.

Maybe she really did want to meditate and prefers to be alone.

"Hey there, Jesse."

Jam's voice startled Jesse and she jumped, slapping her chest. "You scared the shit out of me." She turned to Mary Magdalene. "Sorry, Mary."

"So, were you trying to be a duck or a clam? I really couldn't decide." Jam's dark brown eyes lit with humor.

"I've felt like a clam the last few days, not able to talk to anyone."

Jam's laugh was musical, deep and resonant. She was slender and a bit taller than Jesse. "That must be excruciating for you."

"Even under normal circumstances it would be, but I'm dealing with an unusual issue and Sister Therese wants me to keep it quiet."

"Okay, clam-girl, now you've got me intrigued."

Jesse frowned at the path behind her that Jam had come down. "Wait a minute. How did you get over there," she pointed down the path, "from behind the grotto so fast?"

Jam frowned at her. "I wasn't behind the grotto."

"But I saw you..."

Jesse's heart thumped so hard she was sure Jam could hear it. "Jesus," she breathed.

"What?"

Jesse motioned to the stone bench in front of the statue. "Sit down Sister John Mary. I've got something to tell you."

Jᴇssᴇ ʟᴀʏ sᴛɪʟʟ, listening. This would be her last chance to visit the room on the third floor. Tomorrow she would return home and finish preparing for the first day of school.

Closing her eyes, Jam's face came to mind, her eyes wide with amazement at Jesse's revelation of the ghost in the convent. While Jam hadn't known Sister Rose Marie, she had heard of a sister who'd disappeared. She promised to gather any information she possibly could.

Jesse rolled over and watched the shadows play on the wall beside her. Tonight, the crickets were in full voice, and, though the moon was beginning to wane, it was bright. Not the spooky kind of night that begs for a ghostly appearance. With the rhythm of the chirping and the gentle breeze blowing through the curtains, she drifted off to sleep

Rose Marie. Rose Marie.

She jolted awake. Did she hear the voice or dream it? She held her breath.

Rose Marie. Rose Marie.

A whisper floated from above her.

Despite her many encounters with ghosts, her spine tingled, and a cold sweat coated her skin as she climbed out of bed. Grabbing her flashlight and slipping on her sandals, she crept to the door. As she passed Sister Alphonse's room, loud snoring echoed.

Good. Maybe she won't bother me tonight.

When she reached the room at the end of the third-floor hall, the icy cold seeped from under the door. Sister Rose Marie was in there. Easing the door open, Jesse scanned the room. A shadowy figure glowed with the moon's reflection. She wore the old-fashioned style habit that nuns had worn until recently, a long dress with a large white bib, a black veil with a white wimple around her face.

Desperation.

Like black ink flowing into water, desperation flowed through

Jesse. She fought to maintain her own awareness and not be overwhelmed by Sister Rose Marie's emotions. If nothing else, Maggie's little brother Timmy had taught her that she could be entirely overtaken by the emotion of a ghost who contacted her.

"What do you need?" Jesse had never asked this of a ghost before.

The figure was silent.

"I know you are Sister Rose Marie. I want to help you."

With a gesture reminiscent of the Ghost of Christmas Future, the nun slowly raised her arm and pointed to the black book, still open on the table.

Jesse picked up the book. She'd been so focused on the atlas that she'd forgotten to look at this book.

It was a diary. Holding it toward the moonlight streaming in, she read the last entry dated May 24, 1959.

We focused on the Gospel of Philip today. What a discovery! Mary Magdalene was the beloved disciple. It makes so much sense since she was the first person the risen Christ appeared to. And then he commissioned her to tell the other apostles. How could the Church have maligned her so? I shake with rage when I realize how they silenced her.

I must go to confession and admit my sinfulness. My resentment of the Church fathers for abasing Mary Magdalene for centuries grows with every word I read. I fear they do not respect women since they hold us down from any leadership in the Church. We are relegated to dusting pews and ironing vestments.

And, of course, I must confess my growing attraction to Father Kevin. Each day, my heart soars when we meet. I clasp my hands to conceal their trembling and try not to look into his eyes. When I do, I suspect he may share my attraction. Not attraction—love. The kind of love I renounced when I took my vows. I must pray for strength to resist these feelings. I would distance myself, but we are making so much progress with these codices.

The desperation seeping through Jesse transformed into a red-hot anger. The words surged through her mind: *I shake with rage when I realize how they silenced her.*

Her heart pounding in her chest, the urge to strike out consumed her. She gripped the book in trembling hands. "How could they?!" The words were not her own, yet she had spoken them.

Rose Marie nodded.

Jesse's trembling subsided and other words struck her. Words that twisted her heart. *The kind of love I renounced when I took my vows.*

Jesse looked up at Rose Marie. "Just like Maggie."

Rose Marie sighed, a gentle zephyr on the night air. She faded into the shadows until Jesse stared only at the shadow of the twisted branches swaying on the moonlit wall.

She collapsed into the chair, no longer able to stand. Her hair was damp with sweat, and she still shook. Just as Timmy's ghost had possessed her in his room at Maggie's cottage, Sister Rose Marie had transferred her emotions to Jesse.

She wiped her forehead and tilted her head against the back of the chair. Sister Rose Marie needed her help. Why? Had someone murdered her to silence her? About what? And what was this Gospel of Philip? She had never learned of that one in all her years at Catholic schools from kindergarten at Our Lady of Lourdes elementary all the way up to Nazareth Academy High School. What threat was that gospel?

Or was she killed because of her love for Father Kevin?

One thing was sure, she wanted to find him and ask him some questions.

And she knew exactly who could help her find him.

Chapter Seven

Jesse had one more task to accomplish before she left her "silent retreat." She found Sister Therese in her office.

"Good morning, Jesse." The look on sister's face did not convey the sentiment. Nor did the way she rubbed her fingers over one eyebrow. "I trust you slept well."

Jesse didn't even respond to that statement. "Good morning, Sister. Here's the key to the third floor." She placed the skeleton key on the desk. "Before I go—"

"You aren't really going anywhere, are you?" Sister Therese raised an eyebrow.

Jesse choked back the snarky reply that jumped to her mind. "Since I'm heading home and won't be sleeping here tonight, I thought we should discuss our next steps."

Sister Therese sat back forward and steepled her hands on the desk. "I thought you would have taken care of this...disturbance... by now."

Jesse gripped the back of the chair in front of her to still her angry trembling. "This disturbance, as you call her, is a person in need."

Sister waved her hand. "Oh, posh, Jesse."

"Don't you care that one of your sisters is desperate for peace?

And she won't find it until she gets the answers she is seeking. I need help from you and the other sisters."

"I've told you that I do not want you talking about this to the sisters. We don't need gossip and rumor to run rampant and perhaps even reach the impressionable young girls."

"That already happened, remember? With the ghost of the Seneca woman. You really don't believe the seniors involved didn't tell younger students about what happened? They've probably already started their secret meetings."

"Stop, Jesse! I am ordering you to not speak of this to the other sisters."

"I am not one of your nuns. I have not taken a vow of obedience."

"But you are my employee, and I am giving you an order."

"Fine. You figure out what to do with the ghost of Sister Rose Marie in your attic." Jesse spun on her heel and left.

JESSE HAD FUMED during the entire drive home. But when she turned down the cul de sac and spotted the Cavanaugh House— her house—at the end of it, her shoulders relaxed. Even though this was the site of her first ghostly encounter with Helen Cavanaugh, her home was like a warm blanket that soothed any distress the minute she neared it. And now that Joe had moved in, her home was even more a sanctuary.

Joe's truck wasn't in the driveway, so he wasn't back from the fishing trip with Marty and Jim. They'd be hungry, so she'd make potato salad and sandwiches for lunch.

Just as she finished slicing fresh tomatoes from the garden, Joe's truck pulled into the driveway.

"Hi, Honey, I'm home!"

She could hear the grin in his voice as he called their favorite greeting. A ritual they both cherished.

His Irish heritage was evident with his coppery hair and green eyes. While people described hers as emerald green, his were more like light-colored sea glass polished by the tides. Since he was six-foot-two, she nestled right in at his shoulder, and his body, sculpted by the physical demands of his construction business, made her want to do that as often as possible.

She ran out and into his arms. Then jumped back and wrinkled her nose. "Oh, my word! You stink!"

He laughed. "Nice greeting. You should smell the inside of Jim's Jeep. It's worse than a fraternity house on Sunday morning. We caught fish. Lots of them." He yanked out a cooler and flipped open the top. "What do you prefer for dinner this evening, Madam?" He made a slight bow. "May I suggest the perch or bass, freshly caught in the cool waters of the St. Lawrence River?"

Frowning Jesse scrutinized the fish. "Sir, I yield the decision to your expert palate. First, however, I must insist you bathe."

Joe wrapped an arm around her and kissed her. "You said, 'for better or for worse,' remember?"

She laughed and returned the kiss. "I like the 'better' better."

"Then off I go. Marty will be here soon. He stopped home to shower...at least I hope he did. Jim and Susan will be here shortly, too."

"Great! Lunch is ready whenever you all are."

As Joe unpacked his truck, Jesse smoothed a red checkered tablecloth over the picnic table. After setting it, she brought out the platter stacked with sandwiches thick with ham, Havarti cheese, and lettuce. Beside the platter she put the freshly sliced tomatoes and a relish tray with pickles and olives. Finally, she carried out the bowl of creamy mustard potato salad, then hauled out the cooler packed with Genesee beer and soda.

"Hello! We're here." Her mother-in-law Susan Riley emerged from around the corner of the house followed by Jim Graham. Love had blossomed between them after they'd met through Jesse and Joe. Susan's eyes, more hazel than her son's, revealed her kindness and gentle humor as did the laugh wrinkles around them.

Unlike Joe's coppery red hair, hers was brown with auburn highlights.

As usual, Susan carried a bounty of additional food. "I threw together an apple crisp and a cucumber salad."

Jesse laughed. Susan's generosity and culinary skills were greatly appreciated. "Thanks, Susan." She took the warm pan of apple crisp and sniffed. "Mmmm. Smells delicious. Maybe we should eat dessert first."

"Life is short..." Susan hugged her.

Jim hugged Jesse and kissed her temple. "Hello, sweetie." He was the epitome of the academic with salt and pepper hair, a lean but strong build, and quick intelligent brown eyes. He had been the father Jesse remembered from her childhood, and they were reunited during her investigation of Helen Cavanaugh's death. His wisdom from teaching literature at Hobart and William Smith Colleges often helped Jesse when ghostly appearances disrupted her life.

"Oh, I think you'll want to sample this cucumber salad first. Just right for a warm autumn day." Jim arranged it on the table along with a bottle of Cabernet Sauvignon.

They chatted as they prepared the table.

"Hey, *Bella*!! I brought some Genny 12 Horse Ale and chips." Marty's deep bass rang out.

In one arm he carried a twelve pack, in the other he juggled a large can of Charles Chips. Putting them on the end of the picnic table, he hugged Jesse, then Susan, and shook Jim's hand. Marty's black hair, as usual, stuck up in various places like a poorly mowed lawn in July. He was as tall as Joe, but more solidly built. Keeping up with sheriff office protocols had him in the gym where he tried to work off his grandmother's Italian cooking.

Susan opened the tin of potato chips. "Is Maggie still on retreat?"

Marty quirked his lips to the side. "Yeah."

His eyes reminded Jesse of a lost puppy.

"When is she due back?" Jim opened a beer and handed it to him.

"Soon, I hope. Can't be soon enough." He scrubbed his fingers through his hair, so it now resembled a troll doll more than a messy lawn. He caught Jesse's eye.

"Where's your hubby? Taking a nap?"

"Just finished cleaning up," Joe called out through the screen door. "Be right there. Phone for you, Just Jesse."

Jesse's heart skipped a beat. Even though Joe had called her that endearment since they met, she still smiled. They kissed each other as they passed, she to the phone, Joe to a beer.

"Hello?"

"Hi Jesse, it's Jam. I learned something I thought you might be interested in. Just for kicks I found an old yearbook from 1954. I was leisurely thumbing through it when I came across Sister Rose Marie's picture. It just so happened I was sitting beside Sister Alphonse who saw the page.

"She said, 'Such a tragedy.' Using my innocent voice…"

Jesse chuckled. "You have an innocent voice?"

"…when I need it, yes. I asked, 'Tragedy? Why?' She pressed her lips really tight and started fingering her rosary beads."

"'She disappeared quite suddenly.' she said. I opened my eyes wide and asked, 'Oh, wow. Did she come back?' Jesse, she threw me dagger eyes and snapped, 'It's best if you mind your own business, Sister John Mary.' She was pissed."

Jesse pondered that. "Did she seem sad or angry?"

"Angry. Does she know about Sister Rose Marie's ghost?"

"Not to my knowledge."

"I'm no detective, but her reaction was pretty intense. She knows something about this, Jess. I'm sure of it. And that's not all. Sister Therese came in and noticed what we were looking at and immediately found a task for me to do. Dust and polish the pews in the chapel. She knows something, too."

"She knows that Sister Rose Marie is haunting the convent.

Thanks, Jam. I appreciate your desire to look at old yearbooks just for me."

"Anytime. I'll see what other mischief I can get into."

Jesse rejoined the others at the picnic table. Placing her elbows on the table, she dropped her head in her hands.

"Bad news, Jesse?" Joe took her hand.

They had no idea what she'd been through the last few days. Maggie and Jam had been the only ones she'd confided in. She exhaled. How to explain, especially to Joe, that she was dealing with another ghost? Not on an empty stomach.

She raised her head and smiled. "Not bad news per se. Dig in everyone, it's a long story."

As they ate, she related the events of the past few days since Sister Therese had knocked on her door. She studied Joe's face. His eyes showed concern, but not anger. She breathed a little easier. In the past he would have been angry.

When she finished recounting Jam's message, Susan put her fork down. "I recall Sister Rose Marie." A crease formed between her brows as she called up the memory. "She was vivacious and charming. Very pretty, too. I volunteered on an overnight field trip to Nazareth College with her seniors. She related well to the students." She smiled. "She admitted to them that the annual senior trip was a recruiting tactic for the Sisters of Saint Joseph."

Jesse leaned forward. "Do you remember anything else about her?"

Susan shifted in her seat and folded her napkin. "Rumors circulated about her and Father Murphy. She suddenly disappeared and shortly after, so did he." She took Marty's hand. "I understand now how that could happen." Her voice softened. "I'm sorry I judged them so harshly."

Marty raised her hand to his lips. "Thank you."

Jim snapped his fingers. "I remember Father Murphy. I invited him to speak on a project he was working on." As a professor of the English Department at Hobart and William Smith Colleges, Jim brought in speakers for their annual Writing and the Arts

Festival. "He did a fascinating presentation on the discovery of the gnostic gospels."

Jesse frowned. "Doesn't the Church prohibit us from reading those?"

"Father Kevin was quite open about them. Excited, in fact."

"Is The Gospel of Philip one of them?"

"Yes, it is. Why?"

"Sister Rose Marie referenced it in her journal."

"If she did run away with this priest, what happened? She obviously died if her ghost is haunting the convent." Susan sipped her wine.

Jesse shrugged. "She appeared to me in the third-floor room. It's like a small library dedicated to the study of ancient biblical sites. That's where I found her journal. In it, she admits she was attracted to Father Murphy, but she resisted acting on it."

"But, *Bella*, maybe this guy was upset that she didn't return his advances and, well, things got out of hand."

"Spoken like a true cop, Marty. I'm sure you encounter this kind of thing all the time." She rubbed her eyes. "I can see so many different scenarios. I don't want to jump to conclusions. How about another midnight trip to the criminal records archives?"

"It's a date."

One night when Marty had sneaked her into the archives so she could research the story of Helen Cavanaugh's death, they'd almost been caught. But what she discovered there resulted in the capture of Helen's murderer.

Joe groaned. "Just be careful, Jess, okay?" He rubbed her shoulders.

"I promise. Scout's honor." She crossed her heart.

JESSE HADN'T HAD time to unpack her suitcase when she got home, so she did so before getting ready for bed. Joe came up behind her and wrapped his arms around her. She sank into him.

"You'll be careful?" He whispered against her skin as he nuzzled her neck.

She clasped her hands around his. "I gave my scout's honor."

"Were you ever a scout?"

"Well...no."

"So much for scout's honor." He laughed and turned her around. "I missed you, babe. And I take off for my conference in New York City in a month. I know how these investigations go, and I don't want to be gone while you're involved in one." His lips brushed hers, then he captured her gaze and held it. Passion mixed with concern.

"Joe, I promise I will be careful."

He kissed her and drew her closer. "Let's celebrate my magnificent catch."

She laughed against his lips. "You are my magnificent catch."

"Then reel me in." He yanked back the covers.

"Let me get the suitcase off the bed."

As she lifted the suitcase, a key fell to the floor.

The key she had returned to Sister Therese.

Chapter Eight

Jesse leaned her elbows on her desk and rubbed her eyes. The first day of the new school year had seen its usual bumps in the road for scheduling and class assignments, but nothing too critical. Her students were excited about the new year and their ascent in the pecking order to the next grade up.

She loved the start of a new year, but for the first two weeks exhaustion reigned until she got back into the rhythm. With her eyes closed, head resting in her hands, she could doze right off.

"Hey, Jesse."

She jumped at the sudden greeting. "Hey, Jam! How was your first day?"

"Great. We got new lab equipment, so we'll be able to dissect pigs' hearts as well as frogs this year. Though when I made that announcement, most girls didn't share my enthusiasm and one turned pale as a ghost and had to put her head between her knees." She dropped into the student desk directly in front of Jesse's desk.

Just like Maggie used to do.

God, she missed her best friend. But she planned to visit her this Saturday at Holy Spirit Monastery just south on Seneca Lake.

As if reading her mind, Jam asked, "What do you hear from Sister Angelina—I mean Maggie?"

"She's doing well. I couldn't understand her wanting to leave Marty and go off to spend a few weeks with a bunch of other guys..."

Jam's laugh was contagious.

"...but she's finding a lot of peace at the monastery. And affirmation that she's making the right decision. I'm going to see her this weekend."

"Give her my best."

"Jam?"

Jam sobered. "That's not an 'everything-is-hunky-dory-Jam.' That's a 'burying-the-lead-Jam.' What's up?"

Jesse opened her drawer and produced a key.

Jam's brows creased and her lips twitched to one side. "Yes? A key."

Jesse leaned forward and whispered, "The key to the third floor of the convent."

"MmmHmm...And we're whispering because...?"

"I returned this key to Sister Therese when I left the other day."

"And she willingly gave it back?" Jam joined her in whispering.

"No."

Jam's brows lowered further. "What are you saying?"

"I'm saying that I returned the key, in fact Sister insisted I do so. But when I unpacked last night, this key was in my suitcase."

Jam's eyes widened and her mouth dropped open. "How?"

"How indeed. Sister Rose Marie must have put it there."

"Sure." Jam drew out the word. At Jesse's serious expression, Jam sat back and folded her arms. "Jess, that's hard to believe. You don't really think..."

"Then you explain it. How did a key I returned to the safe keeping of Sister Therese end up in my suitcase?"

"Could she have put it there? Sister Therese, not Sister Rose Marie?"

They stared at each other, then in unison said, "No."

"Jesus, Mary, and Joseph," Jam murmured.

"Rose Marie wants me to go back up to that room, but I don't have a convent key. How am I supposed to get in? And when?"

The sound of the lacrosse team echoed across the grounds as they sat in silence pondering this predicament.

"Compline."

"What?"

"I'll sneak you in right before Compline tonight. All the sisters gather in chapel at nine-o'clock for Compline and pray for about half an hour or so. Just before nine, I'll unlock the back door that leads to the kitchen, and you can come in and head up to the third floor. How long do you need to be up there?"

"I have no idea. I don't even know what I'm looking for."

"How about you take an hour? That will give the sisters time to retire and be all tucked in. I'll meet you and lock the kitchen door behind you when you leave."

"Thank you, Jam! That's a great plan. Would tonight work?"

"Any night. We sisters are creatures of habit." Her laugh rang around the room.

Jesse groaned and then doubled over joining in the mirth.

"That was a good one. I'll meet you at the back door tonight just before nine."

"God bless, Jesse."

Jam's unusually serious tone shook Jesse. She really meant that.

Jesse nodded her thanks. She really needed it.

As she drove up the circular drive to St. Bartholomew's Academy for girls, Jesse turned off the headlights.

"Okay, Bert, here we go." She had named her yellow, 1965 Volkswagen Beetle the day she bought it four years earlier. She patted the dashboard. "Another adventure, Bert." Downshifting into first, she eased along the service road to the back of the convent.

When she got out of the car, the night air was heavy with mist, and the cool humidity clung to her skin. In the distance waves lapped the shore, its earthy smell filling the night. She rubbed her arms, listening to the fugue of crickets and frogs. What would she find in the third-floor room? Where should she even begin?

The bigger question was, how did that key end up in her suitcase? Did Sister Rose Marie really put it in her suitcase? How else could it have gotten there?

She stared out at the dark woods surrounding the school grounds. A slight breeze whispered through the trees, their branches arching toward the cloudy sky like beseeching arms. Rustling at the edge of the trees suggested a large animal moving through the underbrush.

She checked her watch. Eight fifty-five. "Come on, Jam."

An owl hooted just above her. She crossed her arms and moved closer to the building.

The door swung open, and a soft glow spilled out onto the walk.

"Showtime, Jesse." Jam held the door open for her.

Jesse hurried into a small hall with two steps leading up to a door into the kitchen, and a flight of stairs leading down into an ink-black basement. She shivered. *Thank goodness I don't have to go there. Thank you, Sister Rose Marie for picking the third floor instead.*

"I'll be back here at ten-o'clock to lock the door behind you. If you stay in this little hall with the door closed, no one can see you from the kitchen. Just our luck, this would be the night a sister would come in for a bedtime snack. Gotta go."

Jam bolted for the chapel.

Jesse waited until she heard the sweet, clear voices of the sisters singing, "*In manus tuus Domine.*"

She inhaled and whispered, "Well, Lord, I guess I'm in your hands, too."

Removing her shoes, she tiptoed down the hall toward the stairs in the opposite direction of the chapel. The music of their voices floated behind her, and she found some comfort in that.

When she reached the second floor she stopped. What if this wasn't the key to the third floor? What if it was some random key she accidently picked up somewhere?

What if she walked back down the stairs and drove home and into Joe's arms? Was she really the only one who could help Sister Rose Marie? Surely there were other people around she could appear to. People who would know more about the situation and what she needed.

Why me? Life would be so much simpler if ghosts didn't appear to her. Marty's voice drifted to her.

Once they find you, more ghosts will come.

Helen Cavanaugh, the Seneca Woman, and Maggie's little brother Timmy Keegan were no longer searching for someone who could help. She had been the one they chose for help. And now they were at peace.

And Sister Rose Marie needed peace.

Jesse gripped the key and inserted it into the lock. The door squeaked as she opened it, an eerie, shrieking sound. She closed her eyes and inhaled. Far off, the voices of the sisters echoed. When she carefully closed the door, loneliness flooded her.

No one else could help her. She had to do this on her own.

She climbed the steps, grateful that she had installed a new, if dim, lightbulb. At the top of the stairs, the skittering of tiny feet welcomed her.

Her heart pounded. She'd take a ghost over mice any day of the week.

As she stood at the door of the small library, cool air curled from beneath the door and chilled her toes. Sister Rose Marie was in there.

She eased open the door. Beside the open window, the woman's figure glowed in the dark room.

"Hello, Sister Rose Marie. How can I help you?"

A rush of anger flushed through Jesse. Heat pricked at her skin, and adrenalin pulsed through her veins. She trembled, not from the cold ghostly air in the room, but from a feeling of being chained, caught, trapped. Gasping, she fought to breathe.

Sister Rose Marie's shadow wavered, its light flickering. Her hand reached out, but Jesse could barely see her through the dancing starbursts in her eyes. She grabbed the back of the chair, and it toppled over as she fell.

Darkness.

Chapter Nine

"Jesse, Jesse, wake up!" Jam's voice hissed in her ear.

Jesse's eyes fluttered open, and she moaned. Above her, a dim lightbulb swam before her eyes. Her body ached from hitting the floor so hard. She eased up to sitting and scanned the room. It was warm. Sister Rose Marie was gone.

"Where is she?" she muttered.

"Nobody else is here." Jam glanced over each shoulder. "Thank God."

Jesse touched her forehead. "Ow!" A bump was forming on her head.

"I think you hit that chair on your way down."

"I don't remember..."

"Take it easy." Jam helped her up into the chair. "When you didn't show up in the kitchen, I wondered what had happened to you. At least you're still...okay. Kind of."

Jesse closed her eyes, trying to remember. "Sister Rose Marie was here." She nodded toward the corner by the window. "I asked what she needed help with. I was filled with rage, and then I couldn't breathe."

Her head pounded. Her thoughts wouldn't coalesce. What was Sister trying to communicate? With Helen she had experienced overwhelming love. With Timmy, the joy of childhood. With the Seneca woman, overwhelming rage similar to, yet different from tonight. What had made Sister Rose Marie so angry?

And why did she try to kill me? Jesse shivered. She'd promised Joe she would be careful. How did she know a nun would be so violent?

She stood and looked around the room. What was different? Did Sister Rose Marie leave any kind of clue? The atlas was opened to a different page. Instead of Jerusalem and the Dead Sea, now it displayed Egypt.

What could that mean? What about Egypt made Sister Rose Marie so angry?

She inspected the page as best she could under the dim light.

"May I take this atlas with me?"

Jam spread out her hands. "Take whatever you like. Nobody ever comes up here to use any of these books."

Jesse closed the book, committing the page number to memory. One last look around, and they headed for the door.

At the bottom of the stairs Jesse opened the door and came face to face with Sister Therese. Whose face was beet red.

"What is the meaning of this?" Her eyes flashed. Though her voice was low, its anger was powerful.

"Sister, I was only trying to—" Jam began.

"Sister, it's my fault—" Jesse said over Jam's explanation.

A door down the hall opened and Sister Alphonse emerged. Her gray hair stuck out like she'd been in a windstorm, and her eyes blinked against the soft light of the corridor.

"Not you again!" She snarled as she approached. "You are nothing but trouble. Sister Therese, I think it's high time she was let go."

Sister Therese held Jesse's gaze while she addressed Sister Alphonse. "Go back to bed, Alphonse. This is none of your business."

"Perhaps Sister Alphonse could help enlighten me about Sister Rose Marie." Jesse said.

Sister Therese's eyes bulged, and she clenched her fists. Jesse wondered if nuns punched hard. She had taken a risk and probably blown her chances as a teacher at St. Bartholomew Academy for Girls. Also, for discovering what Sister Rose Marie needed.

"Come with me." Sister Therese commanded. She spun around and they followed. So did Sister Alphonse. "Not you, Alphonse. Go back to bed."

Sister Alphonse scowled at Jesse and returned to her room.

Jesse and Jam followed the woman downstairs to her office. As they walked, Jesse pondered the sensations that overcame her in the library. She understood the emotion, that seemed a common thread with her ghostly encounters. But she'd never experienced a physical sensation of choking. This was entirely different.

When they were settled into chairs, Sister Therese clasped her hands on her desk as if she were going to lead them in prayer. But her expression was far from angelic.

"Now, explain exactly what you two were doing."

Jesse took the lead. "I needed to get back into that room, and since you asked me to return the key, I knew you wouldn't let me in."

"So, you recruited Sister John Mary's assistance?"

"I offered to help," Jam said.

Sister Therese turned her glare on the nun. "And just how did you even know about this?"

Jesse leaned forward. "I told her."

"I expressly told you not to speak to any of the sisters, Jesse. You disobeyed me."

Jesse's heart pounded, and so did the lump on her forehead. She tried to hold back her retort, but it slipped out. "As I said, I did not take a vow of obedience." That was probably not the best response.

Sister Therese's nostrils flared. She took a deep breath. "And as I told you, I am your employer, and you are to follow my instructions." She unclasped her hands and spread them out, as if in supplication. "Perhaps St. Bartholomew is not a good fit for you, Jesse."

Jam gasped. "No, wait—"

Sister Therese leveled a cold stare at her, then turned back to Jesse.

"I think it best if you leave us."

All the blood drained from Jesse's head. The room swam and everything turned white.

No. I will not let her get to me. If I get fired, so be it. She took three deep breaths to steady herself.

"Fine. You have five English classes to cover, and you'll need an advisor for the annual Writers' Spring Fling. Oh, and there's the field trip to the Stratford Festival next month. Oh, and then there's the ghost in your attic. That role might be more difficult to fill." She stood up.

Jam covered her mouth and studied the floor.

Jesse grasped the door handle. "Did you wonder how I got up to the third floor, Sister? Where did I get that key? I watched you put it in that top drawer."

Sister Therese glared at her for a moment, then opened the top drawer. She pursed her lips. "Did you take the key?"

Jesse expected her to ask, but it still rankled. "I did not. How could I even get into your office here in the convent?"

Sister Therese raised one eyebrow. After thinking for a moment, she turned her gaze to Jam.

"Sister John Mary, did you take the key."

"That's unfair. Jam—" Jesse exploded.

"Sister John Mary had every opportunity to enter my office and acquire the key."

Jam clenched her fists, trembling. Knowing Jam's tough background, Jesse suspected it wasn't from fear. Jam's lips were pulled tightly together, her eyes downcast. But her brows drew together in a cloud of anger. Jesse could almost see the smoke coming out of her ears.

Look out, Sister Therese.

"You know my background, Sister." Jam's words were measured. "It's not beyond the realm of possibility that I might have stolen a few things in the past. Mostly to feed my younger siblings. But I never lied and I'm not lying now. I did not sneak into your office and steal that key from your desk."

Sister Therese jerked back in her chair as if she'd been slapped. "Of course." She whispered her 'almost' apology.

Jesse held out the key. "This showed up in my suitcase when I got home. I believe Sister Rose Marie gave it to me."

Sister Therese snorted. "Don't be ridiculous."

"Then tell me where it came from."

Sister Therese fell silent.

"And another thing. Tonight, Sister Rose Marie told me she had been murdered."

Chapter Ten

Through the front window, Jesse saw Joe pacing the living room.

Seeing the headlights, he was at the front door in a flash.

"Are you all right? It's after eleven!" He wrapped her in his arms.

"It was quite a night, Joe. Sister Rose Marie appeared, Jam and I got caught, and I got fired."

"Fired? Sister Therese fired you?"

"I might have said some things I shouldn't have."

Joe laughed. "It's your damn red-headed temper."

"Yes, that and Sister Therese's roadblocks everywhere I turn." She brushed back her hair and flopped on the couch.

He sat beside her and gently touched the lump on her forehead. "What happened here?"

She described her encounter with Sister Rose Marie. As she spoke, he got a bag of frozen peas from the freezer.

She held the bag against her forehead. "It was weird though."

"Isn't it always?"

She laughed. "Yeah, I guess you're right. Sister Rose Marie transmitted her emotions to me, but I think she also told me that she had been murdered. Maybe strangled." She explained the sensation of choking and passing out.

"That's new." He agreed. "You're okay though?" His eyes were tender with a mix of concern and love.

"Yes. Besides, if Sister Therese has fired me from St. Bart's, she's also fired me from finding out what Sister Rose Marie needs. I guess I get to sleep in tomorrow."

The phone rang.

Joe checked his watch. "Now, who's calling at this hour?" He went to the hall and picked up the receiver. "Hello?"

He held out the phone. "It's for you, hon." He mouthed silently "Sister Therese."

"Hello?"

"Jesse, this is Sister Therese. I'm sorry to disturb you so late, but I thought you might have just gotten home."

"Yes, I did."

"I spoke in haste this evening. I expect you to be in your classroom tomorrow morning."

Jesse frowned as anger seeped through her. "Are you calling to apologize?"

"Don't make this difficult, Jesse. I was upset and rash in my decision. You are a competent teacher and so should continue at St. Bartholomew's."

Jesse didn't know whether to laugh or scream. Sister would obviously never apologize. This was the best she could do. The thought of sleeping in the next morning had been very enticing, but truth be told, she enjoyed teaching at St. Bart's.

"I will be in my classroom tomorrow morning. But what about Sister Rose Marie?"

Silence.

"Perhaps we've been mistaken. Perhaps we heard the wind whistling through the trees. I think we should let this go."

Now Jesse was furious. She inhaled deeply before she spoke. "I know you're uncomfortable with this, Sister Therese. But you need to face the fact that Sister Rose Marie needs help. It's not the wind in the trees. I've seen her up in that library."

"Stop."

"Perhaps I should take a break from teaching."

"I want you to let this nonsense about a ghost go."

"You were the one who came to me."

"You are correct. Perhaps that was my mistake. I'm asking you to let it go."

"I'm afraid I can't. If a spirit needs me, I will do what I can to help."

"The only spirit I want to hear about is the Holy Spirit."

"Well, Sister Therese, I think they're all holy."

"Do not come into the convent uninvited, Jesse. You are finished with your search."

"If that's what you want." Jesse hung up the phone. She trembled and sank into the chair beside the hall table.

Joe rubbed her shoulders. "That didn't sound good."

"It wasn't. But at least I got my job back." She stood up.

Joe wrapped his arms around her. "That's too bad. I was going to call in sick tomorrow." He kissed her long and full.

Chapter Eleven

After school the next day Jesse found Jam in the biology lab. The classroom doors on either side of the large lab, one hers, one Sister Vincent's, were open. Three students were still in Sister Vincent's classroom listening to her lecture on "proper behavior in a chemistry lab." The girls Jesse glimpsed through the door looked terrified.

Jam's eyebrows shot up. "I thought you got fired last night."

"No, I got an eleventh hour—literally—invitation to stay. I hope you didn't get in trouble with Sister Therese."

Jam rinsed a test tube and nestled it in a rack. "Nah. She scolded me and told me I was a bad girl. I was a bad girl long before I joined the convent. Remember, I grew up in the projects." She winked at Jesse. "She instructed me on the dangers of dealing with the occult. And with you."

"I am quite dangerous." Jesse sat on a tall stool beside a lab bench.

"I know. So, what can I do next to help you?"

Jesse waved her hands in front of her. "Nothing. Sister Therese has her shorts in a knot about this. Thank you for helping last night, but I don't want you to get in more trouble."

"Got it. So, you've encountered Sister Rose Marie's ghost in the library and at the grotto, right? What a coincidence, the grotto is my newest favorite place to pray. I'll listen really closely."

"You're the best, Jam."

"I'm blushing."

From the corner of her eye, Jesse spied a flash of black and heard the unmistakable sound of rosary beads clacking. She jumped at the bellow of her name.

"Miss Graham!"

Sister Alphonse stood before them, trembling, eyes blazing.

"How dare you desecrate Sister Rose Marie with your outlandish rumors! What right do you have to smear her name? To call her a ghost! How fiendish of you. Satan is at work within you, and you're dragging Sister John Mary right down with you. Leave this be..." she stepped so close Jesse could feel her breath on her face, "... or there will be a reckoning."

Jesse stared after Sister Alphonse's fleeing form.

Jam's eyes were wide with wonder. "Her threat sounds vaguely familiar."

Jesse nodded. "Yes, 'a pointy reckoning that will shudder me.' *The Crucible*. You know, she'd fit right in with that story."

"Jess, maybe you'd better back off. You'll suffer the wrath of two women in black robes. That makes me shake a little."

"No way." Jesse lined up pipettes in a neat row. "I've faced worse than the wrath of the nuns. I mean, how dangerous can a convent be?" She frowned remembering the Seneca woman's fury in the underground tunnel not all that far from where she sat. "All I have to do is figure out how to stay in contact with Sister Rose Marie."

"You can meditate in the grotto with me."

Jesse grunted. "The rocks would melt."

AFTER READING THROUGH HER SOPHOMORES' *To Kill a Mockingbird* quiz, Jesse stretched and rubbed her eyes. She loved teaching this book, and the girls seemed to be enjoying Scout and Jem's adventures trying to get Boo Radley to come out.

Staring out the backdoor screen at the dark night, she listened to a barred owl call.

Who cooks for you? Who cooks for you-all?

The owl was free to sing its call.

She thought about people who are silenced. Like Boo Radley and Tom Robinson. People who have no voice. No power. Who are denigrated, ignored, and silenced.

Like she had been by Sister Therese during her "silent retreat."

Like Sister Rose Marie had been by whoever murdered her.

She pulled the atlas she'd taken from beneath the pile of quizzes. She'd only had a brief time to examine the atlas. It had initially been opened to Jerusalem and the ancient Middle East. But then the pages had been flipped to ancient Egypt. By Sister Rose Marie. But why?

Grabbing a magnifying glass, she studied the map closely. A light pencil mark circled an area south of Egypt at a bend in the Nile. What was significant about this location?

Joe came into the kitchen, caressed her shoulders, and kissed the top of her head. "Ready for bed?"

She grasped his hand and kissed it. "I am if you are." She closed the atlas.

They headed upstairs and started to undress. As Joe headed for his side of the bed, he glanced out the window and stopped.

"Uh, I think someone's here to see you."

"What? Where?"

"In the middle of your rock garden."

She stood beside him. Then she laughed. "Joke's on you, Sister Therese."

There, shimmering in the moon light was a figure dressed in black and white.

Joe took her hand. "Don't go down there."

She bit her lip. Joe's concern touched her, but she knew the ghost in their yard was desperate for help or wouldn't be there. "I have to, Joe."

He dropped her hand and sat on the bed.

Jesse slipped back into her sandals and headed downstairs.

She approached the apparition slowly.

Sister Rose Marie hovered just above the boulders at the base of the rock garden Jesse and Joe had created in the early spring.

"Hello, Sister Rose Marie."

The form shifted, the play of shadow and light moving in the darkness.

"How can I help you?"

The scent of roses overwhelmed Jesse. While it started out a pleasant aroma, it increased until it became sickly sweet. Jesse covered her nose with her shirt, but it permeated the fabric. She coughed and gagged, dropping to her knees.

Sister Rose Marie faded and with her the overpowering scent.

Joe rushed out and helped Jesse to stand.

"What was that all about?"

Jesse shook her head to clear it. "Sister Rose Marie just revealed another clue."

Chapter Twelve

The week couldn't end soon enough for Jesse because she was so excited about her visit with Maggie. She and Joe eased into the day with a Saturday morning breakfast of eggs, over-easy, bacon, and thick slices of Susan's homemade banana bread smothered with butter.

"Do you think the walls of the monastery will crumble or get struck by lightning when I enter it?" Jesse bit into the banana bread.

Joe chuckled and wiped a dab of butter off her chin with his napkin. "The walls will stand and welcome you. You don't give yourself enough credit. You are good, and beautiful, and kind. Look at how you're helping Sister Rose Marie. How you've helped others. And not just dead people."

Jesse spewed out her coffee. "That sounded hysterical, Joe."

"Well, hysterical or not, I mean it."

"Hey, you guys got clothes on?" Marty bellowed from the front hall.

"No," they shouted in unison.

Silence.

"Yes, we're decent. Come on in Marty." Joe called.

Marty entered carrying a small bouquet of dahlias. "Hey, I timed it perfectly. What's for breakfast?"

Joe put a plate, silverware, and a coffee mug in front of him. "It's Saturday. We were expecting you."

Marty dove into a plateful of eggs, bacon, and banana bread with gusto. "You're going to see Maggie today, right?"

Jesse's heart melted. The way he said Maggie's name was like a caress.

"Yes. Are these flowers for me?" Jesse reached for the bouquet.

He snatched them away. "*Bella*," he warned. Then he handed them to her. "Will you please give them to Maggie for me?"

Jesse sighed. "I'm not sure I'm supposed to. Her reason for being on this retreat is to ensure her decision to leave the convent is the right choice. Giving her a gift from you could be seen as unfair."

"C'mon, *Bella*. It's me up against God. I think giving her flowers is hardly going to tip the scales."

Jesse laughed. "I'll give them to her, but you'll have to answer to God."

"Thanks." He took a bite of toast. "Hey, Joe, when do you leave for New York?"

"October 3rd." He glanced at Jesse. "If everything is okay here."

Marty glanced from him to Jesse, a puzzled frown on his face.

"Joe's concerned about me tracking down information about Sister Rose Marie. He's worried I'll be in danger." Jesse took Joe's hand.

"You've been in danger with every ghost you've helped. I don't expect this to be different."

Marty finished his coffee. "Listen, maybe I can help speed things up. I'm on night shift next week. Why don't you come in Monday night, and we'll see what we can find in the archives."

"Thanks, Marty. That would be great! Lord knows I can't find out anything at the convent."

"But the good sister did visit you in your rock garden." Joe poured another cup of coffee.

Marty's mouth dropped open. "What? She came here?"

Jesse nodded. "Yes. I guess they can do that. Timmy also left his place of rest and was with me in the cabin in the woods."

"Oh yeah. I remember that now. So, these ghosts can move around."

"And move objects. She deposited a key in my suitcase when I left my 'silent retreat.'" Jesse looked at the clock. "I've got to go. Maggie's expecting me for lunch, and it will take me almost an hour to get to the monastery."

Marty's face was a picture of melancholy.

"You look like a lost puppy, Marty."

"I miss her so much."

Joe swatted his shoulder. "We'll keep busy with manly endeavors today, man."

"Are you going hunting and gathering?" Jesse put her plate in the sink.

"No, we're going golfing." Joe pulled her into his lap and kissed her.

"Okay, folks, let's not make this worse for the lonely, single guy," Marty said.

Jesse straightened and kissed Marty on the cheek. "I will deliver your token of love and tell her of your devotion."

<hr>

JESSE GAPED at the massive stone building that loomed before her. She often envied Maggie's deep devotion and solid belief in God. Jesse, however, had her doubts. Therefore, would these walls collapse when she entered?

I hope Joe's right. These walls are thick.

She parked Bert and scanned the grounds. Lining the hills on the right, rows of grapevines marched up to the crest. On the left, the hill was dotted with white sheep. Soft bleating floated down to her.

She ascended the steps to an imposing oak door with a huge

iron knocker on it. As she reached up to use the knocker, she spied a doorbell. She chose that.

A young man in a hooded black robe opened the door. He had close-cropped hair and a neatly trimmed light brown beard. His intelligent blue eyes glanced at the dahlia bouquet Jesse carried, and he flashed an infectious smile.

"Good morning. May I help you?"

"I'm Jesse Graham. I'm here to visit Maggie Keegan."

He looked puzzled.

"Sister Angelina."

"Ah, yes. I'm Brother Luke." He extended his hand to shake hers. "Please come in."

He led her down a hallway with a stone floor. On the wall to her left were tall leaded windows that arched at the top. On her right at even intervals were icons of St. Benedict holding a staff and a book or a scroll.

Their footsteps echoed off the stone walls. She expected to see knights in shining armor and damsels wearing pointed hennins at any moment.

They entered a kitchen bright with sunlight casting cross patterns on the counters. Two men stood chatting at the stove, one wearing an apron and stirring a large pot. The aroma of basil, oregano, and garlic filled the room.

Jesse's mouth watered. When her stomach growled, she grasped it as if that would silence it. No one seemed to notice.

Maggie stood at a central wood block table peeling carrots. Looking up, she dropped the carrot and peeler on the table. She ran to Jesse and pulled her into a bear hug.

"Jesse! Oh, I miss you!"

"Mags! I miss you so much!"

Jesse held out the flowers and whispered, "So does someone else."

A soft pink glow suffused Maggie's cheeks and her smile widened. "Thank you." She stood on tiptoe to reach a slender glass vase off a shelf. Filling it part way with water, she put the dahlias in it, gently arranging them.

She gestured to the counter. "I'm almost finished here. Give me a minute."

The man stirring the pot at the stove waved his hand. "I'll take care of those carrots, Maggie. You go visit with your friend." He turned back to his task.

"Thanks, Father Kevin!" She untied her apron and hung it on a hook.

Chills prickled Jesse's arms. Father Kevin? Could he possibly be Sister Rose Marie's Father Kevin Murphy? No. Kevin was a very common name. But how many Kevins become priests? Many if their Irish mothers had their way. And he was a priest and not a brother like Brother Luke. It must be him.

She studied the man. He was tall with broad shoulders and brown hair with just a touch of gray at the temples. Beneath the apron, he wore black pants and a short sleeved black shirt. As he stirred the contents of the pot, the other man, dressed in a hooded robe like Brother Luke's, regaled him with a story. Father Kevin laughed, a full belly laugh, showing white teeth and brown eyes that danced with amusement. An incredibly attractive man.

Can't say I blame you, Sister Rose Marie.

Maggie grabbed Jesse's hand, pulling her out the back door. Before them spread an enormous garden. One section held a variety of herbs, the larger part contained vegetables. Beyond that, an orchard stretched in neat rows, the trees laden with almost-ripe apples.

They strolled arm in arm around the side of the monastery until they came to a small grotto. A statue of St. Benedict stood in an arched stone area and dahlias, zinnia, and rose of Sharon surrounded the shrine. But rose bushes occupied most of the space. Splashes of coral, yellow, red, and white roses surrounded them.

Jesse stopped in her tracks. Her head swam and she tightened her grip on Maggie's arm.

"Jess, what is it?" Maggie's voice sounded far off.

Jesse shook her head. "The roses." Anger roiled within her as the floral scent grew increasingly sickly sweet. She held her head, feeling the bump there. "Can we walk somewhere else?"

"Sure." Maggie couldn't disguise the alarm in her voice.

They turned toward the hill where the grapevines covered the hillside. Once Jesse was away from the grotto, her head cleared.

"Jess, what's going on?"

"It's Sister Rose Marie."

Maggie halted, her mouth agape. "What? The ghost? What does she have to do with the roses in the grotto?"

"It's a long story."

"Let's get lunch and you can tell me all about it."

BENEATH A SPRAWLING OAK TREE, they ate salads of fresh vegetables from the garden and homemade bread smothered in strawberry preserves. As they sipped crisp Riesling, Jesse related all that had happened with Sister Rose Marie.

"So, since I left you, you've met a new ghost, had several visits from her, were almost strangled to death, stolen an atlas, gotten fired, and gotten rehired. Nothing unusual for you there."

"Nope. My life is dull and boring." Jesse laughed and sipped her wine.

"I'm glad Jam could help. And I'm glad Sister Therese called to apologize and clarify that you still taught at St. Bart's."

"Oh, no apology was offered. She simply insisted I show up for school the next day. She will never apologize to me or to Jam after accusing her of theft. Sister Therese pulled me into this, and now she just wants it to all go away. Before Bishop Harris arrives. She tried to convince me—and herself—that Sister Rose Marie's voice was the wind in the trees. Ugh!"

Maggie shook her head. "She's in denial for sure."

"Mags, the rumor about Sister Rose Marie is that she ran off with a Father Kevin Murphy. Is he your Father Kevin from the kitchen?"

"Yes. That's Father Kevin Murphy."

"You told me he and Sister Rose Marie visited your cottage, right?"

"He visited often. In fact, I've known him all my life. He's a friend of our family." She put down her salad. "I talked to him after Dad suggested I enter the convent."

"Your father didn't suggest anything. He guilted you into it as atonement for Timmy's disappearance."

Maggie waved away an imaginary fly. "In any event, I wanted to be sure I had a calling. Father Kevin prayed with me and helped me discern my path."

Jesse imagined an impressionable teenaged Maggie being directed by two male authority figures. "Why did you go to Father Murphy? Was he your pastor?"

Maggie glanced at Jesse, then down at her hands. "Dad encouraged me to talk to him."

Jesse kept quiet. *Of course he did. No pressure there.*

"Jesse, I had a call to a vocation. Nobody forced me to enter the convent. And I loved my life as a sister, that's why it's so hard to leave. That's why I'm here making peace with my decision to leave."

"Here with Father Murphy who convinced you to enter in the first place." Suddenly Jesse didn't like handsome, laughing Father Murphy.

Frowning, Maggie shoved their plates into the picnic basket. "You make it sound like a conspiracy." She glared at her. "I do have a brain, you know." She jammed the cork into the wine bottle.

"I'm sorry, Mags. I didn't mean to insinuate anything. It's just that you're here," Jesse gestured to the towering building behind them, "with all this holy influence, listening to Father Murphy's opinion while Marty's not here able to offer his."

Maggie stopped shoving things into the picnic basket. "But, Jesse, Marty is here." She pressed her hand to her heart. "With me every minute, waking and sleeping. I hear his voice. I see his smile. He's making his case quite strongly." Her eyes glistened. "I didn't come here to change my mind. I came here to be the best person I can be in this relationship with Marty. Father Kevin in no way is discouraging me from that."

Jesse took her hand. "Sorry, Mags. I forgot what a stubborn pain-in-the-ass you can be."

Maggie laughed. "Well, don't forget it, Graham." She carefully folded the checkered tablecloth and packed it on top of the items in the picnic basket. "Come on. You need to meet Father Kevin."

Chapter Thirteen

The monastery kitchen was empty, so Maggie left the picnic basket on the counter and led Jesse to the front hall. She rang a bell beside a door leading to the interior of the monastery.

Jesse imagined what the inside would look like. Heavy oak beams? An enormous hearth fit to roast a wild boar? Tapestries on the wall to keep out the cold?

It's not Beowulf, for God's sake.

Brother Luke came to the door. "How can I help you, Sister Angelina?"

Jesse flinched. Apparently, Maggie's decision hadn't made it past this door.

"Brother Luke, I'd like to speak with Father Kevin please."

He nodded, then closed the door firmly.

No girls allowed.

In a few moments, Father Kevin appeared. The apron was gone, and though he wore the black shirt, the opening for the white collar was empty. He smiled and Jesse once again remembered Sister Rose Marie's last diary entry. He would be a man easy to fall in love with. She wondered if he'd ever succumbed.

"Father Kevin, this is my best friend, Jesse Graham."

"Nice to meet you, Jesse." He shook her hand. "Maggie's told me how you connected with Timmy's ghost."

"So now you want to perform an exorcism, right?"

He chuckled, his eyes gentle. "Not at all. Anyone who can help souls to find peace," he glanced at Maggie, "living or dead is A-okay in my book."

"So, you're helping Maggie find peace, right?"

"Jesse..." Maggie warned.

Father Kevin waved her off. "It's okay, Maggie. She's your best friend and it's obvious she looks out for you." He held Jesse's gaze. "I've known Maggie since she was knee-high to a grasshopper. I've never wanted anything but the best for her. But it's never been about what I wanted for her, or anybody else wanted for her. It must be what Maggie wants for herself."

He turned to Maggie. "We're talking as if you aren't right here. You know I only want what's best for you, don't you?"

Maggie smiled. "Yes, I know that." She cocked her head toward Jesse. "She's the one who needs convincing."

A question had been bubbling inside Jesse since Father Murphy opened the door. She could hold it in no longer.

"Did you know Sister Rose Marie who taught at St. Bartholomew Academy?"

Maggie gasped.

Father Kevin reddened.

Was it anger? Embarrassment? Guilt?

The still air closed in on them. No one moved or even seemed to breathe. Church bells pealed above them, and from down the hall she had taken earlier, the aroma of basil, oregano, and garlic floated to her. Cold crept up from the stones beneath her sandaled feet and she fought the urge to shiver.

"Jesse..." Maggie took her arm.

"Yes, I know Sister Rose Marie. We worked together on a project."

The air moved, they breathed, and the bells were silent.

"You know her?" Jesse's ears perked up.

"Yes, but I haven't seen her for years." He broke off his gaze and studied the floor.

The door behind him opened, and Brother Luke stuck his head out. "Phone call for you Father Kevin."

"Thank you." He nodded. "It was a pleasure to meet you, Jesse. I'll see you later, Maggie."

He closed the door softly.

"What was that all about?" Maggie demanded.

"I need to find out what happened to Sister Rose Marie, and I think he knows more than he's saying. Did you notice he used present tense—'I know Sister Rose Marie'—as if she were still around?"

"She is still around though, isn't she?" Maggie crossed her arms.

"You know what I mean." Jesse stared at the door. "Was that an evasive tactic? Does he know she is dead? And how is he involved?"

"You're jumping to conclusions, Jess. You think Father Kevin is guilty of something, don't you?"

"I'd like to hear more about the rumors that circulated when she disappeared."

"They're rumors, that's all. Maybe you'd better leave now. I have to help prepare dinner."

"Mags, I'm sorry. I came here to support you, and all I've done is make you mad."

Maggie's arms were still crossed. "It wasn't the visit I was expecting, that's for sure."

"I wasn't expecting to run smack dab into Father Murphy." She took Maggie's hand. "Can we start over? Do you have time for a walk?"

Maggie shrugged. "I guess so, provided talk of Sister Rose Marie and Father Kevin is off limits."

Jess raised two fingers and crossed her heart. "Scout's honor."

"You were never a scout."

"They wouldn't have me."

They locked arms and walked out into the sunshine.

Jesse looked up just in time to see Father Murphy watching them from an arched, leaded window.

JESSE GNAWED on the end of her pencil. The eraser was long gone and the metal fastener with it. Her seniors' essays on Transcendentalism could not hold her attention, not with the image of Father Murphy seared in her brain. She spit out a piece of yellow paint from the No. 2 pencil as her ambivalent feelings argued.

He seemed so nice.

Why was he watching us?

He's so handsome.

So was Nero.

If Maggie knows and likes, even respects, him, he can't be bad, right?

Why did he turn so red when asked if he knew Sister Rose Marie?

Maybe he loved her.

Maybe he killed her.

So engrossed was she, that the delectable aroma of steaks on the grill didn't stir her. Nor did the approach of a visitor.

"Hey, girl, are you in there?"

Jesse jumped.

The sun illuminated Jam's silhouette in the screen door.

"You look like a saint."

"Well, take a picture, 'cause this is the closest I'll ever get." Jam wore blue jeans and a madras shirt. Her curly black hair was tamed with a red scarf. Slung over her shoulder was a large macrame bag.

"I don't know. You were a saint for helping the other night. Come on in. Would you like a beer?"

"Sure! Saints should hydrate. All those good works."

Jesse laughed and popped the top off a Genny Cream Ale. "I want Joe to meet you."

They headed outside toward the grill.

"Hello!" He waved.

"Joe this is Jam, Sister John Mary."

His face lit up and her stretched out his hand. "Pleased to meet you, Sister. Jesse has told me so much about you."

"Uh oh. That could be good. That could be bad." Laughing, she shook his hand.

Joe unfolded a webbed lawn chair. "Have a seat. Join us for dinner, there's plenty."

"We always cook enough for Marty since he often stops by..."

"Hey, *migliori amici*!" Marty's voice boomed as he rounded the corner of the house.

"...and he's right on time."

Jam lowered her voice. "Oh good. I get to see in action the man who stole Maggie's heart."

Joe unfolded another chair.

Marty waved when he spotted Jam. "Hi."

"Hi," she said.

"Marty, this is Sister John Mary, or as Maggie calls her, Jam."

At Maggie's name his eyes lit up. "Maggie has told me about you."

Jesse smiled. Every time he said Maggie's name it was like a prayer.

"I guess everybody's talking about me. Should I be nervous?"

He held out a hand. "No, I didn't mean she said anything bad. In fact, she said you helped her. A lot. Thank you."

She shook his hand. "You're welcome. She's a special lady."

Marty's grin was as wide as the ocean. "Yes, she is."

"You've got it bad, man." She chuckled.

"Steaks are ready. Let's eat." Joe lifted a sizzling ribeye off the grill and slapped it onto a plate followed by another.

Jesse brought out a salad with garden-fresh vegetables. She hurried to the kitchen and brought out a plate steaming with ears of corn on the cob.

Marty tucked his napkin into his shirt and licked his lips.

"So, Jam, to what do we owe the pleasure of this visit? Which I hope is just the first of many." Jesse crunched into an ear of ripe, yellow corn.

"I had to get away. Sister Alphonse follows me wherever I go. It's really creepy. Sometimes I look up and she's just staring at me."

"What brought this on?" Joe asked.

"She overheard Jesse and me talking about Sister Rose Marie."

"That's your latest ghost, right Jesse?" Marty wiped some butter off his chin.

Jesse sighed. People often called the spirits she encountered "her ghosts." She didn't think of them as ghosts so much as spirits. Those who died with unfinished business. Helen Cavanaugh needed proof that she didn't commit suicide but was murdered. The Seneca woman needed her infant to be buried correctly so he could join their ancestors. Timmy Keegan needed to let his family know where he was and answer their questions about his disappearance.

Biting back a stronger response, Jesse smiled. "Yes, Sister Rose Marie is the spirit I met at the convent."

"And in the grotto." Jam reminded her.

"And in our rock garden." Joe added.

"Your rock garden?" Marty and Jam asked in unison, both staring at it across the yard.

Jesse nodded. "The night Sister Therese fired me."

Marty dropped a pickle on his plate. "You got fired?"

"And rehired. Almost immediately. But I've been banned from the convent."

"So, I'm Jesse's spy." Jam waggled her eyebrows, then shrugged. "If Sister Alphonse will leave me alone."

"I guess you haven't been praying in the grotto then."

Jam patted Jesse's hand. "I will. I promise. But if Sister Rose Marie is coming to you here, maybe you don't need me."

"I want to see her in her own spaces. I don't know why, but I feel like that's important."

Joe nodded. "That's logical if she wants to show you something or lead you somewhere."

Jesse nodded and bit her lip. "I may need you to sneak me into the convent again, Jam."

"No problem. I love living on the edge. I just have to shake Sister Al."

"You'll be sneaking lots of places, *Bella*. Remember, we have a date for the archive room tomorrow night."

"Looking forward to it, Marty."

"Before I forget, the reason I stopped by was to tell you what I found out." Jam reached into the macrame bag and slid out an old yearbook. "1959," she announced. She opened it to a bookmarked page and handed it to Jesse.

Jesse stared at the photograph. A lovely young woman with dark, dancing eyes sat laughing amid several uniformed girls making posters. The caption read "Sister Rose Marie and the Mission Club prepare for the annual carnival." Though she wore the traditional black and white habit of the Sisters of St. Joseph, and the photo was black and white, Sister Rose Marie's energy brought lightness and color to the picture. Jesse's eyes misted.

Jam took the book. "Mission Club has its carnival in early May, so Sister Rose Marie was still alive at the end of the school year. The yearbook comes out at the end of May, so this was probably one of the last photos taken of her."

"This at least gives us a start to a timeline." Jesse sipped her Genny Cream Ale.

Jam thumbed through the pages until she found what she wanted. "There! Check this out."

Jesse leaned in, her eyes widening at the photo. She read the caption below. "Father Kevin Murphy, Chaplain." Here was the man she'd spoken to this afternoon only ten years younger and bearded. His brown eyes held humor, his smile engaging. Forbidden fruit made him more enticing. Father What-a-Waste. She cleared her throat and sat up, heat infusing her face.

"You okay?" Joe asked.

"Yes. Fine." She turned to Jam. "I met him today when I visited Maggie."

Jam raised her eyebrows. "What did you think?"

"What I know is that the rumors that he ran off with Sister Rose Marie are false because he's still a priest and is still here."

"And she isn't." Jam pursed her lips to one side.

"When I asked if he knew her—"

Marty sat bolt upright. "You asked him that?"

"Jesse isn't anything if not forthright." Joe patted her hand.

"What did he say?" Now Jam leaned in.

"He admitted knowing her, even admitted working on a project with her. What was interesting was that he said, 'I know her.' As if he didn't know she was dead."

Marty frowned. "Did he say that to put you off his trail? Try to look innocent?"

"Spoken like a true cop, D'Amato." Joe popped open a fresh beer. "The guy sounds innocent to me."

"I don't know..." Jesse's voice trailed off. "This photo places him on campus, which is opportunity. If they worked so closely together, wouldn't he notice she'd disappeared? I mean, one day she's working beside him and the next day she's gone, and he doesn't notice?"

Marty gestured and Jam handed him the yearbook. "We'll probably get some answers when we check the old case files tomorrow night. Maybe we'll find the date she was reported missing."

Jesse shrugged. "I hope so. But this yearbook from 1959 at least narrows it down. Jam, could you check the 1960 yearbook and see if she's in there?"

"Sure thing. As long as I can shake Sister Al off my tail."

Marty pointed to a photo. "Hey, isn't that Bishop Harris?"

Jesse and Jam peered over his shoulder. Jam leaned closer.

"Sure is." She read the caption. "Newly consecrated Bishop Conrad Harris presides at May Day liturgy before Mission Club carnival."

He stood in the midst of a group of girls in the Mission Club and their moderator, Sister Vincent. The girl in the middle held a dozen red roses. Another photo showed the same girl crowning the statue of Mary with roses.

Jesse gasped. A chill snaked up her spine.

"What's wrong, hon?" Joe took her hand.

She shook her head. "Nothing. It's just...the roses."

"Are you allergic? It's just a photo, Jess." Jam said.

Jesse tore her gaze away from the yearbook. "The last couple of times Sister Rose Marie appeared to me, I was overcome with the smell of roses. I think she's communicating something to me. Somehow roses are tied to her death."

"That gives the bishop opportunity, too. He often visited campus." Marty finished his beer.

"But what would his connection be? What we need is a motive." Jesse sliced into a steaming apple crisp.

"*Bella*, now you sound like a cop." Marty swigged the last of his beer and eyed the dessert.

"There's the rumors about a romantic involvement with Father Kevin, maybe that's the key." Jam said.

Marty shifted in his chair.

Jesse eased his discomfort with a large dollop of whipped cream on his apple crisp.

He didn't touch it.

Jam glanced at him and cleared her throat. "There could be a lot of reasons. And it might not be Father Murphy who did her in."

Joe nodded. "I think you're jumping the gun with your suspicions of him, Jesse."

"You're probably right." She swirled the whipped cream into the apple syrup on her plate, the image of Father Murphy watching from the window searing her mind.

Chapter Fourteen

Just as Jesse opened the door to leave for the police station, the phone rang.

"Hello?

"Hey, Jesse, it's Agent 007 here."

Jesses chuckled. "Hi, Jam. What's up?"

"I snatched a 1960 yearbook and no Sister Rose Marie. And no Father Murphy."

Jesse let that information roll around in her brain for a moment. "So, she must have been killed before the fall of 1959."

"Yes."

"And Father Murphy must have been reassigned. Would they have reassigned him to a Benedictine monastery? He's a diocesan priest, not a priest in an order. It doesn't make sense."

"I can hear the wheels turning. Look, I've got to go to evening prayer."

"Yeah, I'm headed to the police station."

"In handcuffs?"

"No, of my own volition. Marty is taking me to the archive room tonight."

"Good luck. I hope you get some answers. Bye."

"Bye. And thanks, 007."

As she hung the receiver up, Joe covered her shoulders with a light jacket.

"It looks like a chilly rain tonight." He kissed the nape of her neck.

A delightful shiver ran along her spine. "When I get home, I'll need a hot shower and something to keep me warm."

He growled softly in her ear. "I've got just the thing." He wrapped his arms around her, turning her to face him. While one corner of his mouth hitched up in a smile, his eyes were serious. "Be careful, Jesse."

"I'll be with Marty. What could go wrong?"

He pressed his fingers to his lips. "Don't even say that."

———

WHEN JESSE ENTERED the police station, the unusual calm disquieted her. All the desks were empty except Marty's and another officer's in the back corner. The cop sitting there had a smooth babyface. Definitely a rookie.

Am I reaching that age where cops and doctors look too young to be cops and doctors? No. I haven't hit thirty yet.

Next year, lady a nasty inner voice retorted.

Marty caught site of her and waved her over. "Hi *Bella*." He cocked his head toward the young cop, "Wesley can man the floor while we go check out the case files." He grabbed a large key ring, "Hey, Wesley, you're in charge for a few."

Wesley smiled and sat up taller. "Yes, sir."

Even as they descended the stairs, Jesse's unease increased. A shiver ran along her spine. Not a "Joe is kissing my neck" shiver; a what if there are spiders and mice shiver. After all, this was an old building in downtown Seneca Corners. Musty and rich with possibilities of creatures both living and dead.

No more ghosts. One at a time is my limit.

Marty led her to a door with a sign that read "Archives." Flipping through the keys, he found the one he wanted and unlocked the door. Swinging it open, he bowed her through. The last time she'd been here with him, they were more secretive, unsure of who was threatening Jesse's life. This time Marty flipped on the lights with no hesitation.

"You're not taking any precautions, Marty."

"Nah. After all, Sister Rose Marie is at the convent...or I guess in your garden." His eyes darted around. "At least I hope she is."

Jesse patted his arm. "I doubt she'll visit us tonight. You can relax."

"I only met one of your ghosts once, and I don't want to meet one again." He flipped another light on.

She followed him along a row of tall shelves filled with boxes labeled with case names, numbers, and dates.

He clicked his tongue as he ran his fingers along the labels checking dates. "If she disappeared, there might not be any physical evidence." He lowered his arm. "I don't see anything here. Let's check the archive files."

Lined up in rows that extended the length of the room stood tall filing cabinets. They checked dates on each drawer as they passed, Marty reading them softly.

"1959!" He pulled the first drawer open and fingered through the tabbed labels. "Let's start with May just to be sure." One by one he murmured the case name. "Okay, here's June."

Jesse's hopes faded as he repeated the process through June, July, August. When he reached September, he glanced at her.

"Let me recheck." He started at May and continued through August again. He dropped his hands in defeat.

Jesse took a deep breath, her disappointment palpable. Had no one reported Sister Rose Marie missing? How could that be?

"Sorry, *Bella*. Sister Rose Marie not only disappeared from St. Bart's. She disappeared from the face of the earth."

THE PIT in Jesse's stomach throbbed with the rhythm of the windshield wipers as she drove home. She needed answers. Sister Therese blocked her at every turn. Sister Alphonse followed Jam wherever she went. What are they hiding? Were they involved somehow? Surely, they wouldn't kill her, would they? But did they know something that they have covered up all these years? Trying to protect their chaplain?

No matter what Joe said, she had a bad feeling about Father Murphy. Did Father Kevin know that Sister Rose Marie loved him? Did he silence her?

Did one of the sisters do so to avoid scandal?

How could she find answers?

"C'mon, Bert. We're going to the source." She swerved into a driveway and changed direction toward St. Bart's.

Trying to meet up with a ghost on a dark, rainy night was not on her top ten favorite things to do. Especially alone. What had happened to her when she collapsed in the attic room? What will happen if Sister Rose Marie shows up again tonight?

Probably nothing, she reassured herself, one hand on the steering wheel, the other massaging the bruise on her temple.

The rain teemed as she crept up the driveway to St. Bart's. She turned off her headlights, leaving only parking lights to guide her, which made navigation tricky. Another reason to creep along instead of speed. But she was familiar with every turn and bend of this road, so she took her time, preferring to be unobserved.

She parked at the end of the school farthest from the convent and fished around the seat behind her until she found her flashlight.

"Glad I left this flashlight in the car when I left my silent retreat, Bert."

She shut Bert's door as quietly as she could. Pulling up the hood of her rain jacket, she whispered a prayer of thanks to Joe for suggesting she take it along. At least the rain slackened as she made her way along the walk between the school building and the convent. Aiming the beam of light at the ground, she watched for uneven cracks in the cement.

When she reached the back of the buildings, she studied the convent windows. An octagonal extension with stained-glass windows interrupted the straight line of the wall she faced. A light shimmered from the chapel, and she checked her watch. Time for Compline. Through the stained-glass windows she could hear sweet voices floating eerily on the dark, rainy night air. Chill bumps ran along her arms.

If only she still had a key to the convent, she'd hurry up to the third-floor room and wait for Sister Rose Marie to appear. How else could she find out what happened to this sister? Either no one here knew what happened to her—really happened—or they won't say.

When she reached the grotto behind the convent, the rain suddenly stopped. The air was heavy with dampness and the smell of wet grass and early fallen leaves.

Stepping carefully so as not to trip and fall, she wandered to the back of the rock wall that surrounded the statue of Mary Magdalene.

"If you have any power at all, Mary, please keep me safe," she whispered in the gloom.

The narrow passage between the rock wall and the stand of red pine trees behind it was empty. As she peered into the trees, the needles picked at her jacket. Circling around, she returned to the front of the shrine.

"Are you here, Sister Rose Marie?"

Silence.

"I need answers if I'm to help you."

A twig cracked behind her and she spun around. She aimed the beam of her flashlight toward the sound where a raccoon slipped into the black chokeberry shrubs on one side of the shrine. The light illuminated the white blossoms whose delicate almond scent floated to her, but they were overpowered by the scent of the roses. Tonight, it was a pleasant scent...and normal.

A drop of rain splatted on her sleeve, then another. The pitter-pat of another round of showers started, and she pulled up her hood.

Though she hadn't relished another face-to-face with Sister Rose Marie, her heart sank with disappointment. Connecting with ghosts had never been her plan, but the more she did, the more she realized these were desperate souls who needed peace. Once she "met" them, her desire to help was irresistible.

Through the light rain, she peered up at the saint's statue. "I guess Sister Rose Marie is a no-show."

Rain slid down Mary Magdalene's face like teardrops. In the shadows, her expression appeared more disheartened than inspired.

"Sorry you have to stay out in this rain toni—"

She gasped. The scent of roses increased in intensity until her stomach flip-flopped with nausea. Her head swam and the grotto grew and receded as she stared at it.

A soft glow appeared at Mary Magdalene's feet, dimming and shining in rhythm with the movement of the grotto.

"You came," Jesse breathed. She had no strength to do more.

Sister Rose Marie nodded, glimmering through the raindrops.

"I need your help. No one here will help me. And I need to know what you seek." Jesse forced the words out over the stench of rotted roses and the bile that rose in her throat. She held her stomach and closed her eyes, certain she would retch at any moment.

Sister Rose Marie held out her hands in a pleading gesture.

The roses' scent overwhelmed Jesse. She retched in the grass and tried to steady herself, but the dizziness just increased, the smell intensifying.

Her vision faded, everything turning gray. A crack echoed when her flashlight hit a rock as it fell. She followed, her last memory a sharp pain in her temple.

Chapter Fifteen

"Jesse. Jesse!"

From far off, Jesse heard her name. Someone shook her shoulder. She pulled away and tucked further into a ball.

"Jesse, wake up, honey."

Jesse covered her mouth and nose tighter, fending off the stench of roses. Her head throbbed like a frantic drum solo at a rock concert, and she covered her ears to no avail.

"Jesse, please wake up."

Though the voice was distant, she recognized the panic. Her eyes fluttered open and in the glow of a lantern, she recognized Jam. She wore a bright yellow raincoat with a matching hat, rain dripping off the brim. Her eyes were wide with panic, and she held Jesse's hand.

"Jam?" Jesse scanned the garden. "Where am I?" She tried to sit up.

Jam held her down. "Take it easy. We're going to have you checked out before you move."

Jesse's head began to clear. "Sister Rose Marie."

"Yeah, I didn't think you were out here for a picnic."

"How did you find me?"

"Joe called in a panic. He'd tried Marty, but last he saw you was at the police station. I guess he's been running the roads looking for somebody called Bert."

"My car. That's what I call my car. Bert."

"You're not just saying that because you hit your head, right?"

Jesse attempted a smile, but the movement increased the throbbing in her head. "No. For real. I've always called him Bert."

Jam snorted. "Sounds like the perfect man. You give the orders and if he doesn't listen, you shut him down and park him."

Jesse laughed, then groaned and winced.

"Joe called the convent figuring you might have come out to see me. And, by the way, why didn't you include me on this little excursion? He asked for Jam and Sister Alphonse hung up on him. He called again, and she hung up again. He called a third time and asked to speak to the Black sister." Jam's musical laugh echoed in the rain. "She yelled at him, 'She's Sister John Mary, you idiot!' It would be funny if he hadn't been so terrified. Sister Therese just went in to call him and let him know you once were lost but now are found. Were knocked out but now you see."

Jesse smiled. "Amazing, isn't it?"

Jam laughed. "Ah, here come Sister Therese and Sister Vincent. She'll check out your state of health."

The two sisters rushed to them. Sister Vincent bent down to examine Jesse, placing a first aid kit beside her. She felt along her arms and legs, then gently checked Jesse's neck and spine.

"Jesse can sit up," she announced. She nodded to Jam, who helped Jesse sit up.

Jesse blinked as the glow of the lantern split in two and danced in circles. Though the rain had eased to a drizzle, drops seemed to dance before her vision. She closed her eyes.

"I think you have a concussion, Jesse. We should call an ambulance." Sister Vincent poured some water on a clean cloth and wiped the gash at Jesse's temple. Then she took an alcohol swab and gently cleansed it.

Jesse winced. "Ouch!"

"Ouch indeed! What were you doing out here in the dead of

night?" Sister Therese glared at her, but Jesse sensed worry in her expression. Was it for her condition or for what she might have discovered?

Sister Vincent lightly touched the principal's arm. "Perhaps we can ask Jesse her reason for being here later, Sister Therese." She smiled gently at her superior.

Sister Therese nodded and folded her arms.

"Can you stand, Jesse?" Sister Vincent took her arm.

"I think so."

With little effort, Sister Vincent eased her to standing.

"Jesse, Jesse! Oh, babe, are you all right?" Joe pushed past the sisters, Marty behind him.

"Yes, Joe, I'm fi—" Her words were muffled against his shoulder.

He shuddered as he held her close.

"*Bella*, why didn't you tell me you were heading here? I would have come with you, or at least would have known where to look." Marty scanned the area. "What happened, anyway?"

Joe touched the side of her face below the gash. "Who did this to you?"

Jesse raised her hand to touch the spot and Sister Vincent swiped both their hands away. "Let's keep it sterile, please."

"No one did anything to me. I fell."

Sister Therese frowned. "Why were you even back here?"

Jesse glared at her. "Do you really want me to tell you that right now?"

Sister Therese glanced at Sister Vincent. "No. No, not now."

Sister Vincent raised an eyebrow but said nothing.

Joe held Jesse at arm's length searching for other injuries. She wobbled a bit, dizziness overwhelming her, so he held her close again.

"Jesse needs to be seen by a doctor. I think she has a concussion." Sister Vincent shoved the damp cloth and alcohol wipe in her pocket and closed the first aid kit. She stood and threw Jesse a stern look. "And that's an order."

"I'll take her in right now," Joe promised, his voice firm.

She wasn't sorry because now there were ten people instead of five standing around her.

Jam gave her a hug and whispered, "We'll talk soon." Letting go, she spoke so all could hear her. "I know this is a great place for prayer and meditation. It's a favorite of mine, too Jesse, but maybe not at night."

Jesse suppressed a smile. "I'll remember that, Sister John Mary."

Sister Therese rolled her eyes. Sister Vincent's lips twitched the side and she frowned.

THE EMERGENCY WARD was hopping when Jesse and Joe arrived. The smell of antiseptic and fear sent Jesse's stomach into flip-flops.

I hate hospitals.

But given how the room swam, and how a baby's wailing threatened to break her eardrums, she recognized that she needed to be here. Joe steadied her as she walked, and they approached the triage nurse.

After checking in, they sat in puce green vinyl chairs festooned with the crayon designs of a previous occupant. Jesse leaned her head back against the wall and closed her eyes.

Joe had been silent the whole time, but his anxiety and anger floated to her on waves. She wasn't up to the conversation tonight, and she appreciated his silence for now. Despite the noise, she started to doze off.

Someone shook her. "It's best if you stay awake, Jesse."

Jesse peered at the nurse, blinking back the harsh light from the overhead fluorescents. She held her hand above her eyes like a cowboy scout in a Western, trying to see the woman's face.

"Stay awake, hon. The doctor will see you soon."

Jesse gazed around the room at the forlorn and injured crowd. "Right."

Joe took her hand. "Do you want to tell me what happened tonight?" The concern in his voice held a tinge of irritation.

I guess this conversation is going to happen whether I'm ready or not.

She sighed, brushing back an auburn lock that had spilled into her eyes. "Marty and I didn't find anything in the case files at the station. I didn't know where else to turn, so I drove to St. Bart's."

"To ask a statue for help? How very Catholic of you."

Yup. He was angry now that the fear had abated.

"I'd seen Sister Rose Marie in the grotto once, remember? When I met with Jam during my 'retreat.' I thought maybe she would show up again and give me another clue."

"And did she?" He stared ahead.

"Roses."

"Roses?" Now he looked at her. "Are you okay?"

"Remember when Sister Rose Marie visited me in our garden?"

"Yes." He drew the word out. "You got really dizzy and said she gave you a clue."

Jesse nodded. "The overpowering scent of roses. I think it's a clue, Joe. This happened to me when Maggie and I had lunch at the monastery and again tonight. There's something about that scent, but I don't know what it means. Yet. The smell gets so sickly sweet that I get nauseous and pass out. That's how I cut my head. I collapsed and hit a rock."

Joe stared at their intertwined hands. "Jess, you know I support you in this ghost hunting business..."

"Joe, it's not a business. It's a..." She fought for the right word. Gift seemed too full of hubris. Ministry, well, she didn't consider herself a spiritual person which she assumed was required for a ministry.

"Whatever it is, you seem to end up in danger every time. What if Jam hadn't found you? You would have been there all night, bleeding in the cold rain." He drew his lips into a tight line. His voice dropped. "I worry about you." He exhaled sharply. "And sometimes I wish you wouldn't do this."

"That's fair, Joe." She raised their clasped hands and kissed his knuckles. "I wish I didn't have to. But I feel like I have no choice. These spirits need me."

Joe's voice was hoarse. "I need you, too." He wiped his eye.

"Jesse Graham?" A nurse propped open the door to the treatment rooms. "Doctor will see you now."

Jesse stood and weaved. Joe caught her. "I need you, too," he whispered in her ear.

Chapter Sixteen

After a day of lying around the house resting after her concussion, Jesse returned to her classroom. At the beginning of first hour, the fluorescent lights and noisy girls had her wishing she'd stayed home one more day, but by the end of the day, she tolerated classroom life.

At the beginning of sixth hour, a student delivered a message from Sister Therese. When the girl handed it to her, a smirk crossed her face before she turned and left. Jesse noticed the tape that had sealed the message had been pried up and resealed.

"Seniors," Jesse chuckled. She wasn't surprised at the message. A summons.

I would have stopped in to see you in any event, Sister Therese. We have things to discuss.

The bell rang and her students hurried to their seats. Luckily, she had taught the opening scene of *The Great Gatsby* twice already that day, so being distracted by her upcoming chat with Sister Therese didn't interfere with her instruction too much. Plus, as in previous hours, she had them work in small groups for a good part of the hour.

As her students filed out, Sister Vincent entered. The girls gave her a wide berth.

"I see you follow instructions well." She crossed her arms and raised one eyebrow. "Why are you here, Jesse?"

"I got so bored I could hardly stand it. I'm feeling fine...well, maybe just okay."

"Rest is vital with a concussion." The scold in her voice was unmistakable. She moved to sit in a student desk in front of Jesse's but thought better of it and stood. She towered over Jesse, and the desk would have been a tight fit. Not that she was obese, she was large framed with shoulders like an Olympic swimmer.

"Yes, sister." Jesse's response was high and obedient like a student's and they both laughed.

"Seriously, Jesse. You need to take it easy."

Jesse raised her right hand and put her left on her copy of *The Great Gatsby*. "I solemnly swear by the green light at the end of the dock."

Sister Vincent laughed. "Well, that's a pretty solemn promise, Jay and Daisy being the people of integrity that they were. Go home."

Jesse waved the note. "I've been called to the principal's office. After that, I promise to go home."

"Is this summons due to your accident the other night?"

Jesse shrugged.

Sister Vincent studied her. "Why were you really out in the grotto? I don't see you as a meditating-outside-at-night kind of person."

Jesse longed to tell her the reason. Maybe Sister Vincent would know something about Sister Rose Marie. Maybe this sister could offer some information that would help Jesse figure out what happened to her. When she died. How she died. Was she murdered?

But Sister Therese had silenced her. Other than Sister Therese and Jam, no one at the convent was aware of Sister Rose Marie's appearances.

She brought her lips together and looked down at her desk. "I was just out for a stroll."

Sister Vincent snorted. "Yeah. And I'm Twiggy." She sighed. "If you're ever 'out for a stroll' at ten o'clock at night and need help, I'm here."

Shaking her head, she left.

As Jesse walked down the stairs toward the office, she planned what she had to say to her principal. She needed to be prepared because Sister Therese was a force with which to be reckoned and usually controlled any conversation between them.

Well, other forces are at work here, Sister. And I will not abandon them.

<hr>

THE SMIRKING senior walked out the office door just as Jesse arrived. "Good luck," she whispered as she held the door for her.

Ruth, the school secretary caught sight of her and nodded toward the principal's office door. "You can go right in, Jesse."

Jesse pushed through the half door at the end of the counter that separated the students from the principal until they, like she, got called to the inner sanctum. Since the door was open, she knocked on the doorjamb.

Sister Therese looked up from the report she'd been reading. She gestured to the door. "Close the door, please, and have a seat, Jesse."

Jesse did so, realizing that the woman had already taken control.

"How are you feeling? Was it too soon to come back today? You look quite tired."

Her tone was sincere as was the concern in her eyes. Jesse reminded herself they were not enemies. Just two women with different agendas. She unclenched her fists.

"I am a bit tired. It was a tough start to the day but got better as it went along. Being with my students does that. Thanks for asking."

"Good." She leaned her elbows on the desk and steepled her fingers. "What were you doing in the grotto Monday night, Jesse?"

Jesse wasn't sure if she should laugh or get angry. *What the hell do you think I was doing there? Praying? In a downpour?* She reigned in her immediate answer. Honesty was the best policy, right?

"I was waiting for Sister Rose Marie to show up."

Sister Therese collapsed back in her chair and tsked. "You just came by in a teeming rainstorm to wait around for a ghost to show up? And do what? Tell you a deep, dark secret?"

Jesse noted that suggestion. Why say that if no deep, dark secret existed? She waited. Silence was often the more effective defense.

Noises from the outer office drifted through the door. The steady rhythm of Ruth's efficient typing click-clacked as a student begged forgiveness for losing her textbook and promising, "My mother will send the money immediately for a replacement."

Sister Therese sat forward again, folding her arms on the desk. "What did you expect, Jesse?"

Jesse continued to hold the woman's gaze until she broke eye contact and shuffled some papers on her desk. "You put yourself in harm's way." She nodded toward the injury still evident in vivid black and blue on Jesse's temple.

Lurching forward, Jesse splayed her hands out on the desk. "No, you put me in harm's way."

Sister Therese gasped. "Now wait a minute ..."

"You asked me to help you with a ghost in the convent, then prevented any opportunity for me to find out more about Sister Rose Marie."

"I also instructed you to stop your search."

"Too late, Sister. Once a spirit makes contact, they can't rest until whatever is disturbing their peace is resolved. You brought me in, then you sabotaged me at every turn."

The black veil around Sister's face trembled with her anger. "You are to stop." Each word was measured, slow and clear.

"You need to tell that to Sister Rose Marie. You need to go up to the third-floor room and wait for her to appear and tell her to stop."

"Don't be ridiculous." The concern that had been in her eyes now transformed into fear.

"This is not something I initiated, Sister. You did when you told me a ghost was whispering, 'rosary.' I could stop trying to find out what happened, but remember, Sister Rose Marie came to you first. If I'm out of the picture, I guess she'll come back to you."

Sister Therese blanched.

"And another thing. For all your talk of compassion, you are causing her to suffer."

"I just want this to all go away." Sister's voice was plaintive, almost childlike.

"It can if you stop interfering."

Sister Therese stared at nothing and nodded.

Jesse left. Maybe she had controlled this conversation after all. But what was her next step?

———

THE SAVORY AROMA of chicken grilling met Jesse when she opened the door. She followed the scent to the kitchen door and stood at the screen watching Joe and Marty, sitting in identical positions with one ankle resting on the other knee and a beer in hand. She smiled, her heart swelling with love. How blessed she was ... if she believed in that sort of thing.

"Hey, guys." She stepped onto the small back porch.

Joe flipped open the top of a small cooler beside him. "I've got a cold Cream Ale for you, babe." He popped off the cap with the church key resting on the arm of his lawn chair.

"Hey, *Bella*. How you doin'?"

"Much better, thanks, Marty." She kissed Joe, then flopped into the chair beside him. "Except for a brief, but intense, encounter with Sister Therese. I was summoned to the office after school."

"Naughty girl. You're always a rabble-rouser." Marty laughed and clinked his beer bottle with hers.

"I think I made her realize that if I don't continue searching for answers, Sister Rose Marie's spirit might just begin appearing to her again since she was the first to hear 'Rosary.'" She took a deep draught of the beer and sighed. "Maybe now she'll give me free rein to ask the other sisters what they remember about her."

Marty rested his empty bottle on the grass. "I have an idea that might help, too. Since our search of the archives didn't turn up anything, there must never have been a missing person case reported. So, I thought, where else could you find information about members of religious orders? Bingo! *The Catholic Chronicle.* Maybe they have information about her in their files."

Jesse's heart thudded. "Marty, you're brilliant! Do you know anybody there?"

"As a matter of fact, my cousin Flora works there. I'll give her a call."

Jesse bent forward and kissed his cheek. "Thank you."

Joe leaned his elbows on his knees, picking at the label on his bottle. "I wish Sister Therese had won that argument and Sister Rose Marie's ghost had gone back to haunting her."

Jesse's heart sank. She understood Joe's concern because he loved her and wanted her to be safe, but with each ghostly encounter she learned how much these spirits depended on her.

"I'll be careful, Joe. After all, I'm only going to *The Catholic Chronicle's* office."

"Yeah. I seem to remember you saying something like that when you were only going to the archives with Marty. You ended up in ER with a concussion."

She and Marty exchanged glances.

"I need your support in this, Joe."

"And I need you, Jesse."

Chapter Seventeen

Jesse's excitement at meeting up with Marty's cousin Flora at the *Catholic Chronicle* was tempered with painful memories that crowded out all her other thoughts.

As she turned onto Interstate 490 toward Rochester, recollections of good times with her former fiancé Robert, mixed with bad images like walking in on him and her good friend in bed. That had been the catalyst for her move to Seneca Corners.

Her chest tightened at memories of her cruel mother, and of seeing her mother's body splayed across her bed as a warning to Jesse to stop investigating the death of Helen Cavanaugh.

She tightened her grip on the steering wheel, willing the ghosts of visits past to vanish. But they persisted. She turned up the radio, hoping WBBF would block out images she didn't want to see. But even a succession of new Beatles' tunes didn't work.

Finally, she reached the Downtown exit and all her focus had to be on the heavy traffic. *The Catholic Chronicle* was in a small brick building not far from Sibley's department store. She circled the block searching for a parking space, then gave up and parked in the public lot the next street over.

Jesse had called the minute she got Marty's cousin's name and phone number. She jumped at Flora's offer to meet her there on

Saturday. Flora Cipriano's bubbly enthusiasm encouraged Jesse. But she suspected that so much cheerfulness might require a lengthy conversation.

She was wrong.

As she found out when she arrived, it required lengthy and patient listening. And the ability to keep her stomach from doing flip-flops from Flora's overpowering perfume. Perfume that not only caused nausea, but an instant return to the grotto.

Roses.

Was this the clue Sister Rose Marie had been attempting to communicate? That somehow this woman who talked loudly and moved quickly surrounded by a cloud of rose scent would bring answers to Jesse?

Or was heavy rose perfume the reason Flora was banished to the basement room, called the "morgue," that housed old clippings of news articles?

Though Flora was younger than Marty, she resembled her cousin with her dark hair and eyes and beautiful olive skin. Her smile was quick, and her eyes danced with her *joie de vivre*. Like him, she talked loudly and laughed often, as if life were a banquet to enjoy.

She had talked non-stop from the time she'd welcomed Jesse into the building. Her dark curls bounced when she bobbed her head toward an office or an area she was describing as she walked.

"This is the editor's office." Bouncy curls. "Over here are the desks of the copy editors, and over there," bouncy, bouncy curls, "is where the reporters sit to type up and submit their stories." She pointed exquisite, long, red-painted fingernails.

But Jesse liked her—except for the perfume. Flora was sweet and cheerful and trying her best to be helpful.

Jesse hoped she would be extremely helpful since this might be her last chance to find information about Sister Rose Marie.

How would she explain the reason for her visit? She'd told Flora she taught at St. Bart's and was interested in the history of the school. That was fine, but why would she focus on just one sister?

They descended the stairs to the basement, each step causing Jesse's heart to beat faster. Descent to any basement raised prickly goosebumps on her arms and the back of her neck.

When they reached the bottom step, she had a full-blown itching event going on. She rubbed her arms as she followed Flora to a room at the end of the well-lit hall.

Flora spread out her arms and grinned from ear to ear. "This is my domain."

Jesse held a smile for as long as she could, trying to ignore the itching. "Thank you so much for allowing me to enter your domain." She bowed slightly. "I really appreciate it."

"No problem! I love working here, and I love to share my work, though you're the first person who really seemed interested."

"Oh, I am interested all right. Very interested."

"Let's start then." She swept her arm out toward the rows of tall filing cabinets. "These are where we keep all the dead articles. Thus, the name—the 'morgue.'" She giggled. "Down along this wall are the microfiche machines. All our articles have been copied onto film and are searchable there. I always have coffee on, so help yourself." She bounced curls toward a table with a coffee maker and supplies.

"Thanks, Flora, this is great."

"The film is stored on the shelves along the rest of the wall. The boxes are marked with dates. If you need help finding what you're looking for, just holler. Let me show you how to use the microfiche machine." She moved toward a station.

"Actually, I have used them in the past." Jesse recalled her hours spent searching for information about Helen Cavanaugh. She rubbed her eyes just thinking about it. "I think I'm all set."

Flora's face fell. Perhaps she was planning to sit beside Jesse to help her.

And talk.

Jesse took a seat and started the machine. Flora still stood behind her.

Jesse looked up at her. "I don't want to interrupt your work, Flora."

"Oh, sure." Flora scanned the room as if looking for work to do. "Sure." She hurried to her desk.

Once she'd been gone for a couple minutes, Jesse took a deep breath.

But the scent of roses still hung heavy in the air.

While the machine started up, Jesse studied the file drawers, searching for May 1959. Finding it, she threaded the film into the machine and cranked the handle slowly, scanning for any articles about St. Bartholomew's. Since the weekly newspaper served the entire Diocese of Rochester, this was going to be an all-day task. She'd take Flora up on the coffee offer.

JESSE BLINKED her eyes a few times and sat back. Going through the May papers had taken two hours. She yawned and stretched.

"Find what you needed?"

Jesse jumped, not aware that Flora had come up behind her.

"Not yet."

"I'd be happy to help if you're looking for something specific. I know you said you were looking for history of St. Bartholomew's. I went there, so I might know what happened in the 1950s if that's any help."

Despite enjoying the peace and quiet while she was searching, Jesse was tempted to accept Flora's help. Especially if it hurried the process up.

"What year did you graduate?" Jesse's heart sped up.

"1963."

"Did you have Sister Rose Marie?"

Flora screwed up her face and stared at the overhead fluorescent light as if it held the answer. "Hmmm. Nooo, I didn't have her, but I think I remember her. I believe she taught theology and ancient Biblical history."

"That sounds right."

She squinted, searching her memory. "Didn't she leave before I graduated? Maybe when I was a freshman or sophomore."

"Yes. That's probably right." Jesse wanted to give her the exact dates but didn't want to influence what Flora remembered.

Her eyes flew open, and a blush covered her face. "I heard rumors." She whispered, as if anyone else in the empty building could hear them down here.

"Oh?" Jesse raised her eyebrows in invitation. Knowing how Flora loved to talk, she hoped to get useful information.

Looking around, Flora leaned toward her. "They say she ran off with a priest. Father, er...um." Apparently squinting helped her memory. "Murphy! That's it! Father Murphy! They were seen together all over town. Just the two of them. Alone. Suddenly they were both gone." She snapped her fingers. "Like that."

"Do you think that's what happened?"

Flora frowned as if being asked what she thought was a new concept. "I guess I don't know. I mean, it makes sense, doesn't it? If they were together all the time and then they were both gone at the same time..." Her voice trailed off.

Jesse tried to reconcile the disappearance of Sister Rose Marie and the presence of Father Murphy at the monastery with the rumors that ran rampant. Could they have left together and then he changed his mind? Or they had a falling out? And he silenced her? Then Sister Rose Marie returned to the place where she'd felt safe, the convent?

Something about Father Murphy bothered her, and she couldn't put her finger on it. He was handsome, intelligent, polite, practically perfect. Even his white teeth were straight. And his smile. She shook her head.

Flora interrupted her thoughts. "Honestly, I never gave it a lot of thought. I'd heard the rumors so many times, I guess I believed them. But there are other explanations, aren't there?"

She spoke to herself more than to Jesse, but her words tingled along Jesse's spine and the scent of her rose perfume intensified. Flora was delivering a message. A message from Sister Rose Marie.

Flora jumped up, her face flushed with excitement.

"Let's see if we can find anything about Sister Rose Marie in the archives!"

Jesse had to decide how much information to trust Flora with. Certainly, she couldn't tell her about the nun's ghost, but she could narrow their search. She wanted to glean all the information Flora had—if any—before she offered what she already knew.

"Do you remember exactly when Sister Rose Marie disappeared?"

The squinting again, and some face scrunching.

"Let's see. I remember her my sophomore year...no, wait, my freshman year. I graduated in 1963..." She tapped her front teeth. "I thought I would have her for sophomore theology since she was the only sister who taught it that year." She brightened. "I think she left between my freshman and sophomore year. That would be 1959."

This fit with what Jam and Jessie had discerned from past yearbooks.

"Great! Let's start there."

Flora glanced at the roll of microfiche Jesse had just finished with. "May of 1959. Hey, you were really close." She reached for the film, then stopped and studied Jesse. "Why do I think you already knew this?" Flora's demeanor transformed from bubbly to suspicious. "You're not here to do research on the history of St. Bart's at all."

Busted.

Jesse had to come clean as much as she could. Revealing a ghost and a potential murder case couldn't be part of it. Not the way Flora loved to talk.

"You're right, Flora. I got some updated news about Sister Rose Marie, and I thought it would quell the rumors and salvage her reputation and Father Murphy's. I needed trusted, factual resources and Marty thought your expertise with *The Catholic Courier* archives would help."

Flora relaxed.

"I had a window of time to work with, but then to find out you were actually there, well, no source would be better than you."

Flora sat up straighter and smoothed her skirt. She smiled. "I'm happy to help."

Jesse patted her hand. "Thank you."

Flora jumped into action. "You've searched through May issues. Let's look at June."

Though Jesse hadn't wanted a co-researcher, this was the only way to mollify her. And she had been generous to open the archives to her.

"Yes. Why don't you do the search."

Flora grinned. "Okay." She packed the May microfiche in its small white box and returned it to the shelf. Pulling out the next box, she deftly fit it into the reader and started to search.

Jesse couldn't believe that Flora could chatter so much and read the articles at the same time, but Flora pulled out the essence of each story in a nutshell, dispensing diocesan gossip as she went.

"They always post the reassignment of the priests in the June issue. Maybe they had something in here about sisters being reassigned." She stopped. "Here it is!" She read the headline: "Three Sisters of St. Joseph Reassigned for Mission Duties."

Black and white photos showed three smiling nuns. Two pictures were candid shots as the sisters packed their items. Sister Rose Marie's was the one Jesse had seen in the St. Bart's yearbook.

Jesse leaned in, reading the story as Flora read it aloud, using her index finger to keep her place. Jesse read faster. She grabbed Flora's pointed finger and drew it down two paragraphs.

"Look."

Sister Rose Marie Winston, SSJ was transferred from her teaching assignment at St. Bartholomew Academy for Girls in Seneca Corners to join other Sisters of St. Joseph working with the

African American community in Selma, Alabama. Sister Rose Marie taught theology and history of ancient Biblical cultures.

FLORA CLAPPED HER HANDS. "There it is! There's your proof that she did not run away with Father Murphy."

Jesse forced a smile. "Yes, there it is. The truth in black and white."

She fought down the anger roiling inside. No one, including Sister Therese, had ever mentioned Sister Rose Marie moving to Selma. Here was a cover-up if she ever saw one. Who started the rumor about her affair with Father Murphy? Was it a smokescreen? And why did people believe it if this was in *The Catholic Chronicle*? Did they sense a cover-up at that time, too?

Flora babbled away as Jesse pondered the implications of this story. One sentence caught her attention, and she focused in on Flora's chatter.

"...and Sister Alphonse said she'd wanted to go to Selma with the others, too, but her request was turned down at the last minute..."

"When was that?" Jesse interrupted Flora's monologue.

Flora blinked and stopped talking. "When was what?"

"When did Sister Alphonse request to be transferred to Selma?"

"Ummm." Flora donned her thinking face again. "I had Sister Alphonse for homeroom when I was a sophomore, so it must have been right around the time Sister Rose Marie left."

Jesse's mind raced.

Left or was killed?

Chapter Eighteen

"I'm springin' ya' from this joint." Jesse folded Maggie's kerchief into a neat square and tucked it in her friend's suitcase. She took the sweater Maggie held. "You won't need this. This afternoon is going to be as warm as July."

Maggie sighed and gazed around the small room she had occupied in the guesthouse of the monastery. "The peace and quiet has been lovely, but I'm ready to leave." She sat on the bed.

Jesse snapped the suitcase closed and studied her best friend. "Are you, Mags?"

Maggie studied her hands clasped in her lap. After a minute she rubbed her hands together. "I came here to confirm I was following the path God intended for me." She smiled at Jesse. "I'm sure now, but had I not taken this time, I wouldn't have been sure. And that uncertainty would have cast a shadow over my relationship with Marty." She bounced off the bed. "I can't wait to see him!" She grabbed her suitcase and hurried to the door. "Let's go, Graham! Get the lead out."

Jesse chuckled, following her out.

As they drove toward the Keegan cottage, Maggie grew quiet.

"Wondering how your dad is going to greet you?"

"You read my mind. Although he said he accepted it when I

announced my decision to leave the convent, he's also had time to think it over. He wasn't gung-ho then, and I have a feeling he'll be even less so now."

Jesse glanced at her, then back at the road. "You're not the thirteen-year-old he can dictate to anymore. It's your life. You get to call the shots now."

"I know, but it's not that easy." She viewed the scenery passing by her window. "I want to please Dad. I don't like dissension in our family. And I want to..." She shrugged. "I don't want to disappoint him."

Jesse let that thought hang in the air.

"Silly, I know, but it's true." Maggie sighed.

Jesse reached for her hand. "Not silly at all. If I'd had Jim in my life while I was growing up, I'm sure I'd want to please him, too." She returned her hand to the wheel while she navigated a sharp curve. "But not at the expense of my happiness. And what I believe is right for me."

Maggie nodded. "I feel like I'm having to choose between Dad and Marty." Her breath hitched.

"What if it comes to that? I mean, not to be cruel, but we're about ten minutes away from you possibly having to make that decision."

Maggie didn't answer. She fiddled with the hem of her blouse. "I would hope that Dad loves me enough to want me to be happy."

Jesse didn't verbalize her thoughts. It would be too unkind.

Your father stuck you in the convent for penance for his own guilt over Timmy's death. That's not looking out for your happiness.

Instead, she squeezed Maggie's hand. "Of course he does."

Maggie exhaled and nodded.

They pulled into the dirt road that led to the Keegan cottage.

Maggie's knuckles were white. "Marty and I thought it would be best if I greeted my fath...family first, so he'll be here later."

"I think he's picking up Joe."

"Oh, good. Dad likes Joe."

Again, the unspoken words were left unsaid.

As Jesse pulled into the driveway, Siobhan Keegan drew back the curtain and broke into a grin that said "mother love" loud and clear. The curtain dropped, the back door flew open, and Maggie was in her mother's arms in a heartbeat.

"Oh, sweetie! It's so good to see you." Her eyes searched her daughter's, and in that moment, Jesse believed in unconditional love.

Maggie beamed at her. "Hi, Mom."

Siobhan tore her gaze from her daughter and smiled at Jesse. "So good to see you again, Jesse." She pulled her in for a hug. "You're just in time for dinner."

"Hey, Mrs. Keegan. It's great to see you, too." Jesse kissed her cheek, surprising them both. In all the years she'd been coming to this cottage, since ninth grade, she had never kissed Mrs. Keegan. It must have been that unconditional love moment.

"Come in. Come in." Laughing, Siobhan swiped at them with a dish towel.

"Hey, Sis." Sean Keegan was tall and built like a swimmer with broad shoulders and a slim waist. His hair and eyes were dark like Maggie's, and his smile increased his handsome rating by ten. He hugged her and whispered loudly, "Should I still call you 'Sis' even if you're not a sister anymore?"

Maggie laughed and whispered loudly back, "But I'm still your sister, so you can call me Sis."

In unison they said, "As long as you don't call me late for dinner." They laughed and hugged again.

"Hey, Jess." Sean grabbed her into a bear hug.

Jesse returned the hug. "A little birdie told me you just went to Woodstock. How was it?"

His eyes grew wide. "When Jimi Hendrix played 'The Star-Spangled Banner,' the whole place went nuts!"

She laughed. "That must have been awesome. Freshman year, big man. How do you like St. Bonaventure?"

"He loves it." Liam Keegan stood behind his son, placing his hands on his shoulders. "It's exactly where he belongs."

Jesse raised her eyebrows but said nothing. When she'd visited the previous summer, Sean had his heart set on Cornell University.

Sean forced a smile. "It's great. My swimming coach is awesome."

"Atta boy," Liam patted his shoulders. Hard.

Jesse smiled and Sean looked away.

"Hi, Dad." Maggie's voice was soft, tentative.

"Hello, Sister...I mean Margaret...Maggie." His form of address changed with each lowering of Siobhan's eyebrows.

Maggie stepped forward, reaching out to hug him, but only managed to kiss him on the cheek. His hands still grasped Sean's shoulders.

Way to show your favoritism. Jesse bit her lip to avoid speaking it aloud. *Your son who follows your directives gets the contact, but not your "fallen" daughter.*

"Dinner is ready, so let's sit down and eat." Siobhan shooed them to the dining room table.

"Hi, all." Courtney Keegan burst through the door. "Sorry I'm late, but I had to stop for gas." She hugged Maggie. "Hey, Sis."

Jesse's mouth dropped open at the change in Maggie's sister.

Before Jesse discovered what had happened to Timmy Keegan all those years earlier, Courtney barely spoke to her family let alone hugged any of them. Especially Maggie since Liam held her up as the paragon of virtue. Maggie had entered the convent. She was the saintly one. The obedient daughter. How could Courtney live up to that? Not to mention she had been hearing Timmy's ghost for years but realized her family would never accept that.

Now she turned to Jesse and hugged her, too. They had bonded over Jesse's saving Courtney's life and affirming for her that, indeed, she did hear Timmy and was not crazy.

"Hey, Jesse. So good to see you."

Jesse warmed at her sincerity.

"Great to see you, too."

Siobhan passed a heaping bowl of mashed potatoes to Jesse and nodded her head toward the table where Sean already sat.

"What can I help with, Mom?" Maggie asked.

"Here, sweetie." Siobhan managed to get in another hug and a kiss on the forehead as she handed a basket of steaming dinner rolls to Maggie.

Again, Jesse's heart swelled at the demonstration of unconditional motherly love. Something she never had. She blinked back stinging tears.

They sat in their usual places with Liam at the head of the table. He kept his eyes downcast as Maggie sat to his left between him and Sean. In the past, he would ask "Sister Angelina" to say grace. Today he started it himself, eyes still downcast.

"Bless us oh, Lord..."

The others joined in.

Though Sean and Courtney kept the conversation light with his stories of starting as a freshman at St. Bonaventure University and hers of starting as an adjunct professor at Hobart College, an underlying tension filled the room. Liam hadn't looked at Maggie, and she focused on her siblings.

Jesse noticed how pale she was despite her laughter at their jokes and questions she posed. She probably kept asking them to keep the conversation going, which was wise because eventually silence descended.

Liam cleared his throat. "Have you decided to go back to the convent where you belong?"

"No, Dad." Maggie's voice was soft, but firm.

He slammed his fist on the table. "Damn it, Margaret. God called you. Are you turning your back on God?" His voice thundered.

Jesse winced, aware of what was coming. Though Maggie had a gentle nature, she also had Irish heritage. She was about to blow up. She started softly.

"I have just spent almost a month at a monastery praying for discernment...."

"And you didn't listen to God—" Liam shouted.

Maggie's fists were balled on the table, and she leaned forward.

"I listened, Dad. And I heard."

Liam fell back in his chair.

Her voice rose with each word. "I listened to God tell me that I was on the right path. Do you remember when you told me I should enter the convent, Dad? I was your sacrificial lamb offered up because of Timmy. Well, that reason for entering didn't hold up." Her face was as red as the geraniums in the vase behind her. Her voice softened. "Just because I love Marty doesn't mean I don't love God. Or you. My heart overflows with love. There's enough to go around."

Liam gaped at her. The lines on his face deepened, and his hands slumped helplessly on either side of his plate.

"Hello! Am I early?"

Jesse recognized Father Kevin's deep baritone.

When he entered the room, everyone sat frozen in place. Jesse thought they must look like a museum tableau. Maybe in an exhibit about the Inquisition.

"Oh, well, er, perhaps I should return later." He stumbled over his words.

Siobhan stood in a flash. Was this because she was a gracious hostess, or because she was so grateful something happened to end this exchange?

"Sit down, Father. You're just in time for dinner."

His gaze flitted from Liam to Maggie to the almost empty dishes on the table. He held up his hands.

"I've already eaten dinner, but thank you, Siobhan."

She rattled dessert plates and the coffee carafe in the kitchen. "Then join us for dessert."

The priest glanced again at Liam who nodded and indicated an extra chair next to Sean.

"Please, Kevin. Have a seat." His voice didn't sound pleased.

Jesse figured he had planned to rebut what Maggie had said and strongarm her into relenting. For a brief moment she was glad to see Father Kevin. Then she took in his perfect tan, perfect white teeth, and his perfectly pressed slacks and her defenses shot back up. What was it about him?

Father Kevin smiled at Siobhan. "Maybe later, I'm still full from dinner. Hey, Liam, let's take a walk. I want to talk to you about the parish festival coming up."

Liam grunted and rose from the table. Glancing at Maggie, he tossed his napkin onto his plate.

The two men left.

Siobhan put a tray of brownies down in front of Maggie. "Have some dessert, honey. You'll feel better."

Maggie's hands shook as she passed the plate across the table to Jesse. "I don't think brownies will help right now, Mom. Thank you though."

Jesse took a brownie and passed the tray to Sean, but Courtney intercepted it. "Me first. Sean will take them all."

That broke the tension a bit and they laughed.

"You shouldn't have spoken to your father like that." Siobhan reached for Maggie's hand, but Maggie clasped hers in her lap. She started to speak, but Courtney cut her off.

"That's exactly how she should have spoken to Dad. Does he only respect her when she has a habit and veil on? He needs to respect her decision and the fact that she's an adult with a brain... and a heart."

"But he's her father."

"And she has always given him the respect he deserves. But he didn't deserve it today."

Maggie held up her hand. "Hello! I'm right here. I can speak for myself." She took a deep breath. "I have made my decision. No one, not even Dad, is going change my mind. I'm sorry if I've disappointed him...or anyone, but this is my life."

Sean glanced out to the beach where Liam and Father Kevin stood talking. "Wait a minute. Did Dad ask Father Kevin here to help him try to change Maggie's mind?"

"Father Kevin helped me while I was on retreat at the

monastery. He is very supportive, and I doubt he's here in cahoots with Dad."

Siobhan shrugged. "He might have invited him thinking he would help convince you."

Jesse studied the two men at the water's edge. They stood in the same stance, one arm folded supporting the other, a hand at their mouth. Two men in agreement on something.

She wondered just what it was.

Chapter Nineteen

A knock on the backdoor brought Maggie to her feet. Jesse followed right after her.

"Marty!" Pure joy replaced Maggie's anger.

"Maggie!"

For as long as Jesse had known Marty his voice was loud, sometimes gruff, usually joking. But not when he said Maggie's name. So soft it sent shivers through Jesse every time.

He swept Maggie into his arms, one eye on the entrance to the dining room.

Joe stepped around them to embrace Jesse.

Her heart pounded and her body tingled with warmth even though it hadn't been weeks since they'd been together. Maybe it was the memory of how he'd awakened her that morning.

Picking up on Marty's discomfort, Maggie patted his chest. "Dad's outside. Things didn't go too well when I got here today."

"*Che cavolo!*" Marty swept his hand through his hair, causing it to resemble a corn stalk. His worried eyes studied Maggie. "What do you need me to do? Leave?"

"No, stay. Dad will have to get used to seeing us together." She smoothed his hair back in place, then took his hand and pulled him toward the dining room.

Siobhan rose to greet him, wrapping him in a bear hug. "Welcome, Marty. It's good to see you again."

Marty's shoulders relaxed. "Thank you, Mrs. Keegan. It's nice to see you again, too."

Sean held out his hand. "Good to see you, man."

"Thanks, Sean." Marty shook his hand vigorously.

Courtney kissed his cheek. "You're a brave man." She glanced at Maggie. "And a good one."

Marty's smile was crooked, and his face was the color of a pink carnation. "Thanks, Courtney."

Joe and Jesse had hung back partly to give the Keegan family time to show their support of Marty, and partly to stay in an embrace.

Marty turned around. "Hey, get a room, you two." At a look from Siobhan, pink carnation blossomed into the reddest rose. He cleared his throat. "Sorry, Mrs. Keegan."

"Don't be. I was thinking the same thing. Come on everyone, it's extremely warm for September, so the lake should be bearable. Did you guys bring your bathing suits?"

Joe held up a paper bag. "Yup. Maggie gave us a heads-up that swimming would be expected."

"Nice beach bag, Joe," Courtney, teased.

"You can change in the upstairs bedrooms." Siobhan pointed to the stairs.

She didn't say Timmy's room. Not since he'd found peace and so had they.

Marty stared at the two men standing on the shore. He drew in a deep breath and headed toward the stairs.

AFTER CHANGING into her bathing suit, Jesse relaxed in a dark green Adirondack chair on the shore. She smiled at Maggie and Marty floating on two blow-up rafts, their clasped hands keeping them close. Occasionally Maggie's musical laugh and Marty's booming voice echoed across the water.

She checked the front yard for Mr. Keegan, but he was still out back getting Joe's expert opinion on building an addition to the cottage. Jesse smiled contentedly and returned to her book. She'd start the seniors off with Shakespeare. *Hamlet.*

"The play's the thing..." Father Kevin eased down into the chair beside her. "...wherein I'll catch the conscience of the King."

How odd that he would quote such an appropriate line from the play. She studied him, wondering if she would catch his conscience. Get him to reveal information about Sister Rose Marie.

"I get the feeling you don't especially care for me, Jesse." He held her gaze with his deep brown eyes.

She broke the gaze, glancing out at the lake. "How could I dislike you? I don't even know you." She raised one eyebrow at him.

He cocked his head but said nothing.

Jesse felt like she was a kid in the principal's office, or worse yet, the pastor's office.

Damn, silence is powerful.

She wanted to return his gaze and out-stare him, but she was pretty sure she'd lose that contest. He'd had way more practice.

She set her book upside down on the arm of her chair and turned to him. "Did Maggie's father invite you here to join forces with him and try to convince her to return to the convent?"

He smiled. God, he could be a movie star. *The Sundance Kid's* Robert Redford had nothing on him.

"He did, actually."

She almost fell out of her chair. Sean was right. She glared at him. "I hope you were unsuccessful."

He shrugged. "Depends on what your version of success is."

Oh, he was frustrating.

"Did you or did you not support him in trying to convince Maggie to return to the convent?"

"You know I have the seal of confession. I don't reveal what people say to me." His mouth quirked up at the corner.

Stop! Sister Rose Marie didn't stand a chance against his charm.

"You're teasing me."

"It's so easy to get your Irish up." He held out his hand. "Sorry. Am I forgiven?"

She ignored his hand but had to chuckle at the thought of her absolving a priest. "I don't think I'm allowed. The Vatican would frown on that."

"Touché." He eased back and leaned his head against the chair. "Liam did invite me here to talk Maggie into returning to the convent. I did not agree to, and Liam got angry." His voice softened. "It might have disrupted our years of friendship."

Jesse leaned back, watching a cloud float across the sun. He sounded sincere, but something within her didn't want to believe him. What was it?

"So, you've sided with Maggie and now I'm supposed to like you?"

"Aha! I was right! You don't like me."

Her cheeks flamed. She walked right into that. "I don't know you enough to like or dislike you."

"Would it help if I told you I supported Maggie's decision, even knowing the wrath of Liam would fall upon me. And if you'd ever golfed with him, you'd know his wrath." He chuckled.

"I suffered his wrath when I stayed with them and discovered Timmy had never left his bedroom. He kicked me out."

"Ouch. I think what you did to help the family move on in their grief was wonderful. Especially Courtney. She's a changed woman."

"Thanks." She almost didn't say it. She didn't want to be nice to him. The topic of Timmy's ghost brought to mind the ghost of Sister Rose Marie.

"Tell me about Sister Rose Marie." She blurted it out without even realizing it.

He didn't move a muscle. Did he even breathe?

She glanced sideways at him.

He was stone.

"I know about the rumors." He sat up, placing his elbows on his knees, hands clasped. "Is that what you want to know about?" His tone scolded her.

"No, I—"

"C'mon, babe. Time for a swim." Joe scooped her into his arms, but his gaze fell on Father Kevin.

Jesse laughed and kissed his cheek.

Calm down, Joe. Nothing going on here.

"The water looks cold."

"It'll be great. I'll race you to the lake." Setting her down, he grabbed her hand, pulling her along, but not before she saw the priest gesture to her to wait.

But waiting wasn't an option. Joe's grasp held fast.

What was Father Kevin going to tell her about Sister Rose Marie?

Chapter Twenty

Jesse tried to loosen her blouse from her sunburned back. She and Joe had joined Marty and Maggie on rafts out on Seneca Lake, and the suntan lotion didn't tan her skin. She was lobster red. Joe wasn't much better off. They cursed their pale Irish skin all night as they tried to get comfortable enough to sleep.

Lack of sleep and tender skin made Monday seem like a week. As her sixth hour seniors filed out, her note-bearing friend from the office appeared.

"Summons for you, Miss Graham." The girl smirked.

Jesse reopened it—the student's ability to hide her snooping was poor—and read the message. It was a mimeographed copy addressed to the whole faculty.

Bishop Harris will visit on Friday. Classes will be shortened, and luncheon will be served at 11:30 a.m. We will have Mass immediately following and students will be dismissed after that. Please sit with your homeroom and take attendance. A reception will be held for Bishop Harris in the social room.

Between the lines was "attendance is mandatory." The order was as clear as if Sister Therese had said it before folding the memo and the words floated out upon opening. Early dismissal of students usually meant extra time for planning or grading.

"But not on Friday." Jesse sighed and noted the change on her calendar.

"What's that I just heard? Was an expletive embedded in that sentence?"

Jam leaned on the door frame, arms folded. She pushed off and sauntered to the student desk in front of Jesse. She eyed the note as Jesse crumpled it up.

"Hey, he always gives us a day off when he visits."

Jesse tossed the note in the waste basket. "Maybe then I can catch up with grading."

"Already? The school year just started."

Jesse pursed her lips to the side. "Welcome to the world of the English teacher."

"Hey, I learned something about Sister Rose Marie."

Jesse leaned forward. "Tell me."

"She left here to work with other Sisters of St. Joseph in Selma."

"Who told you that?"

"Believe it or not, Sister Alphonse." Jam paused and gazed out the window. "But how can that be if she's showing up here in the convent every night?"

"That's the same story I read in *The Catholic Chronicle*." Jesse tapped her pencil while she pondered this. "I thought it was a cover-up, but maybe she did go to Alabama and returned. Or maybe she died there, and her spirit is haunting a place that felt like home. Or where she thought someone might help her."

"Then she should have shown up at your door. No one around here seems to want to talk about her let alone help her."

"Ahem," Sister Therese coughed softly. "Forgive my intrusion."

Jam rose to leave, but Sister Therese motioned her to sit back down.

Her eyes bored into Jesse. "Bishop Harris has requested a word with you while he is here on Friday, Jesse."

Jesse leaned back in her chair, the springs squeaking in protest. "Me? He doesn't know me from Adam."

Why would he want to see her?

Conrad Harris had been installed as bishop of the Diocese of Rochester ten years earlier in 1959. Aside from being in the pews while he presided at liturgy, Jesse had never been near him let alone exchanged a word with him.

Sister Therese arched one eyebrow. "I'm sure I don't know. But be prepared for his summons throughout the day." She turned on her heel and left.

Jam and Jesse stared at each other.

"What the hell does the bishop want with you?"

Jesse suspected it might just have to do with hell.

FRIDAY MORNING DRAGGED on even though Jesse had to cram six hour-long lessons into three hours. Because of the shortened day, her students' focus was on what fun they were planning for the afternoon.

Jesse dreaded the afternoon.

To her dismay, the afternoon dragged on, too. She'd expected Bishop Harris to approach her—or rather, as Sister Therese had put it, "summon" her—during the luncheon. But he was busy basking in the attention of the sisters and the serving staff who fawned over him.

Over her coffee, she studied the man. In his early sixties, he was not much taller than she, but he walked with a presence that insinuated stature. Silver ran through his dark hair, and he had piercing blue eyes. He walked erect and his movements were sudden and direct.

She thought of a hawk.

He chatted with Sister Therese and other sisters at his table, but his eyes travelled the room. Until they settled on her, a chill-inspiring steely blue scrutiny.

This is it. This is when I get the call.

But his gaze continued on, sweeping the room like a lighthouse beacon. Or the eye of Sauron only blue.

She let out a breath she didn't know she was holding. Why did he affect her so? She wasn't beholden to him. Well, maybe her job... but he had no control over her. She remembered sitting in her fourth-grade class when an earlier bishop visited. In this moment, she realized the fear she experienced that day was directly infused from her fourth-grade teacher Sister Amata like an IV drip. The woman could hardly speak. The man only had power because Sister Amata gave it to him.

Jesse wasn't about to do that. She got up and left the room. She could feel the intelligent blue eyes piercing her back.

She went to the ladies' room and stayed until she was sure he'd be dressing in his vestments for Mass. When she gathered her homeroom students and led them into the chapel, they were the last to be seated. As expected, only the last rows were available. Everyone wanted to be close to the front for the bishop's blessing.

His voice filled the chapel as he celebrated Mass. Now his movements were seamless, a wave on which his voice floated, mesmerizing.

She barely heard him read Luke's Gospel about Mary Magdalene having seven demons, or his homily about her being a reformed prostitute. The homily was a warning about the sins of the flesh. Probably the only topic that would hold the attention of teenage girls. Stifled giggles produced angry stares and "shushes" from the sisters.

After Mass, she joined the sisters and other faculty members for the reception. She and Jam stayed in the back of the room. Maybe he'd forget about wanting to talk to her. She had her back to him but could tell by the widening of Jam's eyes that he was approaching.

"Miss Graham?" His voice held authority, and the scent of incense he had used at Mass clung to him.

When she turned to him, his gaze was as mesmerizing as his voice had been.

"Yes. How do you do, Bishop Harris?" She extended her hand. No way she was going kiss his ring. Of course, not all the sisters had, either.

As they shook hands, his engulfed hers with warmth, his grasp firm but not hard.

He smiled. His face was transformed with softness and welcome. The change put her off balance and she wobbled. He held her steady, then released her hand.

Behind him stood a priest who had assisted him at Mass and instructed the wait staff on the bishop's needs. He was younger, balding with a small moustache. His eyes bulged behind strong glasses.

"Would you please come by my office next Tuesday at..."

The priest checked the already open calendar. "Four o'clock, Bishop."

The bishop nodded. "At four o'clock? Would that give you enough time to finish your teaching day?"

At least he was considerate. Jesse mentally scanned her own calendar. Tuesday after school she often went to the gym. Could she deny his request or negotiate a time? Somehow, she didn't think so. Plus, she was extremely curious.

"Of course, Bishop Harris." She resisted the instinct to bow.

"I look forward to chatting with you then." He nodded and the priest swept him away.

Jam grinned. "Well done, Jesse. You didn't kowtow to him at all."

Jesse stared after the man. "Why does he want to meet with me?"

Chapter Twenty-One

Jesse smiled as she scanned the faces encircling her round oak table. *This is how I love it.*

On her right sat Joe who winked at her. Beside him Susan, his mother, chatted with Maggie who sat across the table. Jim sat between them, listening intently. Marty rounded out the group on Jesse's left. He concentrated on his pot roast.

"I've accepted a job with Canandaigua Academy. I'll be teaching math to juniors and seniors." Maggie fanned herself. "I suspect it will be quite different from teaching at St. Bart's."

"Congratulations, Maggie." Susan put her fork down. "Different, but somehow easier?"

Maggie nodded. "Yes. It would be too difficult to return to St. Bart's. Sister Therese and I discussed it at length." She lowered her gaze to her hands resting on the table. "I think she was relieved to see me go, but unenthused about finding another math teacher."

Jim took another slice of garlic bread. "How long a drive will that be?"

"Not too bad. At most on a snowy day maybe forty-five minutes from our cottage."

Marty looked up from his plate. "I can give you a police escort if the weather's bad." He turned to Jesse. "How did your search at *The Catholic Chronicle* go?"

Jesse chose her words carefully. After all, it was Marty's cousin who had helped her.

"Flora was extremely helpful. We found an article that said Sister Rose Marie was leaving St. Bart's to work with the other Sisters of St. Joseph down in Selma, Alabama."

A mix of expressions circled the table. Confusion, skepticism, and doubt. She waited while they all took this in.

Susan spoke up first. "So perhaps she traveled to Selma for a while and then returned?"

"Or could she have died there and her ghost now... not lives... exists... here?" Joe offered.

"Or it's a cover-up." Marty spread his hands out as if showing the obvious.

Jesse nodded. "I've considered all these things. We know ghosts can travel because, sorry Mags, Timmy followed me out to the cabin in the woods. But I think that's because he was sort of attached to me."

"Then Sister Rose Marie must have attached to you because she showed up in our garden that one night." Joe took a swig of his Genny Cream Ale.

Maggie nodded at him. "But she also must have attached to Sister Therese since she's the first one to hear the ghost."

Jesse pondered that. What else was that woman not telling her?

JESSE SNUGGLED into Joe who curled against her, his arm encircling her. She smiled at the thought of her "family" gathered around the table. Family isn't always blood relatives. Closing her eyes, she drifted in and out of sleep. She pulled away from Joe and lay on her side facing him. His gentle breath tickled her hair. Sleep eluded her and she rolled to her back.

Staring at the ceiling she tried a relaxation method she'd learned.

Relax my toes. Relax my feet. Relax my ankles...

Nothing was relaxing. In fact, her body tensed with each passing minute.

Then the scent of roses drifted through the window.

Sister Rose Marie.

She eased out of bed so as not to awaken Joe. Padding to the window in her bare feet, she tucked the curtain aside and scanned the yard.

Sister Rose Marie stood by the rock garden.

Jesse's heart thudded in her chest so hard she thought it would indeed awaken Joe.

"Wake the dead," she murmured, slipping on her sandals and grabbing a sweatshirt.

Joe mumbled a response, then snored gently.

She didn't want to go out there. She didn't want ghosts in her life. She didn't want mystery and secrets. Joe's arm remained where she had lain, inviting and warm. Why not just crawl back into his arms? Why not let all this go?

Because they need me. These spirits need to find peace. And for some reason, I'm their only hope.

She hurried downstairs and into the backyard. The cool fall air grew frigid as she approached the rock garden.

Sister Rose Marie faded in and out, a wisp of smoke against the black night. Like a dark cave, her mouth moved as if she spoke.

"What is it, Sister Rose Marie? What do you want to tell me?"

The ghost's arm raised in a gesture of petition. Then she pointed to her veil.

"Yes, I'm trying to help you. Please help me to understand." Jesse stepped closer.

The pungent scent of roses as she neared the ghost overwhelmed her. Though her heart continued pounding with fear, Jesse's skin crawled with anger. A desire to lash out overtook her.

"What do you want?" Her voice echoed through the night.

She threw her arms out, begging. Her body shook as she stumbled closer. "What do you want?" Rage rushed through her.

She wrestled a rock from the edge of the garden and threw it across the yard. She stomped her foot. "Tell me."

Bending, she tugged on a bigger rock, but couldn't budge it. "Shit, shit, shit!" Her voice sliced the breeze.

Strong arms encircled her, dragging her away from the rock garden.

"Shhh, Jesse. Quiet babe. It's okay. Everything is okay." Joe's voice was soft in her ears.

She fought him at first, but the anger gradually dissipated. She struggled for a minute, then collapsed like a rag doll in his arms.

Joe eased her down in the grass, cradling her in his lap. He brushed her tangled hair from her face all the time whispering reassurances. "Quiet now. I'm with you." He scanned the yard. "And I think Sister is gone."

As he rocked her, she burrowed into him. "I was so angry, Joe."

He kissed her temple. "I noticed."

"The anger was hers—Sister Rose Marie's. I need to know what she was so angry about."

"How do you plan to find that out?"

She sat up and met his gaze. "From the only person who knew her well back then. Father Kevin Murphy."

He drew back and frowned, dropping his arms. "What about Sister Alphonse? Or Sister Therese. Didn't they know her?"

"Sister Alphonse won't give me the time of day. And Sister Therese wants to stick her head in the sand about this. Every time I ask for her cooperation, she sends out more roadblocks."

She searched his face. Trouble shaded his hazel eyes, and did she detect fear? Reaching for his hand, she pulled him closer.

"There's nothing to worry about, Joe."

His eyebrows shot up. "Nothing to worry about? You think this guy killed Sister Rose Marie. Now you're digging all that mess up. If he did kill her, why not you? Tidy things up a bit."

"Joe..."

"Why wouldn't he? I would think a first murder might be hard, but once you get the hang of it, why not do it again?" He stood up.

She stood and held his gaze. "That's not all, is it? You're jealous of him."

He folded his arms. "Why should I be jealous? He's old."

"Some would say he's handsome."

"Would you say he's handsome?"

She shrugged. What was it about that man? Yes, he was handsome. Everyone loved him. Why did he set her teeth on edge?

"I see." Joe stalked off to the house.

"No, I don't think he's handsome. Well, maybe he is a little. But I'm not attracted to him." She babbled as she followed him. "In fact, I don't like him, but I don't know why."

He spun around almost knocking her down. "Is it because you fear him? Because of what he might have done? Or is it because you don't trust yourself with him?"

"Now you're being ridiculous. He's way older."

"You just made my point. So, you're afraid of him?" Joe's red hair glistened in the back porch light. He stood, arms folded, feet planted wide.

Now Jesse was angry. Comfortable angry. Her own anger, not Sister Rose Marie's out-of-control anger. Arms akimbo she leaned toward him.

"You listen to me, Joseph Reilly. I do not fear that man. I am not attracted to that man. I just plain don't like that man."

"Why not?"

Jesse puffed out a breath. "I don't know. But I know I need to talk to him."

"Do you want me to go with you?"

"Don't you trust me?"

Joe ran his hands through his hair, making it stand up on one side. Which was adorable and caused Jesse to want to wildly kiss him and head back to their bed. What had been their warm, inviting bed.

"You aren't making this easy. I'm trying to support you here."

Her anger had completely dissipated now. She took his hand. "Thank you, Joe."

"One mystery is what happened to Sister Rose Marie. The other is your intense dislike for that guy." His voice was soft as he stroked her cheek with his thumb.

In the moonlight, beneath the star-spattered sky, she realized he was right. Was Sister Rose Marie communicating to her this aversion to Father Kevin? That didn't fit with what she wrote in her journal. But if he killed her, she would carry that anger to her grave.

Hell hath no fury like a woman scorned.

Maybe Joe was right. Maybe meeting with Father Kevin to talk about Sister Rose Marie could be dangerous.

Chapter Twenty-Two

A woman who must have been a marine, judging by her rigid posture and severe expression, met Jesse at the reception area in the diocesan offices.

"Hello, Miss Graham. I am Bishop Harris's secretary. He is expecting you."

She marched Jesse to a sweeping staircase with intricately turned oak balustrades on either side. As they ascended the stairs, the secretary's back remained stiff, not a hair out of place, the seams of her stockings flawlessly straight. The lining of her skirt generated a *swish-swish-swish* cadence.

At the door at the end of the hall, she turned sideways, and Jesse waited for her to salute. Instead, she opened the door to a thickly carpeted office. A large mahogany desk sat sentinel by the door to an inner office. The woman indicated a chair and took her own seat at the desk. Perched on the front edge stood a name sign in black with gold lettering: Agatha Stern.

Jesse smiled. *Fitting.*

Though the high oak wainscoting, and mullioned windows gave a regal effect, the thick carpeting muffled any noise in the stuffy room, stifling Jesse. Icons of Jesus, Mary, and the saints stared down at her from the walls. One saint in particular caught her eye.

A woman with streaming ginger hair and swathed in a scarlet robe held a red egg. Jesse stared and pondered which saint she might be. Patron saint of poultry farmers?

A faint scent of incense tickled her nose. As she grabbed a tissue from her purse, an image of the bishop swinging the thurible around his desk every morning came to mind, and she chortled. When the secretary looked up at her, she coughed into her tissue and nodded an apology.

Any Catholic would be intimidated in this space. But she was not going to let the bishop have his power play. Whatever it was he wanted, she would stay strong.

She jumped when a buzzer sounded on the secretary's desk.

So much for staying strong.

Agatha Stern smirked.

"Bishop Harris will see you now Miss Graham." Never losing her good posture, the secretary rose and opened the inner door for Jesse.

This office was twice as large with even more saints staring at her. She looked around for the one with the egg but didn't spot her in a quick inspection.

On the wall behind his desk, photos of the bishop with community leaders, at various parishes, and attending school functions peppered the wall. One photo was identical to the picture she had seen in the 1959 yearbook. He would have been on St. Bart's campus when Sister Rose Marie taught there.

And died there?

Bishop Harris sat behind another mahogany desk that dwarfed his secretary's. He stood and shook Jesse's hand when she finally reached his desk.

"May I offer you coffee or tea?" His baritone voice rang around the room despite the thick carpet and heavy drapes.

Jesse glanced back to see the woman still standing in the doorway. "Yes, coffee would be great."

She didn't normally drink coffee this late in the day, but she was going to take as much control here as she could.

Bishop Harris nodded, holding up two fingers. The door closed softly behind her.

"Please, have a seat."

He was nothing if not courteous.

She was just plain curious.

When she was seated, he resumed his seat. Her chair seemed a bit lower than his. Or was that an illusion? He certainly sat higher. Maybe both he and his secretary attended the same posture academy.

Jesse sat taller in her chair.

Bishop Harris pushed aside a thick ream of papers that had been centered on his desk. He gave her his full attention. Dark eyebrows arched above steely blue eyes. They reflected no warmth, though his smile was polite. Folding his hands on his desk, he cleared his throat.

"Are you enjoying your teaching assignment at St. Bartholomew's this year?"

A strange question since the year had just begun. Was this a casual conversation starter or a veiled threat? She maintained her straight posture though her back muscles began to protest.

She smiled. Politely.

"Yes, very much, thank you, Bishop Harris."

He let that hang in the air.

Apparently, a threat.

"I've been told you've been curious about Sister Rose Marie."

Ice ran through her veins.

The marine knocked softly and entered with a silver coffee service. She positioned it before the bishop and poured his coffee adding the correct amount of sugar and cream. Of course she would know that, but the action seemed so intimate.

Jesse watched, fascinated.

"Sugar?"

A faint memory of Jim balancing her on his shoulders and calling her "Sugar" floated to her mind. Had this woman just called her Sugar? She startled out of her reverie.

"Excuse me?"

The woman arched an eyebrow. "Would you care for sugar? Or cream?"

"Oh, just cream, thank you."

After settling them in with their coffees, the woman left.

Jesse sipped hers. "Mmmm," she murmured. The rich flavor danced on her taste buds. She was not a coffee connoisseur, but if she had been, this would have passed the test with flying colors.

"Do you like it? It's fair trade from South America."

"Fair trade?" Jesse wasn't familiar with that term.

"Yes, we buy it directly from the grower so there's no middleman and the grower receives a fair price. We try to do that with many of our foods." The bishop sipped his drink. "It's a win-win. We get better coffee; they make a better profit."

Against her will, she liked this guy a little more. But he didn't call her up here to discuss coffee. She waited.

"Did you know Sister Rose Marie?" He cocked his head and raised his eyebrows.

"No."

"Then why this interest?"

A pit formed in Jesse's stomach. Something was off here.

"How did you know I was interested?" She clung to her pledge to stay strong. Who would have told Bishop Harris about her interest? Sister Therese? No, she wanted to keep this haunting hush-hush. Father Kevin? Probably not since he now lived at the monastery rather than being assigned to a parish. Jam? Jesse snorted a little.

"Did I say something funny?"

"No, sir. Bishop." Was she supposed to call him "your eminence?" Well, she wasn't going to. It made her look weak.

"Not at all." She sat taller. "Who told you I was interested in Sister Rose Marie?"

Sitting back, he steepled his fingers and propped them beneath his chin. A researcher pondering a particularly interesting specimen. Clouds moved across the sun that had been shining on the silver streaks in his dark brown hair.

Jesse forced herself not to shift in her seat. She appreciated the power of silence. She used it with her students. It wasn't comfortable on the receiving end.

"If you didn't know Sister Rose Marie, why are you interested in her?" He wasn't going to reveal his source.

"I never knew Sister Rose Marie or anything about her until someone had a special request."

"And who made that special request?"

"I'm not at liberty to say." The pit grew in her stomach.

Bishop Harris lifted the stack of papers and retrieved a folded newspaper. He settled reading glasses on his nose and scanned an article. The sun broke through and glinted off Bishop Harris's lenses.

Jesse recognized the headline and photo at the top of the paper. The edition she and Flora had found in *The Catholic Chronicle* archives. His source must have been Marty's cousin Flora. She was the only person aware that Jesse was researching her. But Flora didn't seem to be high enough up the diocesan food chain to have an in with the bishop.

"Here's an article of interest." His voice was smooth, condescending.

Now he was playing cat and mouse with her. He knew perfectly well she had seen this article. She wasn't going to play his game.

"Yes, the one reporting Sister Rose Marie's transfer to Selma. She left St. Bartholomew's that summer." She held his gaze.

A look of surprise flickered in his eyes before he shoved the newspaper back under the stack. "Sister Rose Marie was a valuable member of our team down in Selma."

"Oh? How long was she there?"

He spread out his hands. "I don't recall. And I'd really prefer you drop this little investigation or whatever you're doing."

"Where did she die?" The words came from nowhere.

The bishop's mouth dropped open.

Jesse was as surprised as he that she had spoken them.

He leaned forward, placing his arms on the desk, folding his hands. "I am asking you to drop this research."

She was certain "asking" meant "telling." She was right; something was fishy about Sister Rose Marie's death. If not, she wouldn't be sitting in this chair with damp armpits.

Now the bishop's voice was soft, almost musical.

"I hear you have a... proclivity... to deal in the occult."

Jesse jerked back. Where did this come from? She recovered and sat up, her mind racing. Who was this source? The same as the one who told him of her research?

"I certainly hope you're not introducing these beliefs to our young Catholic girls at St. Bartholomew's." He removed his glasses, his brows two angry slashes above his piercing eyes.

There it was again. The threat. *Shape up or you're gone. No room for "witches" in our sacred school.*

She would not be intimidated. "I teach English, Bishop. Not religion."

A muscle in his jaw twitched. "It's best you stick to punctuation and classic literature. Leave occult dabbling alone, Miss Graham. And curb your curiosity. Snooping into things that are none of one's business can be quite dangerous." He rose. His own punctuation. The meeting was over.

Full stop.

Jesse tried to hide the trembling in her legs as she rose. So many questions raced through her mind. How did he know all this? What was he hiding? And what was he afraid of?

He'd threatened her, no doubt about it.

Was Joe right? Was it time for her to be afraid?

Chapter Twenty-Three

"Your cousin Flora ratted on me to Bishop Harris." Jesse stood, hands on hips, glaring at Marty.

Marty paused, the coffee pot poised above his mug. "What?" His face was scrunched up as if his grandmother was speaking to him in lightning-speed Italian.

"Flora. She must have told the bishop that I was digging through the archives of *The Catholic Chronicle* for information on Sister Rose Marie."

He poured the coffee into his mug then replaced the pot on the burner. "You think Flora called up Bishop Harris and said, 'Hey, Conrad, I've got some hot info for you?'"

"Well, not exactly like that." Jesse flopped into the chair across her kitchen table from him. "I wish I'd thought to call him Conrad in his office."

Marty stopped, his cup an inch from his lips, and stared at her. "You were in the bishop's office?" His voice dripped reverence.

Jesse rolled her eyes. Raised by Italian Catholic parents in a household ruled over by a devoutly Catholic grandmother, of course Marty would be in awe of the bishop. If he'd been in the hot seat with Conrad, he would have melted into a puddle.

"Yes. I got called in on the carpet for investigating Sister Rose Marie's disappearance. But it wasn't a disappearance, she simply moved to Selma, Alabama." Jesse raked her fingers through her hair, rested her elbows on the table and cradled her face in her hands. "I asked him where she had died."

Marty's eyes were deep brown saucers as he stared at her. "You asked the—" his voice cracked—"the bishop where a ghost died?"

Was he looking at her with reverence or fear? It didn't matter. She stuck out her chin. "Yes, and I'd do it again."

She hadn't thought it possible for his eyes to get any bigger, yet they did.

"But would you really, *Bella*?" His voice was soft.

"Marty, he's hiding something, and I want to know what. Sister Rose Marie will never find peace unless I discover what it is she seeks. And he might just know a piece to that puzzle."

"What puzzle is that?" Joe entered and deposited his lunch box on the counter. He bent and kissed Jesse, lingering for a minute.

"That's my signal to leave." Marty rose.

Jesse pulled him back into his chair. "Marty, will you check with Flora and ask if she talked to the bishop?"

He nodded.

"So how did your meeting with the bishop go today?" Joe grabbed a mug and finished off the coffee.

"Not well." Jesse brushed stray curls off her forehead. "For one thing, he knows I was researching Sister Rose Marie at *The Catholic Chronicle*."

Joe's gaze moved to Marty who held up his hands in protest.

"I didn't tell him."

Joe chuckled. "I didn't think you did. But would your cousin... what's her name?"

"Flora," Jesse and Marty said in unison.

"Yeah, would Flora go to the bishop about this?"

Marty brushed his hands through his hair creating its usual disarray. "Flora is a lowly archivist. She doesn't know the bishop.

And I doubt she'd randomly call him up and say, 'Hey, Bish, I've got some news for you.'"

Jesse put her hands on her hips.

Marty held his hands up in surrender. "I know. I know. I will ask her. But I think you're barking up the wrong tree."

A car door sounded at the front of the house and Marty stood up so fast he almost spilled his coffee. "That's Maggie."

Jesse laughed and smoothed down Marty's hair.

"Hello, everyone." Maggie addressed them all, but she only had eyes for Marty.

He took her by the hand and kissed her gently.

"Maybe this is our signal to leave," Joe said.

Marty didn't hear him, his eyes lingered on Maggie.

She beamed back at him.

"Okay, kids, back to earth."

Maggie laughed and took the chair beside Marty's, but neither let go of the other's hand.

Joe looked at the clock. "Too late for more coffee. How about a Genny?"

Marty and Jesse gave him a thumbs up.

Maggie demurred. "I have to drive home, and I wouldn't want to get stopped by a cop."

Marty made a low noise in his throat. "I could stop you, maybe put you in handcuffs..."

Joe held up a hand. "Okay, stop. Whatever you two do on your own time..."

"We never!" Maggie's face was as red as the tomatoes on Jesse's counter. She frowned at Marty who looked like a scolded puppy.

"Sorry, Maggie."

"Ginger ale for me." She shot him a smile.

"Jesse was just telling us about today's meeting with Bishop Harris." Joe popped a cap off a bottle of Genny Cream ale and handed it to Jesse.

"Oooh, how did it go, Jesse?" Maggie sat forward.

"You mean aside from the thinly veiled threats that my job is at risk if I don't drop this investigation of Sister Rose Marie?"

"Shit," said Joe.

"Holy shit," said Marty.

"Holy Mary," said Maggie.

"I don't know who even told him I was curious about her. Let alone who would tell him I went to *The Catholic Chronicle* to find information."

Maggie stared at Marty.

He held up his hands again. "I know, I know. I'll talk to Flora tonight. But I'm telling you that's like me going to President Nixon to tell him I gave somebody a traffic ticket."

Jesse wrinkled her nose. "I wouldn't want to go to him and tell him anything."

"You get my point. Flora has no pull, no sway. Why would she do that, anyway? Didn't she help you search?"

"Good point." Jesse nodded. "But still..." She stopped, a puzzled look on her face.

"I'll ask her."

"Thanks, Marty."

"Who else knew besides us?"

They pondered that in silence.

"Helloooo!" Susan's voice rang out from the hallway. Preceding her was the aroma of lasagna.

Marty's stomach emitted an epic growl.

Susan set the casserole on the counter, bent to kiss Joe and then Jesse.

Jesse's heart warmed, unused to the sweet attentions of a loving mother.

"What's got all of you so somber?"

Joe poured her a glass of merlot. "Jesse met with the bishop today."

Susan's eyes widened. "With the bishop? Jesse, you're moving up in the world."

"Down is more like it. He tossed out a few veiled threats and a direct order to stop investigating Sister Rose Marie. One wrong step and I'm probably finished at St. Bart's."

"Oh my." Susan's hand fluttered to her mouth.

Jesse filled them in, remembering the conversation in detail.

"Then he mentioned my, and I quote, 'proclivity to deal in the occult.' How does he know these things? Who even talks to him about me?"

"Maybe it's through the grapevine." Maggie sat forward. "Maybe nobody you know went directly to him with all this information. Maybe somebody told somebody who told the bishop."

Susan nodded. "Or mentioned it to someone on his staff who then told him." She slumped in a chair next to Joe.

"What's up, Mom? You've got that look on your face."

She smiled at him, then glanced at Jesse. "I was going to ask if you'd help serve at the Bishop's Banquet, but I doubt you'll want to see him after that meeting."

Jesse shook her head. "No, thank you!" She sat up. "But wait a minute... Yes, I will. He's not going to dictate what I do and where I go. And he's not going to silence me."

Joe grinned and hugged her. "That's my Just Jesse."

Susan clapped her hands. "Okay. I'll let Agatha know."

Jesse's eyes blinked, as that familiar pit hit her stomach. "You know Agatha Stern?"

"Yes, we went to school together."

"And you talk to her all the time?"

"Not really. Just recently because I'm chairing the regional Bishop's Banquet fundraiser."

Even though they continued talking, it was white noise to Jesse.

Susan knew Agatha Stern? Could she have mentioned Jesse's interest in Sister Rose Marie to the bishop's secretary? Is that how he found out? Blood pounded in Jesse's ears.

Joe took her hand. "You okay?"

She started. "Uh, yeah. Sure." She forced a smile.

Could Susan have unwittingly put Jesse into this situation? Where her job had been threatened. Where *she* had been threatened? From now on she would be more careful about what she revealed to Susan.

"Hello, all!" Jim entered with a freshly baked apple pie and a bottle of wine.

"Everybody's here!" Marty shouted.

Joe gave him a quizzical look. "You okay, man?"

"Yes! A-okay. I've been waiting until we were all here." He took Maggie's hand.

She flashed a radiant smile.

He stood and grinned from ear to ear. "Maggie has agreed... Maggie..." His words tumbled as he choked up.

"We're engaged." Maggie's finished for him.

Everyone jumped to their feet in a wild scramble to embrace them, exclaiming congratulations.

Jesse's heart swelled to bursting with happiness for her best friend. This had been a long journey for Maggie. She was happy it led to their future as husband and wife.

For a moment, she forgot that her mother-in-law might have inadvertently betrayed her.

JESSE'S MIND still reeled from Susan's revelation. She pulled on a tee shirt and opened the window a couple of inches. The cool September air floated into the room, stirring the curtains. A movement caught her eye.

An eerie light wavered in the rock garden. Sister Rose Marie.

"I'll be right back. Sister Rose Marie is in the yard." She called loud enough for Joe to hear her above the noise of the shower. Grabbing a pair of sweatpants, she hopped into them as she headed toward the stairs.

The night smelled of fallen leaves and bonfires, and clouds scudded across the moon. Beneath her sandals, dead leaves crackled. As she neared the wraith, it took more distinct form.

"Hello, Sister Rose Marie." Each ghost had guided Jesse to be more comfortable. She recognized that they were spirits searching for peace, and the only way they could find it was through someone on this side who could make things right. Despite the Seneca Woman's wrath that had often put Jesse in danger, the spirit sought peace for herself and her infant.

The pale form of Sister Rose Marie pulsed gently. She held out her hand to show Jesse a rose. Then she raised another hand to show an oval shaped object.

Jesse shook her head. "I don't understand."

"Jesse? Jesse? Are you out here?"

Joe's voice boomed in the hollow night. Sister Rose Marie faded and was gone.

He ran up to Jesse and pulled her close. "What are you doing out here?" He glanced toward the rock garden. "Oh." He dropped his arms. "I was scared. After what the bishop said..."

"I told you I was coming out here."

"When?"

"When you were in the shower. Didn't you hear me?"

"No."

Fear and anger played across his face.

"I'm sorry I worried you."

He pulled her close again. "A part of me wants to agree with the bishop. Ghosts usually bring danger to you, even if it's not from them. They stir up events from the past and it usually pisses someone off. And they go after you."

"I'll be careful, Joe. I promise." She probably sounded like a broken record. But she was sincere.

"I know you have to do this. I know you're helping them, but I always worry that..."

He left the obvious unsaid. That she would end up a ghost herself. He wrapped her in his arms. "Did she give any hints?"

"She showed me two objects. A rose and some kind of ball."

"Do you know what they mean?"

"No idea. But I need to visit Father Kevin again. He seemed to know her better than anyone."

Joe grunted.

"I know. I have a funny feeling about him, too." Jesse kissed his cheek.

"The feeling I have about him isn't funny at all." Joe frowned.

Chapter Twenty-Four

The imposing stone monastery rose before her, and Jesse envisioned knights in shining armor riding forth from it. On the grounds, the vegetable garden sprouted pumpkins and zucchini, and the sheep grazed on the hill. The bucolic scene filled her with peace, and on some level, she could understand the draw of the monastery.

Yeah, Graham, you wouldn't last a week.

She chuckled. So true.

This time she looked askance at the iron knocker and remembered the doorbell. Once again, Brother Luke answered.

Is this his sole responsibility?

He held a sheaf of paper with musical notes dancing across it. Ah, he did have more responsibilities.

"Good evening, Miss Graham. Peace be with you and yours. Father Kevin is expecting you."

Jesse didn't know whether to bow to this blessing, or make the sign of the cross, or curtsy. She nodded. "Peace be to you, Brother Luke."

He smiled. Apparently, she nailed it.

As their footsteps echoed along the corridor, another sound joined in A mesmerizing sound. Chanting voices floated from the chapel in harmony so sweet it squeezed her heart. She wanted to stop and just listen for a while. The singing seeped into her soul like a soothing balm, bringing a deep sense of peace.

Peace. This is what Sister Rose Marie and the other ghosts she'd met sought. She breathed in this moment with holy music flowing over her like warm water. In this instant she believed in God. How could she not?

She hadn't realized she'd stopped. Brother Luke waited, his eyes cast to the stone floor as if he understood what she was experiencing. She took a deep breath and let it out slowly.

He smiled kindly and stretched out his arm, indicating where she should follow. He stopped beside a wooden door and knocked.

"Enter."

Father Kevin's office looked like that of an English professor at Cambridge. Books lining the shelves with other books resting atop them, books piled on tables, books stacked on floors. He stood at a table filled with papers scattered about.

But instead of paintings of literary giants, the walls were covered once again with icons. Jesus, Mary, St. Benedict, and the woman with the red egg. Yet, in another picture she held a white jar.

"Hello, Jesse. It's good to see you again."

Though he smiled, his greeting was cool.

"Thanks for agreeing to see me, Father Kevin."

He studied the pages before him. "Are you here to sling more arrows at me?"

"No. I'm here because I think you were closer to Sister Rose Marie than anyone."

Now she had his attention.

"Why this interest in her?" His face grew hard, a muscle twitched in his jaw. "Do you want to hear a sordid story about a priest and sister?" His face softened. "No, you're sympathetic to Maggie, not judgmental." He peered at her, his brown-eyed gaze intense. "Why are you here, Jesse?"

She pondered what to tell him. He'd been told about Timmy's

ghost, so he wouldn't be surprised that she encountered another. But if he cared for Sister Rose Marie, even just as a dear friend, it would rattle him. She wouldn't tell him. Not yet.

"I know she was at St. Bart's when you were the chaplain. I know she left in 1959 to work in Selma, Alabama."

She waited.

He frowned. "Yes, that can be confirmed anywhere. Why come to me?"

"When did she die?"

His face blanched. He studied the pages on his table.

"Who said she's dead?"

Jesse shut her eyes. He didn't know.

"When was the last time she contacted you?" Her voice was soft.

He slammed his fist on the table, making her jump. He thundered, "Who are you to come here and ask me these questions?" His hands shook, and his eyes misted.

"I've seen her ghost," Jesse whispered.

He stared at her, mouth agape as if ready to ask a question. He said nothing, just stared at her as if trying to comprehend what she'd said. Finally, he sank into his chair and stared toward the mullioned window, appearing to see nothing in the present, but many things in the past.

The chanting reached them, slow and melodic. Soft against her painful words. Rising and falling, ethereal and fragile against the harsh reality Jesse had revealed.

He rubbed his eyes. "I wondered..."

Jesse waited.

As though talking to someone at the window, he continued. "She left for Selma so suddenly. Never even said goodbye..." He clasped his hands in his lap, staring at them. He shrugged. "I wrote, but she never answered."

Jesse's heart broke for this man. He no longer looked commanding and handsome. He looked lost.

"And now you say she's..." His gaze returned to the window.

"You were in love with her." Jesse's voice was almost a whisper.

The chanting filled the silence, rising and falling like ocean waves. Like life itself with its joy and sorrow. Right now, Father Kevin was in the falling music, the decrescendo that sometimes never resolves.

Jesse sat as still as one of the statues along the hallway, letting him absorb this tragic revelation.

He took out a handkerchief, wiped his eyes, and blew his nose.

The chanting ended on decrescendo fading into the stone walls of the monastery.

Father Kevin rose. "The rumors about us weren't true, though I did love her. But I also was—am in love with someone else." He tapped the manuscript. "I am in love with her." He pointed to the first page. "*We* were in love with her."

"You and Sister Rose Marie??

He nodded.

Jesse read the title. *Gospel of Mary.* She frowned. "Someone wrote a gospel about Mary?"

"Not the mother of Jesus. Mary Magdalene."

Her eyes widened. "You're in love with a prostitute?"

Exhaling a breath that sounded like a pressure cooker, Father Murphy scrubbed his hands across his face. "Oh, what the Church has done." His expression held a mixture of exasperation and anger, but his warm eyes showed sadness. "Mary Magdalene was not a prostitute."

Though his words were soft, they struck Jesse with the force of a shout. They buzzed around in her head like a swarm of bees in a garden. She drew them into the order he'd said them, but still they did not make sense. The voice of her high school religion teacher rang in her brain.

"But I've always been told...." Her words faded into the air as the truth of his sank into her heart. "She wasn't?"

His soft smile chased the sadness from his eyes. Now they expressed compassion. "No. In fact, she was wealthy and helped finance the ministry of Jesus. And she followed him."

Jesse let his words sink in. All she'd been taught about this woman collided with what Father Murphy described. She shook her head slightly trying to merge these opposite ideas. She caught him studying her.

"If this is true, why have I been fed such an ugly lie?"

He sighed. "I don't know, Jesse. Power. Control." He stared at his hands. "It started in a sermon given by Pope Gregory way back in 591 when he implied that she was a prostitute. The Church never corrected this misinformation. I guess they used her as an example of someone whose sins were heinous but still could be forgiven."

Jesse's stomach flipped over. The Church's treatment of women had always rankled her. But to totally destroy a woman's reputation and never repent or correct it made her sick.

Father Murphy placed his hand on the manuscript as if he were protecting it. "Who did Jesus first appear to after his death? Mary Magdalene. Then he charged her to tell the other apostles about his resurrection." His eyes met hers. "Yes, Jesse, it makes me sick, too."

She swallowed. *Am I that transparent?* "You and Sister Rose Marie were not only studying this, but you were also going to present it, right?"

"Not only present it, but include it in the high school religious education curriculum. We also planned to include other gnostic gospels such as Thomas and Philip."

"Wait. Who? I've never heard of those gospels."

"Intentionally. The Church has made the word gnostic sound like heresy. Actually, gnostic is from the Greek *gnostikos* which means "knowing" or "able to discern.""

"Then why aren't they included in the Bible?"

"Because they were buried in the desert near Nag Hammadi Egypt..."

Jesse stiffened. That's why that area was circled on the map in the atlas.

"... and not discovered until 1945, long after the canon of the

Bible had been determined. Some of the codices discovered at Nag Hammadi pre-date the four gospels in the Bible. That means some were written much closer to when Jesus lived, written, perhaps, by his followers."

Now Jesse stared out the window, tapping her fingers, the memory of her mother telling her on the way to her first day of kindergarten that Santa didn't exist.

Eileen Graham's eyes had never left the road while she delivered the news. "By the way, Jesse, don't embarrass yourself, or me, by talking about Santa Claus. It's a lie. I probably never should have started that nonsense in the first place."

Her red-tipped fingernails brought a cigarette to her scarlet lips. Jesse was always fascinated by how the end of the cigarette would light up when her mother did that. After that day, the lit tip of a cigarette just made her sad.

Like that day, another deep belief she'd held fell into the hole of deception. How could she have been so naïve?

Because someone you trusted led you down the garden path. In this case a garden with thorns, weeds, and snakes.

"Jesse?" Father Murphy's soft voice brought her back to the present. "Are you okay?"

Jesse dragged her gaze from the window to his gentle eyes. She could see why Sister Rose Marie had been drawn to this man. She nodded.

"Why?" That was all she could muster. She had already stopped going to church except when required at St. Bart's. Rules of the church for women were very different than for men. Women couldn't be priests or deacons. Women had to cover their heads in church with a hat, or a scarf, or a little round chapel veil that looked like a lace doily off the coffee table in the living room. It wasn't unusual for a forgetful woman to have a facial tissue bobby-pinned to her hair. And all the prayers were for men.

And they did this to a woman who was obviously a close follower of Jesus.

She repeated, "Why?"

He shrugged. "As I said, power, control. Maybe feeling threatened that Jesus held a woman in such high esteem. Philip's Gospel clearly says that."

"And Sister Rose Marie knew all this?"

He nodded. "She had all the resources I have here."

Jesse thought of the third-floor room at the convent. How could she get back there?

Chapter Twenty-Five

When Jesse entered Jam's biology lab, two students were washing beakers and test tubes. At a different sink, Jam had her sleeves rolled up and wore rubber gloves and an apron. She picked up a bloody metal pan and immersed it in a tub of soapy water. The red oozed into the soapy water turning it pink. The clinking of glass and the clang of metal on metal echoed in the large room.

"Pig heart day?" Jesse asked.

Jam laughed. "Yes. The glamour of teaching biology. Getting your hands bloody and covered with viscus. There's nothing like holding in your hand the organ that keeps something alive."

"You're serious." Jesse raised her eyebrows.

"As serious as can be." She rinsed the pan. Her eyes sparkled. "I love this sh—stuff." She glanced at the students who were too busy whispering to hear her.

"I have a favor to ask." Now Jesse glanced at the girls.

"Okay, ladies. I'm turning you loose. No more passing notes in class, all right?" She rinsed off her gloves, hanging them on a rack to dry.

"Yes, Sister John Mary," they said in unison. One was the smirking note bearer. She smirked again and Jesse took some comfort in knowing she wasn't the only one on the receiving end.

"Shoo now. Shoo, shoo." Jam flapped her towel at them.

They left, giggling.

"Love those two. They're just like I was—always skirting the edge of acceptable behavior, usually in trouble. Spirit! That's what they have. They'll make great nuns someday."

Jesse chuckled. "I doubt it."

"What can I do for you?"

They sat at a high lab table. The metal chair was cold against Jesse's butt and back. She shivered.

"Too much gory talk?" Jam asked.

"No, your chairs are so damn cold."

"Keeps the students alert. How can I help you...with the favor, not the cold chair. I'm not touching your butt."

Jesse chuckle. "Thank you for that. I need to get into Sister Rose Marie's room again."

Jam sat back, folding her arms. "That didn't turn out very well last time as I recall. We both got called on the carpet and you got fired."

"But I'm back," Jesse sing-songed, grinning.

"Stop that. You look like Lucy flirting with Schroeder."

Jesse settled her elbows on the table, cradling her chin. "I'm more worried about getting you in trouble again."

"Sister John Mary in trouble? Why do I not find that hard to believe?" Arms crossed, Sister Vincent leaned against the door-frame between her classroom and the lab.

Jesse' face burned. How long had she been standing in the door listening? How much had she heard?

The woman entered and pulled up a chair beside Jam. "What's up, ladies? You two look like you got caught with your hand in the cookie jar."

"We were talking about pig hearts," Jesse said.

"We were talking about naughty students," Jam said.

Their words tumbled over each other.

Sister Vincent studied them. "Thou shalt not lie."

They were silent.

"How can I help keep Sister John Mary out of trouble? And how is it related to Jesse's little escapade in the grotto?"

Jesse inhaled deeply. She was tired of fighting a losing battle to find out information about Sister Rose Marie. Sister Therese wanted her to stop. The bishop wanted her to stop. Father Kevin's words came to mind, *As I said, power, control.*

She was tired of being silenced.

"Did you know Sister Rose Marie?"

Sister Vincent fell back against the chair as if she'd been slapped. "What?"

"I need to know about Sister Rose Marie."

"Why?"

"I'll explain that after you tell me about her."

Sister Vincent shifted in her seat and looked from Jesse to Jam and back.

"She was an excellent theology teacher with a vast knowledge of ancient texts and the Gospels. I taught with her here until she left to work at Good Samaritan Hospital down in Selma, Alabama."

"Did she ever come back to St. Bart's?"

The woman thought for a moment. "No."

"Do you remember how she left?"

"Left St. Bartholomew for Selma?" She shrugged. "I suppose she took a Greyhound bus."

"I need to get into her third-floor study."

Jesse felt Jam's gaze burning into her. Could she trust Sister Vincent with the truth of Sister Rose Marie's appearances? Would she see it as "of the devil" as Sister Therese did? Would she inform Sister Therese of Jesse's request to visit the study?

She glanced at Jam, who nodded imperceptibly. Green light.

"Sister Rose Marie was murdered. I've seen her ghost."

Sister Vincent's face went as white as the wimple that surrounded it. "That's impossible," she whispered.

"Jesse sees ghosts all the time. She even communicated with Maggie's—Sister Angelina's—little brother." Jam sounded like a proud mother.

Sister Vincent gazed from one to the other, her eyes wide.

Jesse explained about Sister Rose Marie's appearances and her visit with Father Kevin. As she spoke, Sister Vincent's expression altered from disbelief, to astonishment, to fear.

Jesse understood. Ghosts scared her at first. She shivered as she recalled first meeting Helen Cavanaugh in the attic room of her house. She studied Sister Vincent as the woman contemplated this news. Judging by the shock on Sister's face, most likely Jesse would be called into Sister Therese's office and fired in the morning.

"This is insane. Ghosts aren't real." Sister Vincent looked to Jam for confirmation. "We're scientists, not magicians, right? We don't pull rabbits out of hats or ghosts out of thin air."

Jam's silence was enough.

"You believe this nonsense?" Her eyes darkened with anger.

Jam nodded. "Others have seen her, too."

The noise of the girls' volleyball practice filled the silence. Sneakers squeaking on the wood floor of the gym. Shouts as the ball bounced. The coach's whistle.

"Sister Therese?"

Jam nodded.

"That was why you came here on the silent retreat." Sister Vincent nodded slowly.

"Yes."

"I thought that was kind of strange. A newlywed leaving her husband two weeks after they were married to hang around with a bunch of sisters."

"I'm not supposed to tell any of the sisters, but Sister Therese brought me in to investigate the ghost in the convent."

Sister Vincent stared at her hands clasped on the table, her knuckles white.

"Sister Rose Marie needs peace. She's come to me to help her, but I've been silenced. I'm certainly not supposed to be talking to you about it."

Sister Vincent tapped her fingers on the table. Jesse could almost hear the wheels turning.

The tapping stopped. "Why do you need to get into her study?"

"I need to see her notes about what she and Father Kevin were working on."

At his name, Sister Vincent frowned. "Does he know about this?"

Jesse nodded.

"I wouldn't trust that man as far as I could throw him."

"He seemed deeply moved by what I told him."

Sister Vincent snorted. "I'm sure he did. Did you know he was an actor before he was ordained? Some of his homilies are quite dramatic. He gave quite the performance as Hamlet."

Jesse thought about his reaction when she told him about Sister Rose Marie. His outburst, his trembling, his misty eyes. Had that been a performance just for her?

Sister Vincent stood. "I'll get you into Sister Rose Marie's study."

Chapter Twenty-Six

Jesse winced. This wouldn't be an easy conversation.

"Jesse, no. Please don't go back to the convent at night again. It didn't end well the last time." Joe took his arm from around her shoulders and sat up on the couch.

"Joe, Sister Vincent will know I'm in the convent. I won't be alone." She hugged his arm to her.

"Will she be with you? Or is she going to unlock the door and disappear? What if something happens to you up there? What if Sister Rose Marie goes on a rampage?" He dislodged his arm and paced the room.

"Let me go with you."

"They don't allow men in the convent—especially in their bedroom area."

"Sister Therese no longer allows you there either, but that doesn't stop you."

Jesse wiped her brow. "I have to do this alone. You know I do. If there's a chance for Sister Rose Marie to appear and offer any more clues, I must be alone. Otherwise, she won't show up."

Joe swatted at the back of a chair as he passed. "I don't like this," he muttered.

"All I have to do is gather up her research on Mary Magdalene and the gnostic gospels."

He halted, his eyes wide. "That's all? You told me about all the books and papers in that room. How long will it take you to find what you need? You'll have to sneak back down while they're eating breakfast. Sister Therese will wipe the maple syrup from her lips so it's crystal clear when she says, 'You no longer work here, Jesse.'"

He knelt and took her hands. "But that's not what worries me. I worry that you'll be injured again. This whole situation is getting more and more dangerous."

"Sister Vincent..."

"I don't give a rat's ass about Sister Vincent. I want to make sure you're safe. Some things even Sister Vincent can't fix." His eyes misted.

"I love you, Joe." Jesse's voice was soft. "Thank you for being so concerned about my safety." She kissed him.

"But you're still going to do it."

"Yes. I have to."

THE FULL MOON hid behind heavy clouds as Jesse waited beside the back porch of the convent. Why were nights in September so dark? At the sound of a barred owl, she pulled her jacket closer.

The door opened. She waited to make sure it was Sister Vincent. She was about to step forward when the flash of a lighter lit the face of one of the postulants. The young woman inhaled deeply and blew a stream of smoke into the dark night. Another postulant, holding a glass of water, joined her and the first postulant lit her cigarette. They chatted quietly as they sat on the bottom step.

Jesse took short, quiet breaths as she burrowed into the shrubbery next to the steps. Soon, the women stomped out their cigarettes and tossed them into the glass of water. They walked toward the garbage cans just next to Jesse. Her heart thundered in her chest. Two more steps and they would see her for sure.

The back door opened, throwing a shaft of light across the porch and along the steps. Sister Vincent stuck her head out. "Bring your cigarette butts here, ladies."

One step away from discovering Jesse, they froze and looked at each other.

"I know you have them. I want to make sure they are sufficiently snuffed out before you throw them in that garbage can and start a fire."

With heads hanging, they retreated toward the kitchen door. Sister Vincent looked past them as they stepped inside. The shaft of light disappeared leaving Jesse in the shadows.

Doubling over, she let out the breath she'd been holding. In a few minutes the kitchen light went out and Jesse stood in complete darkness.

The owl hooted again, and she jumped.

"Maybe I should have listened to Joe," she whispered.

The night sounds closed in around her. The whoosh of the owl's wings as it flew past her, and the terrified squeal of a feral cat. Another animal crawled through the woods just beyond the vegetable garden. She prayed it wasn't a skunk.

Shivering, she pulled up her collar.

After an eternity of waiting, the kitchen door opened.

"Jesse? Are you there?" Sister Vincent whispered as she swept the flashlight across the yard.

"Here I am." She emerged from the bushes.

Sister Vincent's eyebrows shot up. "That was a close call."

"Indeed." Jesse climbed the stairs and followed her into the convent.

They crept through the dining room into the front foyer. Sister Vincent stopped and cocked her head, listening. Nodding she ascended the stairway to the second floor. Just before the landing, the stair she stepped on let out a creak that echoed through the hallway.

Jesse was surprised earlier steps hadn't protested the woman's hefty size.

They waited for a moment to ensure no one came out of their bedroom, then continued up the stairs.

Sister Vincent bent and removed her shoes. Jesse did the same. Tiptoeing, they passed Sister Therese's room. Before they took two more steps, the sonorous sounds from Sister Alphonse's room assured them they didn't have to tiptoe.

Reaching the door to the third floor, Sister Vincent fished in the pocket of her habit and brought out a large keychain. She handed Jesse the flashlight.

Jesse aimed it at the ring of keys as Sister Vincent searched for the right one. She held it up and then inserted it in the keyhole. The door eased open seamlessly without a squeak.

Sister Vincent leaned toward Jesse's ear. "I oiled it this morning."

Jesse smiled. "Thanks."

Jesse climbed the stairs crablike, her feet treading on the ends of the steps where creaks were fewer. Reaching the end room, she stopped and bent over, tucking her fingers beneath the door. The air in the room was cool, but not the frigid cold that signaled Sister Rose Marie's presence.

Her heart slowed and her breathing returned to normal.

Upon entering, she switched on the light and turned off the flashlight. She scanned the room wondering where to start. The table. That would have been where Sister Rose Marie would have been working last.

Her head blocked the dim glow from the lightbulb, so she switched on the flashlight again. Neatly stacked papers huddled in one corner of the table, a notebook and pens rested opposite. Tucked alongside the table was a leather courier bag.

Jesse picked up the stack of papers and studied them. They were typed notes describing Jerusalem and Palestine during the time of Jesus. In the middle of the stack was a copy of the manuscript Father Kevin had shown her.

She ran her fingers across the print as she read it again. *Gospel of Mary*.

She read the gospel the opening lines.

Mary questioned her Master, "At the end of an aeon, will all matter be destroyed?"

As she continued, her mind filled with sounds from the past. Bleating donkeys, voices in a marketplace, shouts of vendors. Then the stillness of a meadow. Birdsong and leaves tossing in the breeze.

Icy air tickled her toes through the sneakers she wore. The cold surrounded her until her breath puffed out in tiny clouds.

Sister Rose Marie had arrived.

In the corner of the room near the window she glimmered and flickered in the soft light. Her image solidified and faded as if a mirage. She held nothing this time. No egg. No rose. No jar. Instead, her hands clutched her throat, her mouth gaping as though struggling for breath.

Jesse couldn't breathe either. Her throat was encircled by unknown hands, squeezing, and squeezing until her eyes swam with tiny dots and all vanished into blackness. She held the edge of the table, but couldn't balance, couldn't see. Dropping to her knees, she gasped trying to get air into her lungs.

As suddenly as the choking hands gripped her, they released her, and she collapsed to the floor. She lay there, shivering with the icy cold and the fear of dying. Tears slid down her face as she stared at the ceiling. What had Sister Rose Marie endured, being strangled like that? Did she tremble with the same fear Jesse just experienced?

Suddenly, Jesse's tears weren't caused by fear alone. She cried for Sister Rose Marie and how she suffered in the final moments of her life. Gripping the table, she hauled herself to kneeling, then to standing.

Sister Rose Marie shimmered in the corner, no longer gripping her throat. Tears glistened on her cheeks, and she nodded.

Jesse clasped her hands in a promise. "I will find out who did this to you."

Sister Rose Marie nodded, a slight smile crossing her lips. Then she pointed to the table.

Jesse lifted the courier bag, setting it on the chair. Scooping up the papers and the notebook, she nestled them inside. Then she turned to Sister Rose Marie.

"I will take good care of your research."

Sister Rose Marie raised her arm, ready to point to something else, but stopped.

Sister Vincent stood in the doorway, eyes wide, mouth agape as she stared at Sister Rose Marie.

"No. No it can't be. It can't be!" She shook so that her veil trembled about her head, the rosary beads tied to the rope belt at her waist clattered. With a thud she dropped to her knees and made the sign of the cross. Then she hid her face in her hands.

Sister Rose Marie faded until the corner where she had stood was shrouded in shadow and some warmth returned to the room.

Jesse knelt beside Sister Vincent, wrapping an arm around the trembling woman. "It's all right. Sister Rose Marie is gone."

She helped the woman stand, steadying her. "Just let me get the bag."

Jesse picked up the courier bag and hefted it onto her shoulder. "Let's go." She switched off the light and aimed the flashlight beam down the hall. Placing Sister Vincent's arm across her shoulders, she supported the woman as they walked.

How was Jesse going to get her to her room and exit without being caught?

Sister Vincent whispered as though praying a litany. "It can't be. It can't be. It can't be."

It must be, she thought.

Chapter Twenty-Seven

Sister Vincent wobbled, and her legs gave out. Jesse tried to hold the woman up, but she couldn't. Not that she was obese, more like she was solidly built. And heavy. She slid down along Jesse more than fell on the floor.

"Come on, Sister. You must get to bed."

Glazed eyes stared at her. "How am I supposed to sleep with that devilish apparition one floor away?" She drew her hand across her eyes. "My God. Who would believe..."

With the convent so quiet, Jesse was sure she would hear if anyone below was up and about. She tugged on Sister's arm. "Perhaps you could say the rosary until you fall asleep."

The woman nodded. "Yes. Prayer. Prayer's the thing."

"In which to catch the conscience of the king." Jesse whispered, echoing Father Kevin's Shakespeare quote.

"What?" Sister Vincent's voice was hoarse. "What did you say?"

"Nothing. It was what someone else said."

Sister Vincent reached for the banister and started down the stairs. "Never in all my years did I imagine..."

They reached the second floor and Jesse paused. "I will need to go out the kitchen door. It won't lock behind me."

"What does it matter if the kitchen door is locked? 'Hell is empty and all the devils are here.'" Sister Vincent hissed.

Jesse shuddered. *Another Shakespearean quote. This certainly is a tempest.*

She left Sister Vincent at the door of her bedroom and continued to the kitchen. All clear. The night air hit her like new life. Fresh breath. No choking. And not nearly as icy cold as the room had been.

A LAMP GLOWED through the front window as Jesse pulled into her driveway. After turning off the ignition, she stared at the two windows of the attic room. Where she first met Helen Cavanaugh. Where she found out the secret of the Cavanaugh House. Where a life was taken, and hers was almost as well.

Would her life be in danger once again?

Walking into her house was like walking into a warm blanket. This is where she found Joe. This is where she found family. Despite the heinous act that had occurred here, this house was now full of love.

When she reached the top of the stairs, she tiptoed to the bedroom lest she awaken Joe. She needn't have bothered. He lay bare-chested, one arm crooked behind his head, gazing at her.

"I thought you'd be asleep."

"Not until you were safely home." His voice was soft.

Things were okay with them. She smiled. "I'm safe."

She shed her sweatshirt and unbuttoned her blouse.

His eyes followed her every move. He motioned for her to sit beside him. He tugged off her blouse and wrapped his arms around her to reach her bra clasp.

"You're awfully cold. She showed up, huh?"

"Yes, and scared Sister Vincent to death."

After she wriggled out of her jeans and dropped them to the floor, Joe pulled her in next to him under the blankets.

"I need to warm you up." He kissed her shoulder.

"Yes, please."

He nuzzled against her neck. "I'm glad you're home, Just Jesse."

"So am I, Joe. Very glad." She pulled him closer. "Let me show you how very glad I am to be home."

Chapter Twenty-Eight

Jesse heard the familiar knock at the back door as she poured steaming coffee into their mugs.

"C'mon in, Marty." She grabbed a third mug.

"Morning, *Bella*." He accepted the coffee and sat down. "Can't stay long. I'm picking up Maggie to shop for wedding stuff."

Jesse grinned. He still blushed when he mentioned her name.

"You are so smitten."

"Don't I know it." He stirred sugar into his coffee. "She's amazing."

Joe entered. "Who's amazing? Who could you possibly be referring to?" He punched his best friend's arm playfully.

"Hey, your trip is coming up next week. All set with your presentation? Pretty big stuff, my man."

Joe twitched his mouth to the side, avoiding Jesse's gaze. "Yeah. Pretty big."

Marty put his mug down. "I'm here to tell you that I talked to Flora. She never said anything to the bishop about your research. But she did mention it to her editor, Ed Roth. Maybe he told the bishop."

Jesse nodded. "That would make sense. But why would anyone care?"

Joe shrugged a shoulder. "Could have been a casual conversation. 'What's new at the *Courier*?' 'Oh, just some trouble stirred up by some pesky redhead.'"

Jesse swatted him. "But you're right, Joe. If they know each other, it could've happened something like that. Minus the redhead remark."

Knowing Flora told her editor Ed Roth about Jesse's interest in Sister Rose Marie was a huge relief. That meant Susan most likely wasn't the culprit. She'd said she only met with Agatha Stern occasionally, so there was no reason for them to discuss Jesse at all. Except that Jesse had just been called into the bishop's office. And they were in touch recently to plan the banquet. But did Agatha even know Susan was her mother-in-law? She hadn't taken Joe's name.

I imagine Bishop Conrad Harris vetted me pretty thoroughly.

She sipped her drink, relishing the warm, sweet taste of the coffee. Relishing the warm, sweet atmosphere of her home. Relishing the warm, sweet company of her husband and her friend. And somewhat relieved that perhaps it hadn't been her mother-in-law who ratted her out.

Though she wasn't as afraid of ghosts as she had been at first, each encounter left her drained. As her ability to take on their emotions grew, she found it difficult to disassociate from their fear, anger, and turmoil. Even after making love with Joe the night before, she lay awake trying to push away Sister Rose Marie's distraught emotions.

"Jesse?"

Joe's voice brought her back to the conversation. "Sorry, I was thinking about my encounter with Sister Rose Marie last night."

"She showed up again?" Marty's eyes bulged.

"Yes. And once again she communicated that she'd been strangled." Jesse rubbed her neck. "Communicated it exceedingly clearly."

Joe tightened his lips.

"Sister Vincent also saw her and really freaked out. You know, she told me Father Kevin had been an actor before he was ordained. She said not to trust him.”

“Mom might know about that. You could ask her.” Joe put his cup in the sink. “Oh, she called to remind you of the bishop’s dinner tomorrow night.”

Jesse nodded. “Yes, I remember. I ask her about him then.”

Marty folded his hands on the table like a schoolboy. “You’re going to serve the bishop?”

“I doubt I’ll serve him particularly. But I wonder what he’ll think when he sees me there.”

Joe chuckled. “He’ll probably ask for a food tester.”

* * *

SMIRKING girl handed Jesse a note at the beginning of sixth hour. Again, the tape had been picked at and resealed. Jesse wasn’t about to give her the satisfaction of confirming she knew the girl had opened it.

“Thank you.” She looked at the girl expectantly.

Crestfallen, the girl left, no longer smirking.

“You aren’t going to get a rise out of me,” Jesse whispered to her back. She put the note, unopened by her, on her desk.

“Good afternoon, ladies.”

“Good afternoon, Miss Graham.” Their response was robotic. They’d been doing this ritual for years.

“This afternoon I want you to write about a time you had something to say, and you were silenced. Or a time no one believed what you said. Or a time someone twisted what you said. How did that make you feel? How did you handle it?”

“Oh, good! We’re finally going to read *The Crucible*,” the girl in the front seat of the center row said.

Jesse smiled and glanced at the clock. “You’ve got ten minutes.”

The girls opened their notebooks and Jesse opened the note. She didn’t need to read it. Sister Therese wanted to talk to her. Yup. Right at the end of sixth hour.

JESSE MADE her way to the office. Sister Therese was waiting for her behind the counter. Sister Therese never waited for anyone. Usually, you stood at her desk while she finished whatever she was, or appeared to be, working on. It was a control tactic Jesse recognized.

Her heart beat a little faster.

"Good afternoon, Jesse. Please come in."

This was going to be bad. None of this was Sister Therese's *modus operandi*.

When they were seated, Sister Therese leaned her elbows on the desk and steepled her hands, not as in prayer, palms together, but palms apart, fingers touching. A grounding posture.

Jesse's palms began to sweat.

"I looked at your course curriculum. You're scheduled to teach *The Crucible* next."

"Yes, I did a preliminary lesson on it today. The girls are really excited about it."

"I'm sure they are, but you are not going to teach it."

"What?" Jesse shook her head in disbelief. *The Crucible* was required in St. Bart's literary canon. And the most popular book for her students. What student could resist teenage girls involved in witchcraft? And a love affair at that.

"Instead, you will teach *Moby Dick*."

"*Moby Dick*?" That was an interest killer. Teen girls didn't relate to a man chasing a whale. "But why?"

Sister Therese played with the pen on her desk. She rolled it, then tapped it, then clicked it, and finally put it down. "I don't want it taught."

"Sister Eleana just finished teaching it to her class."

Sister clasped her hands on the desk. "I don't want it taught by you."

Jesse bristled, sitting bolt upright in her chair. "Because I 'dabble in the occult' as you say?"

"Precisely."

"You're afraid I'll convert the girls to become Satan worshippers." Jesse's voice rose a tad.

Sister Therese's eyes were trained on her pen.

Jesse clenched her fists. "You saw Sister Rose Marie. Do you think she worships Satan? Because she's a ghost? You saw her. You heard her yourself."

"I heard something, yes."

"So now you're trying to convince yourself it was the wind? Or a creaking board? Too late. You asked for my help and now you're going to punish me?"

"Not me." She continued to stare at the pen.

"What do you mean by that?"

"Bishop Harris has instructed me that you are not to teach anything that smacks of the occult."

Jesse gasped as if she'd been punched in the gut. She blew out a gust of air. "Bishop Harris...?"

Sister Therese met her gaze. "I'm sorry."

"Were you the one who told him about my interest in Sister Rose Marie?"

Sister Therese raised one eyebrow. "Do you really think I would mention this to him?"

"Well, somebody did because that's why he 'summoned' me. And he threatened me."

"Careful, Jesse..."

"Well, he did. And he's following through. I'm silenced again. First, I can't talk about Sister Rose Marie, now I can't teach a book that has a tremendous impact on my students. Wow."

The girls' cross-country team ran past the window. Their cheeks were rosy, some chatting as they ran, ponytails swinging with each step. Jesse recognized a few of her students. Students who were going to be very disappointed on Monday when she handed out *Moby Dick*.

Chapter Twenty-Nine

Jesse tilted her face to the sun aware that this would probably be one of the last eighty-degree days of the year. She loved early fall when the sky was azure and the tips of the maples hinted at color. The only difference was the crispness of the breeze making a September eighty-degree day just that much cooler than a July one.

While tonight she'd have to see Bishop Harris at his dinner, today she would forget about what he said. She would forget about being silenced, and by his silencing her, silencing her students who would forfeit the opportunity for their voices to be heard while discussing the heinous treatment of women and girls in Salem, Massachusetts in 1692.

Today she would ignore *Moby Dick*, too.

With Joe out on a construction site with his men, she had the day to herself. She sat in the webbed lounge chair, a small table beside her, careful not to spill her iced tea on the reams of paper from Sister Rose Marie's study. She'd been itching to get to them since Thursday night.

Balancing her notebook on her legs, she picked up her copy of the *Gospel of Philip*.

Of all his disciples he loved
his companion, Mary Magdalene,
the most, and kissed her.

Jesse sat bolt upright. Papers flew through the air as adrenalin zinged through her. Stunned, she shivered despite the warmth of the sun. How could this be? It was evident from this writing and from the *Gospel of Thomas* that Mary Magdalene worked closely with Jesus as an integral part of his ministry. Certainly, this was a time when women were oppressed and given little consideration. But Mary Magdalene understood Jesus's message and mission better than any of the other apostles.

And that's why they silenced her.

How dare a woman presume to know the Master's teachings better than the men? Clearly that was Peter's attitude as well as most of the other apostles. Who silenced Mary Magdalene? She practically disappears after the death of Jesus in the canonical gospels of Matthew, Mark, Luke, and John.

Jesse understood Sister Rose Marie's rage. No wonder she was silenced. This would shake the patriarchal Church to its foundations.

Suddenly, strong hands encircled her throat. Gasping, she grabbed at them, trying to loosen the person's grip, but to no avail. Bracing one foot on the ground, she clawed at the hands to wrench them away, but her head swam as the trees above swayed in dizzying circles.

The grip tightened around her neck as hands squeezed tighter. A cloth covered her nose, and a sickly-sweet odor invaded her senses. Roses? No, something else. She struggled for breath, but none came. Just as none had come the other night when Sister Rose Marie appeared in the study.

She could barely keep her hands on her attacker's as drowsiness overcame her. The azure sky faded to black. The buzzing in her head had nothing to do with bees. She was dying.

She was silenced.

BUZZING CONTINUED. And crackling. And breathing was difficult, but she was breathing!

Rubbing her aching throat, she struggled to stand up. When she took a deep breath, thick smoke gagged her. She coughed so hard her sides hurt, and her eyes stung with the haze. A metallic taste coated her mouth, like the time in preschool when she tried to eat a shiny new penny.

Beside her flames blazed in the fire pit, sending orange sparks and charred streamers into the air.

"Oh no! Oh, my God, no."

Her stomach lurched at the sight of papers curling into black ribbons in the flames. Pulling herself up, she lurched toward the trees. She grabbed a hefty stick and thrust it into the fire, pushing the papers to the edges of the fire pit away from the flames.

"No!" She poked at flames licking the pages as they turned to ash. The wind shifted, blowing thick smoke in her face. "No," she croaked, then fell to her knees, overcome with smoke and weariness.

Crawling to the other side of the pit, she resumed her frantic attempt to save Sister Rose Marie's research. A loud crack split the air, and the wood collapsed trapping the remainder of the papers beneath it.

Jesse knelt beside the blaze unable to speak, gasping for breath. Tears streamed down her face as she thought of Sister Rose Marie.

"I'm sorry," she whispered.

SHE STOOD, arms hanging limply at her sides, as the hot water streamed over her. No amount of water could stem the burning of her eyes. When the hot water ran out and cooled, she stepped out of the shower and into a thick towel. Though she lifted her arms to dry her hair, the effort was too much, and she sank to the lid of the toilet.

Slumped, she stared at the black and white octagonal tiles on the floor. They had been here when Helen Cavanaugh stepped out of the shower. They had been here when someone strangled her in the attic room all those years ago. And now, here she was, almost strangled, almost killed.

How was she going to tell Joe? Did she have to tell him? Yes, because of the angry bruises on her neck. Yes, because of the charred papers on the kitchen table. Yes, because when you love someone, you don't lie to them. Even if it means they'll be angry as hell at you.

Gathering all her strength, she draped the towel on the rack and crossed to her room to get dressed. She considered wearing a turtleneck. To hide this from Joe? No, but perhaps to ease into the story before he noticed the evidence of her attack. But the sun still shone, and the windows were open to the balmy fall air.

No, a turtleneck would look ridiculous. And as if she were trying to hide something. That would make it worse.

His truck door slammed and then he called, "Hi, Honey, I'm home."

A smile was in his voice at their favorite ritual. Often dinner was delayed for a while as they celebrated their reunion at the end of a long day. She closed her eyes and wished that would happen today. But it would not. She would not be silent about this.

He called up to her, "I'll get us a beer. It's too beautiful out not to grill." The refrigerator door closed. "Hey, are you grilling me dinner? Or are we going to roast hot dogs and marshmallows?

She'd descended the stairs as he talked.

He was looking out the window at the fire pit, the slanting sun rays highlighting his red hair with golden tint. God, he was beautiful. She didn't want to spoil this evening.

"Hi...Joe." Her raspy voice broke with each word.

He turned to her. "Hey, do you have a sore throat?" As he

approached her, his eyes widened. He held her shoulders. "My God! What happened to you?"

Jesse tried to speak, but another croak was all she could manage.

Joe's shock morphed into rage. He glanced at the fire, then held her gaze. "Who did this to you?" His voice was low and quiet, almost a whisper.

He was at his boiling point. Shouting would have been better.

"I...don't...know." Her throat burned.

He pulled her into a fierce hug. "I'll call Marty."

Jesse nodded as best she could against his shoulder.

When he released her, she slumped into a chair and trembled. The possible consequence hit hard. She crossed her arms on the table and cradled her head on them as tears dampened her sleeves.

Joe's shaking voice echoed from the hallway. "Hey, Marty. I need you to come here right now. Oh, okay. As soon as you can then. Thanks, man."

He returned to the kitchen and sat across from her. Stroking her hair, he lapsed into silence.

Jesse finally raised her head, wiping her tears on her sleeve. "I ... know ... you're angry."

He rubbed his hand across his mouth.

Jesse waited for his wrath. It was deserved.

Instead, he took her hand, his eyes glistening with tears. "This is why I hate you being involved with ghosts. I can't lose you, Jesse." Leaning forward, he hugged her, burying his face in her damp hair. "I know you have to do this, but it scares me to death."

How she relished his arms around her, strong and loving. She caressed his back, the muscles straining against his shirt. "I love you, Joe." She inhaled, her throat burning. "Even if I wanted to...be done with ghosts, I don't think...they'll leave me alone. I certainly never asked for this... gift or curse? And I don't know how to resolve it." She took another shaky breath. "I would end these appearances... if I could. I would stop asking... all the questions."

He pulled her onto his lap and held her. He was her haven, and she snuggled into his arms around her.

Joe leaned back against the chair. "Ask the questions. Help them find peace. This is your gift. I will never ask you to be silent."

The dam broke and Jesse shuddered with sobs. Fear, relief, love for this amazing man flowed through her.

Joe held her as she cried. "Marty will be here soon. He's out on another call." Settling her back on her chair, he rose and put on the tea kettle.

Jesse smiled. He understood what comforted her. A steaming cup of chamomile tea.

As she hugged the cup of tea to herself, they walked out to the fire pit. Wisps of smoke curled into the air and red-orange embers glowed through the blackened pages.

"Those were Sister Rose Marie's copies... of her research and the gnostic gospels." Her heart ached. All Sister Rose Marie's work destroyed by someone who was threatened by it. Probably her killer. Jesse rubbed her throat.

And could have been mine.

"Hey, what's up?" Marty called. He joined them at the fire pit.

Jesse explained what had happened, and as she spoke, Marty's expression darkened with concern.

"*Bella*, are you okay? Do you need to go to the hospital? I can get you there fast in my squad car."

Jesse shivered at the thought of the hospital. "No. I'm fine. Just a little shaken."

Marty examined the marks on her neck. "Hmmmm. Whoever he was, he was strong. You're lucky to—"

"Thanks, Marty." Joe scowled at him. "What should she do? File a report?"

"Absolutely. And we'll photograph that bruising." He studied the fire pit. "I'll call in a forensics team to check out the scene of the..." He cleared his throat. "Let's move inside so we don't disturb the scene. They could find evidence here."

Jesse smiled at the change in Marty when he was performing

official duties. He was in command, no nonsense. "Good idea. I need to get dressed for the bishop's dinner anyway."

They headed for the kitchen, but Marty stopped.

"Do you think this is connected to your ghost hunt?" Back to the Marty she knew.

Jesse twitched her lips to the side and nodded. "Yes."

Marty stared at her, his mind at work. "You need to be very careful, *Bella*."

"Yes, I can see that."

Chapter Thirty

Maggie burst through the door. "Jesse! Jesse, are you all right?" The panic rang in her voice.

Jesse emerged from the kitchen into the arms of her best friend.

"Marty called and told me what happened to you. I've been frantic." She held Jesse at arm's length and looked her up and down.

Unlike her usual jeans and a sweatshirt outfit, Jesse wore a cream blouse and a cream and sage plaid skirt. When Maggie's gaze landed on Jesse's throat, her brown eyes widened in fear. "Oh, sweet Mary, what happened to you?"

Jesse shrugged. "I was surprised from behind by someone who wanted to scare me. The worst thing is they burned all of Sister Rose Marie's research sources."

"No, the worst thing is they tried to kill you."

Jesse remembered the grip on her neck. She shook her head. "No, Mags, if they'd wanted to kill me, they could have. I think they just wanted to scare me."

"Always the optimist, Graham. But why? Could it have been a random act?"

"Why would someone do this to me? If it had been random, it

would probably be someone who wanted to rob me. This guy wanted to burn the material I got from Sister Rose Marie's room."

"But who..." Maggie's voice trailed off.

Jesse had a suspicion. "Only one other person was remotely interested in that material."

Maggie's eyebrows drew down in anger. "You mean Father Kevin."

Jesse said nothing.

"You don't know him like I do, Jess. He is a kind and generous man."

"Then who else?"

Maggie pursed her lips. Finally, her eyes lit up. "Bishop Harris! You said before that he's interested in your investigation."

"So, you think Bishop Harris left his cushy, tastefully appointed office to drive to my house and strangle me so he could burn those papers?"

"Well, would Father Kevin leave the comfort of the monastery to do the same?"

"I don't know. Maybe he wants to publish his findings. Or create a new curriculum. Something that would make him famous, or a noted scholar. He used to be an actor after all. Seems to enjoy the spotlight."

"Yeah, that's why he secluded himself at the mona—"

The front door flew open, and Susan and Jim rushed in.

"Jesse, are you—" Jim's eyes locked on her throat. "I can see that you are not."

Susan gasped and covered her mouth.

"I'm fine. Everyone can settle down." Jesse led them to the kitchen.

As they gathered around the table, Susan, a nurse, examined Jesse's neck. "Hard enough to knock you out, but not to kill you."

"They also used something sweet smelling to knock me out." A fleeting touch of dizziness recurred as Jesse remembered the smell.

"Probably chloroform," Susan said.

"You didn't see him?" Jim asked as he opened a bottle of wine.

"No, nor did I hear him approach."

"It just doesn't make sense. Who would do this to you?" Susan took Jesse's hand.

Jesse and Maggie locked eyes.

Jim looked from one to the other. "So, you have an idea who." He poured the Cabernet Sauvignon into their glasses.

"Jesse thinks it was Father Kevin." Maggie said softly.

Susan's eyebrows shot up. "Father Kevin? Whatever reason would he have?"

Jesse described what she found in Sister Rose's research documents.

Jim scratched his chin as only a professor can. "In academic circles, a find like that would be gold. Not that much has been published about it yet. But Father Kevin could have begun publishing it years ago if that's what he wanted to do. I don't see where you're a threat there."

Jesse related his emotional response when she said she'd seen Sister Rose Marie's ghost. "He seemed so sincere, but I was told he was quite the actor before he was ordained."

Susan nodded. "Yes, he was. I saw him in several performances, including Shakespeare."

"Hamlet." Jesse sipped her wine.

"Yes, I think it was."

Jesse intended to keep her thoughts to herself, but the idea rushed out. "I also wonder if it was the bishop."

"Bishop Harris?" Susan's voice rose in surprise, her wine glass poised halfway to her lips.

Jesse squeezed her eyes closed realizing how ridiculous both suggestions sounded. "Ugh. I know it sounds crazy, but who else even cares about Sister Rose Marie's research? In fact, who else even knows about it? And if not those two, then who?"

Silence fell at the table as they all pondered this.

"I guess I could ask Bishop Harris at his dinner tonight. 'Hey, Bish, did you try to strangle me earlier today?'"

"Not funny, Graham." Maggie picked up her wine glass. "But I do see your point."

"Speaking of the dinner, we need to scoot." Susan stood. "Are you up to this, Jesse?"

"Sure am." Jesse picked up a sage scarf that she'd hung across the back of her chair. "I tried a turtleneck for tonight, but the weather is still too mild. Who can show me what to do with this scarf to hide these bruises?"

Maggie shrugged. "I'm afraid my wardrobe repertoire is quite limited. Now if you had a veil and wimple, I could help you."

Susan chuckled. "Here let me try."

After a few tries, Susan had covered Jesse's throat with an attractive scarf style. "There! You look like Audrey Hepburn."

"No, that would be Maggie." Jesse examined herself in the hall mirror.

Susan chuckled. "That may be, but you look like a movie star yourself. Off we go."

Jesse hesitated.

"What is it, Jess?" Maggie asked.

"Why do I feel like Daniel walking into the lion's den?" Jesse swallowed.

<hr>

THE BANQUET ROOM at the Cathedral Offices building glittered with candles in sconces reflecting the shiny gold filigree in the wallpaper. Tall pillar candles on the tables illuminated the faces of the guests. Crystal goblets tinkled as wine was poured, and polite conversation punctuated with soft laughter filled the room.

Soft music floated above it all, liturgical, of course. Jesse scanned the room looking for the source and gasped. Sitting at the piano with impeccable poise sat Father Kevin. He was dressed in his black clergy suit with its white collar at the base of his throat.

Light from the sconces cast golden highlights in his brown hair. He smiled at the woman chatting with him. Handsome, charming, an accomplished musician. Just like Robert. Robert whom she'd loved. Robert who had cheated on her. Not only hurting her but humiliating her.

She clenched her fist and her jaw. What if she punched him in those teeth that gleamed like a toothpaste commercial? Her stomach roiled, and she stood frozen at the sight of him.

"Are you okay?" Susan touched her elbow to lead her into the room, but Jesse didn't move. "Jesse, are you feeling all right?"

Susan's voice brought her back to the present. She looked around as if seeing the room for the first time. "Yes, I'm fine."

Jesse caught Bishop Harris staring at her. The man speaking to him looked over his shoulder at her and nodded. The bishop turned his gaze to the man but glanced at her once more.

"Susan, who is the man talking to Bishop Harris?"

Susan followed her gaze. "That's Ed Roth. He's the editor of *The Catholic Chronicle*. Let's head into the kitchen and get ready to serve the dinner."

Jesse scanned the room. Mostly men. The women would be in the kitchen, of course.

Organized chaos reigned when they went through the swinging doors. Marine sergeant Agatha Stern gave orders like a drill sergeant, and women hustled about like an army of ants. Agatha spotted Susan and waved.

Her posture didn't slump an inch as she crossed the floor to them. "Hello, Susan. Thanks so much for offering to help toni..." She finally noticed Jesse and raised one eyebrow.

Mr. Spock would have been impressed. Jesse waited for her to say, "Live long and prosper."

Instead, she flared her nostrils and nodded curtly. "Miss Graham."

"Miss Stern." Jesse forced a smile.

She sure doesn't like me. Why? She hardly knows me.

"Give us our orders." Susan picked up an apron and tied it in back.

"We're replenishing the hors d'oeuvres trays." She glanced at

Jesse. "Perhaps Miss Graham could wash up empty trays as they come in."

Jesse almost blurted, "Afraid I'll poison the bishop?" but instead she simply nodded as she tied her apron.

Once appetizers were finished, Bishop Harris's voice echoed through the speaker system.

"Welcome to all of you this evening. I want to thank you for your generous, and hopefully, continuing, contributions to the Diocese of Rochester..."

Jesse turned on the water to wash the last of the trays and block out his voice. Since he forbade her to teach *The Crucible,* thus silencing her, she would silence him the only way she could. She turned the faucet on high.

All the other women were gathered at the door, peeking out at him and the party they weren't invited to attend.

Hearing applause, Jesse turned off the water and dried a tray.

Agatha Stern examined the clean trays carefully. She nodded, satisfied. "Miss Graham, I need you to wait on table fourteen."

Oh brother. Jesse bit her lip.

Susan was about to remove her apron when the door swung open. A few women gasped.

"Thank you, ladies, for all your hard work. It means so much to us." Bishop Harris beamed at the group.

Agatha stepped forward as if receiving an award. "You're most welcome, Bishop Harris."

"Agatha, please join us for dinner." He smiled at the other women and held the door for Agatha.

"When do we get to eat?" Jesse whispered to Susan.

"After we finish cleaning up." Susan winked.

"Even dogs get scraps from the master's table," Jesse mumbled.

Susan laughed and handed her a tray of plated dinners. "Show time."

Jesse had served some of the dinner parties her mother, Eileen Graham, threw, so she was well-trained in "serve from the left, remove from the right." She'd also waited tables in some of

Rochester's finer restaurants during college summers, so she was quite comfortable in this kind of crowd.

Father Kevin finished playing "Now Thank We All Our God" on the piano, then took his seat.

At table fourteen.

As Jesse placed the last plate in front of a buxom woman with bluish hair, he accidentally jostled her arm. A dinner roll slid off the plate, landing in the décolletage of the lady's dress.

"Oh, excuse me, Jesse," Father Kevin apologized.

"I'm terribly sorry, ma'am," Jesse said.

They spoke in unison, and as one, reached to retrieve the errant bun, then as one, pulled their hands back.

"Oh, my word!" The woman secured the roll and set it on her plate. But her gaze never left Father Kevin, and her blush confirmed she wished he'd not withdrawn his hand.

"It was totally my fault. I bumped into Miss Graham."

"No apology necessary, Father."

Did she really bat her eyelashes at him?

Jesse straightened and caught Bishop Harris glaring at her, the pulse in his temple throbbing. If he hadn't tried to strangle her the other day, he appeared to be ready to do so now.

JESSE WAS USED to being on her feet all day in her classroom, but she was out of practice carrying large, heavy trays. She arched her back and grasped the dish towel in both hands to bring her arms above her head and stretched.

"That was the last dish. Are you ready to head home?" Susan asked, hanging a soaked towel on a rack.

"Yes, let me run to the ladies' room and I'll be all set."

She pushed through the kitchen's swinging door right into Father Kevin.

"I was coming to find you and apologize for bumping into you earlier." His brown eyes showed concern.

"You mean the roll that landed 'where no man has gone before'?" She clamped her lips realizing what she'd just said to a priest.

He threw his head back and laughed. "Oh, Jesse, that was a good one."

She let out a breath. "Sorry, Father."

"No, you made my night." He wiped at his eyes. "I'm not a big fan of stuffy affairs. The woman who was supposed to play tonight broke her wrist yesterday. I was 'invited' to play in her stead."

"Your playing was lovely." Jesse was glad it had only been liturgical music. His style was so like Robert's. He was so like Robert.

She gasped. That's why she didn't like him!

It struck her like lightning. He was handsome, charming, well-dressed, smooth. Just like Robert. Robert whom she'd loved. Robert, her fiancé. Robert who cheated on her. She inhaled deeply, remembering that pain.

But he wasn't Robert.

"Are you okay?" Father Kevin reached for her hand.

"Yes, yes. I just remembered...er...something I need to do." She withdrew her hand and fumbled with her scarf.

Father Kevin's eyes widened. "Jesse—" His gaze was glued to her throat.

She quickly adjusted her scarf as best she could.

He scrutinized her. "If you ever need to talk, just call me. Anytime."

"No, it's not what you think. I need to go. Now." She ran to the ladies' room.

She felt his eyes boring into her back.

Chapter Thirty-One

Jesse hit the snooze button on her alarm clock, and lay with her eyes closed, thinking about her encounter with Father Kevin at the bishop's dinner the night before. He genuinely looked shocked at the sight of the bruises on her neck. But could she believe him? He was so smooth and charming.

Too smooth and charming.

Robert had been smooth and charming, and she had trusted him. Loved him. And look where that had gotten her.

Joe stirred beside her. He rolled to her, cupping her against him.

Yes, look where it had gotten her. She smiled.

Thank you, Robert.

But if Father Kevin was her attacker, he was an excellent actor, too. Oscar winning.

"Good morning." Joe's words were muffled against her neck. He moved against her. "I'm assuming you hit the snooze for a little lovin' time."

She snuggled closer. "Mmmmm."

She hit the snooze again ten minutes later.

AFTER SCHOOL JESSE headed to Jam's classroom. When she entered, her head spun and her eyes watered.

"Oh, my God." She grabbed for the counter beside the door. Spots danced before her eyes.

"Jesse, what's wrong?" Jam took her arm and led her to a seat at one of the lab tables. "Jesse? Are you all right?"

Going to the sink, Jam poured a glass of water and brought it to her.

Jesse gratefully accepted it. "The smell."

"It was lab day. We were studying...well, I don't think you want to hear about that. We used chloroform on the drosophila flies. That reminds me, I need to order some more." She patted Jesse's back. "You're white as a ghost. No pun intended...not that that was a pun..."

Jesse's head cleared. She took a long drink of water. "It's what I smelled the other day."

"Where in the world did you smell chloroform?" Jam sat on the stool beside her.

Jesse tucked a finger at the top of her scarf and pulled it down.

"Good God in heaven!" Jam almost fell off her stool. "Who did that to you?"

"I suspect it was whoever killed Sister Rose Marie. Based on what I've experienced during encounters with her, she was strangled." She adjusted her scarf to cover the bruises.

"She can communicate with you?" Jam screwed up her face in disbelief.

"All of the ghosts who have appeared to me communicate their emotions. That leads me to follow breadcrumbs to whoever harmed them. Once justice is done, they go away."

"And that's where the chloroform came in?"

"Yes. He strangled me until I almost blacked out, and then he covered my mouth and nose with a cloth doused with chloroform. When I walked in here, I relived those moments."

"Sister John Mary, where did we put that new box of pipettes?"

Jesse startled at the sound of Sister Vincent's voice.

"Hello, Jesse. How are you today?" Her gaze fell to the scarf. "Looking quite fashionable."

Jesse fingered the scarf, hoping the bruises were concealed well enough. She didn't feel like explaining all this to anyone else.

"Oh, I adore Audrey Hepburn, so I thought I'd give this look a try."

"Hmmm." Sister Vincent squinted at her.

"I have the box here in this cupboard." Jam opened a floor-to-ceiling oak door to reveal neatly arranged supplies for the lab. All the boxes were labeled with contents and a date. She tugged a box off a middle shelf and handed it to Sister Vincent. Then she recorded it on an inventory sheet taped to the inside of the door.

"Thanks." Sister Vincent turned to Jesse. "Did you find what you were looking for the other night?"

"The other night?"

Sister Vincent frowned. "Yes. The other night when...when I let you in." Her face drained to chalk white.

The night Sister Vincent met Sister Rose Marie in the library. Her first ghost. No wonder she blanched at the thought of it.

"Yes. Thanks so much for your help."

The nun studied her.

Jesse shifted after a moment.

"Are you feeling all right?" She positioned the box of pipettes on the table. She had that "Let me take your blood pressure" look that nurses often have.

Jesse's gaze flicked to Jam. "Yes. Yes, I'm fine."

Sister Vincent nodded, retrieved the box, and left.

Jesse's hand flew to her throat. "Was my scarf covering the bruises?"

"Yup. You're fine."

Once again, Jesse wondered how much Sister Vincent had heard of their conversation. She lowered her voice.

"Whoever did this burned all the papers I'd taken from Sister Rose Marie's study. That's why they knocked me out and didn't..."

"Kill you," Jam finished for her. "Geez, you need to be careful.

If this person killed Sister Rose Marie, your life could be in danger, too."

A chill skittered up Jesse's spine. "I know. But I can't stop. Now I'm convinced Sister Rose Marie was killed because of her research. And I've lost it all."

Jam rested her elbow on the lab table and propped her chin on her hand. "She didn't make copies?"

"I never looked. Her study is packed with books and notebooks and papers." Jesse frowned. "But I know who has copies."

"Who?" Jam sat up.

"Father Kevin Murphy."

"Can you go to him and ask for copies?"

"No."

"Why not?"

"Because I think he's the one who did this to me."

As Jesse closed the curtains on the front window, she froze at the sight of a black sedan gliding below a streetlight. Two hours earlier, when she'd lit the reading lamp beside this window, that same car had driven slowly past her house.

Hers was the last house on a dead-end street.

No cars came down this far unless they were visiting her or her neighbors on either side of the street. Occasionally, a lost soul would have to turn around in her driveway, but they didn't appear after that mistake.

This car had driven past the previous night as well. Now the driver turned around in her neighbor's driveway.

"Joe, do you recognize that car?"

He joined her at the window catching sight of the rear of the car as it drove away.

"Hard to see in the dark, but it looks like a Ford Galaxie. Why?"

"That's the second time it's driven by this evening. And I saw it last night, too."

Joe frowned. "I can try and catch up with it."

She gnawed her bottom lip. "He's probably long gone. But I'm going to watch for him."

"We'll watch for him." He scooped her into his arms. "I'm with you, babe."

She melted into him. Sometimes she forgot how afraid for her he was. "Thanks, Joe."

JESSE HAD PLANNED to watch for the strange car after dinner the previous night, but Maggie had called so she was on the phone in the hall and missed her chance. Tonight, she and Joe changed into blue jeans and black sweatshirts and headed out to the front yard.

The sun had set an hour earlier, and Jesse had noted the time of the car's arrival previous nights. Eight-thirty. At eight-fifteen, they stationed themselves beside the large lilac bush near the road and waited.

The night was still, and the waning moon played hide and seek with high feathery clouds. In the woods behind the house, twigs cracked as a family of deer moved through. When the moon peeked out, in its glow, Jesse checked her watch. Eight-twenty-eight. Her heart thumped faster as her eyes strained down the road.

Minutes passed and still no car. At last, an engine grew closer, but her heart sank when a neighbor down the street pulled into his driveway. She shifted from foot to foot, growing disheartened.

"Wouldn't you know he's a no-show tonight." She checked her watch again.

Joe wrapped an arm around her, hugging her close. "Let's give him a little more time." He stopped, listening. "I think this might be him."

The car eased down the road and slowed in front of their house, turning just in time to pull into the neighbor's driveway.

Jesse could barely make out the license plate with its orange numbers against the dark blue background. She squinted, then wrote numbers on the palm of her hand with a black magic marker.

Joe whispered near her ear. "Yes, it's a Ford Galaxie. Probably a '68."

She nodded.

The car swept back down the road.

Jesse's knees wobbled and her body shook. Grabbing Joe's arm, she tried to walk. "It was him, Joe. It was whoever strangled me."

He picked her up and carried her inside. In the lamp glow of the living room, his brows were drawn together, his lips taut. Gently, he settled her on the couch and brushed a lock of hair out of her eyes. He didn't have to speak his concern or his love for her. His green eyes shone with both.

"We know what car he drives. Now what?" His face was grim.

Jesse opened her hand. "We call Marty and have him trace this license number. I got some of it."

Joe took her hand and grinned. "You're amazing, babe."

He gathered her into his arms, stroking her hair.

His warmth and strength renewed her.

Finally, he stood and helped her up. "Ready for bed?"

Tugging his hand, she headed for the stairs. "C'mon, I'll help you finish packing for the builders' convention."

He pulled her back. "I'm not going."

"What?"

"I'm not going." He dropped her hand.

"But you've been looking forward to this trip to New York City all year. And you're one of the main speakers. You've got to go."

He folded his arms. "Do you really think I'd leave you after what's been happening? And now this..." he glanced at the road, "... somebody is stalking you." He shook his head. "No, babe. I'm staying right here."

She raised her arms in frustration. "You can't!"

Having Joe miss this opportunity because of her tore a hole through her heart. But she had to admit, she'd feel much safer having him here. She dropped her arms, slapping her legs in anguish.

"Please, Joe..." Her words floated out, thin and pleading.

The stubborn look in his face answered. His brows arced down. "How could you think I would leave you at a time like this?"

"There must be a way. I couldn't live with myself if you missed this opportunity."

He stared at her, the irony of her words hanging in the air between them. Then he brushed by her and headed upstairs.

She flopped on the couch, hugging one of the throw pillows. Rubbing her eyes, she tried to ease the pounding in her head. There had to be a way that Joe could leave her and know she was safe.

Her eyes flew open. She smiled at the water-tight plan she devised.

Chapter Thirty-Two

Jesse stood at her mailbox in the main office. She flipped through offers from encyclopedia companies, tossing each in the waste basket. As she scanned the weekly memo from Sister Therese, an exaggerated cough sounded from behind.

Turning, she was face to face with Sister Alphonse.

"As usual, you are blocking access to my mailbox."

If looks could kill…

"Excuse me, Sister." Jesse sidestepped her, but students were milling near the counter, so she couldn't move completely out of the way.

"Jesse, could you please reach my mail and hand it to me?" Sister Vincent called from across the counter with a wink and a smile.

Apparently, Jesse wasn't the only one who found encounters with Sister Alphonse unpleasant. She grasped her own mail with her right hand and pulled out the mail from Sister Vincent's mailbox with her left.

Sister Alphonse spotted the numbers written in marker on her hand. She grabbed it, causing Jesse to drop Sister Vincent's mail. "What have you done? Your body is a temple of the Holy Spirit and you have defiled it." She held Jesse's hand up. "Do you see what she's done?"

Jesse felt like Hester Prynne. She'd have more empathy the next time she taught *The Scarlet Letter.* She yanked her hand away, but not before Sister Vincent and Sister Therese also saw the numbers.

Two of the students squatted down and retrieved Sister Vincent's mail. One of them made a fist and tucked her hand into her uniform blazer, but not before Jesse spied a number written on her hand. Students did it all the time. She hoped they never got caught in Sister Alphonse's classroom.

"Jesse, in my office please." Sister Therese stood at her door.

She couldn't believe this. She was going to get dressed down in the principal's office like a student.

Sister Alphonse sneered at her and left.

Giggles came from the girls retrieving the fallen mail, then Sister Vincent's quiet reprimand, "Enough, girls."

Sister Vincent walked through the swinging door and put her hand on Jesse's shoulder. "Sister Alphonse's response was antagonistic, but her message was true. Your body is the temple of the Holy Spirit. Do not desecrate it. Stop by my lab. I may have a solution that might erase the ink."

"Thanks." No way would Jesse erase this ink until she got answers.

Arms crossed, Sister Therese tapped her fingers against her black sleeve, waiting.

Jesse followed the principal into her office.

Jesse flopped into the seat in front of Sister Therese's desk, ready for another lecture about the temple of the Holy Spirit.

Sister Therese sat across from her, folding her hands on the desk, her eyes downcast.

Jesse waited. And waited.

Wow, this is going to be some lecture.

Sister Therese inhaled deeply. "The voice is back."

This threw Jesse off guard. "The Holy Spirit's voice?"

Sister Therese frowned in confusion. "What?"

Jesse held out her palm. "Didn't you call me in here to lecture me about my body being the temple of—"

"Good Lord, no." She waved the idea away. "The voice saying 'rosary' is back."

Jesse sat back and closed her eyes. "She's saying her name. Sister Rose Marie."

"No. I refuse to believe that."

"Then what—"

"This is occult, Jesse. I'm going to call in a priest to exorcise the convent."

That might not bode well for Sister Alphonse.

Jesse almost chuckled but caught herself.

"So, you think Satan is on the third floor of a convent whispering 'Rosary, rosary?'" Jesse folded her arms. "I think he'd find a different message."

Sister Therese sat back in her chair, with a loud sigh. "I can't believe this. How can a ghost appear in such a holy place?"

"If humans are present, no place is completely holy. Humans are human."

Sister Therese's eyebrows drew down, her nostrils flared. "Are you insinuating that someone here is...is...invoking this ghost?"

"Not at all. Face the obvious fact. Dehumanizing the ghost isn't going to help. It's Sister Rose Marie and the sooner you come to terms with that, the sooner I can help her, and she will find peace. And so will you."

The principal, always in charge, always in control, wiped her brow in surrender. "What do you need to do?"

"First of all, you need to understand that Sister Rose Marie was murdered."

The nun stood. "No. That can't be possible. You need to stop spreading violent stories."

Jesse lowered her scarf.

Sister Therese stared in horror. "Oh my God."

"Whoever killed Sister Rose Marie also attacked me and burned all of the research I found in her study."

Sister Therese sank back into her chair. "What research? How did you find her research?"

"Confession time." Jesse made the sign of the cross. "I snuck back up into her study. I had to sneak because you have blocked me every step of the way."

Sister Therese tightened her lip. "You disobeyed me."

"'Oh, necessary sin.' Yes, I did."

"How?"

"That's irrelevant. This is the decision you need to make right now. Do you want 'the voice' to continue or are you willing to allow me what I need to help Sister Rose Marie? That, Sister, is the only way you will be free of her."

"I will pray about it."

"You do that. Hopefully, 'the voice' won't interrupt your meditation."

Sister Therese drummed her fingers on the desk. "All right. What do you need?"

"I need access to her study. And I may need to make copies of some things, ideally when no one else is in the copy room."

Sister Therese nodded. "I'll get the keys you need."

Jesse pulled her scarf back up to cover the bruises. "Thank you."

She's the one who should be thanking me.

When she opened the office door, Sister Alphonse jumped and pretended to study the bulletin board. "Oh, it's you. I hope you got a significant penance."

"I did. Twenty rosaries said on my knees on a cold, stone floor."

Sister Alphonse's eyes glittered. "So, you add lying to your list of sins."

"As do you, Sister. Eavesdropping."

JESSE GRABBED a couple of Genny Cream Ales from her ancient refrigerator that growled into a hum, protesting being disturbed. She opened the bottles with the churchkey and handed them to Marty and Maggie.

"I have a big favor to ask." She caught Joe's eye. He nodded.

"Okay." Marty tipped his bottle toward her. "Ask away."

Maggie didn't speak.

"As you know, Joe is supposed to be in New York for several days. With all that's happened…," she glanced at Maggie and didn't add "to me," "… Joe doesn't want to go."

Marty nodded. "I get it."

Jesse held out her hands like a supplicant. "But he's supposed to be a presenter at the annual builders' convention. He's been so excited."

Marty nodded again. "Ow. That's a tough one."

Joe kept his eyes on the table and shifted in his seat.

She continued, "He wants me to be safe. Who could keep me safer than you, Marty?"

Maggie's eyes grew wide.

Marty nodded with a smile. "So, you need a babysitter with a gun? I can do that."

She met Joe's gaze. He gave her the half smile that always started heat spreading through her body.

"Thanks, Marty," they said in unison.

Marty scratched his chin, squinting his eyes at Joe. "Aren't you going for, like, a week?"

Joe shook his head. "Change of plans. I leave tomorrow, give my presentation Saturday night, and will be home as soon as possible on Sunday."

Jesse's heart sank. Joe had been like a little kid at Christmas, looking at the conference brochure and picking out his sessions. Now he'd miss all those plus seeing the vendors with their latest equipment and tools.

Joe squeezed her hand as if to reassure her.

Marty's face darkened. "*Bella*, you should have reported that attack. We could have gathered evidence. And then we could follow up on the car sneaking around."

Maggie stared at her bottle.

"I have part of his license plate number." She opened the palm of her hand.

Marty read the numbers. "Eight, Five, Six." He rubbed his chin. "I'll see what I can do."

"It was a black Ford Galaxie." Joe took Jesse's hand and rubbed the numbers, as if doing so could erase the threat. The numbers didn't disappear. Neither did the threat.

"That helps a lot. Thanks." Marty took Maggie's hand. "Everything okay?"

Jesse's heart hurt at the sadness in Maggie's eyes because of her. Because she believed Father Kevin was her attacker. Jesse didn't pray very often, but right now she prayed she was wrong.

Maggie shrugged. "I'm worried about Jesse." She continued to stare at her bottle.

"Mags, I don't want it to be Father Kevin." Remorse coursed through Jesse.

Maggie glared at her. "Don't you? You've made every argument that he's the one who murdered Sister Rose Marie. And now you believe he's trying to kill you."

"Mags, he would have killed me if he'd meant to—"

Maggie slammed her fist on the table. "Maybe it wasn't him. Maybe someone else is after you for whatever reason. I can't believe you'd think this of him."

Jesse bit her lip. She wanted to yell, "Then who else would it be?" She grasped at something to say to pacify Maggie and remembered their previous conversation about this. "Maybe Bishop Harris."

That suggestion sat heavy in the silence of the room.

The radio on the counter played a Beach Boys tune softly in the background. Outside a lawn mower engine roared in the distance.

Jesse picked at the label of her bottle.

Finally, Joe cleared his throat. "I think the main thing here is to keep Jesse safe."

Marty nodded. "I'll track down this license plate number and see what I can find."

A single tear trickled down Maggie's cheek.

Jesse reached for her hand. "I'm sorry, Mags. I just don't have any answers."

"Why don't you visit him with me. You can ask him yourself."

Joe sat bolt upright. "No, I don't think that's a good idea. I really don't want Jesse anywhere near him."

Maggie stood. "Then I guess we have nothing more to talk about." She walked out.

Marty stood with a mournful look. He watched her leave, then looked at them, his eyes pleading.

"It'll be okay, Marty." Jesse didn't like to lie.

"I'll get back to you on this license plate number."

"Thanks." Her stomach flip-flopped. Now she would know who was stalking her. And almost strangled her.

Chapter Thirty-Three

Jesse drove Bert up the driveway to the convent, extinguishing her headlights as she got close. Joe had left that morning for New York. A perfect opportunity to revisit Sister Rose Marie's study.

Right before he left, Joe kissed her with the passion of a man who knows he might lose his beloved.

You're not going to lose me, Joe. The words didn't assuage the pang of guilt at returning to the convent behind his back.

Marty had called to say he'd be late. The cop pulling night shift called in sick, so Marty had to cover for him until another cop filled in. He wouldn't be at her house until eleven.

Jesse convinced him that she'd be safer at the convent until later since each night the stalker had been showing up around eight-thirty.

She checked her watch. Evening prayer would just be starting, so she could sneak in unobserved. Reaching into the back seat, she grabbed her satchel then walked to the back of the building, excitement at the prospect speeding up her heartbeat. What a relief that Sister Therese had finally relented and given her the keys she needed. The key to the kitchen door worked without a squeak.

From the chapel, soft chanting echoed down the hallway. She stopped to listen, inviting the soul-soothing melody to fill her. With that sound, she could almost become a believer. For a moment she envied the sisters' steadfast faith. But people in her past had robbed her of that belief. And somehow Bishop Harris and Father Kevin didn't strike her as being quite as devoted to God as these sisters were.

She climbed the steps to the second floor, pausing to listen for any sound. She was so accustomed to hearing Sister Alphonse snoring at this point that her precaution was automatic. But all the sisters would be in the chapel right now.

The third-floor door opened easily with its recent oiling. She closed the door behind her. Flicking on the dim light, she climbed to the third floor. The chanting drifted up, calmness tamping down her excitement. Despite losing all the research she had found, she hoped she would find something that would help her discover what had happened all those years before.

When she reached the door, she pressed her hands against it. It was cool, as was the corridor, but not icy cold. Sister Rose Marie was not here. At least not right now.

The half-moon shone brightly through the window, unhindered by clouds. But tree branches painted a spidery shadow on the wall behind the table. A skittering of tiny feet behind the wall across the room sent shivers up her spine.

Be brave, Graham. You're bigger than that little mouse.

Her pep talk didn't help, and she quickly turned on the soft light. Her hands shook as she picked up a book off the table and thumbed through it.

The air turned icy. Sister Rose Marie was here. But she didn't appear by the window as usual. Her ethereal form shimmered beside the bookshelf.

Jessie didn't want to approach her. Not only because she didn't want to scare her away, but that was where the sound of skittering paws came from. She'd hoped she could find answers from this one book on the table farthest from that wall.

So, I'm more afraid of a mouse than a ghost? That's not normal.

Sister Rose Marie held a white jar in one hand and with the other gestured to a large book lying on its side and tucked into the bookcase. When Jesse didn't move, she gestured again.

Jesse didn't move because of the flash of white fur that ran across the floor. Instead, Jesse hopped on the table and sat frozen as the mouse sniffed along the floorboard. The icy chill faded as did Sister Rose Marie's image.

She jumped off the table. "No, please don't leave. I just have this thing about mice."

But it was too late. The ghost vanished.

"Damn!"

The mouse squeezed into a hole between the floor and the wall and disappeared.

"Just like Tom and Jerry." She let out a long breath.

As she approached the bookcase, something red caught her eye. Stunned, she picked up a fresh red rose lying in front of the book Sister Rose Marie had pointed to.

The book dwarfed the others on the shelf, and she recalled a librarian once referring to this size as quarto. Jesse had found that size book useful in high school study hall for concealing the mystery she actually was reading.

She hefted the tome off the shelf and a sheaf of papers fluttered to the floor. As she gathered them, she read the title: *Gospel of Mary*.

She blinked. And blinked again.

Her hands trembled as she sank into the chair unable to believe what she was reading. She shuffled through the pages, anxious to take this home and read it in good light.

"What do you think you're doing?"

Jesse jumped from the chair, knocking it over. She clutched the manuscript to her chest.

Sister Alphonse flew into the room, veil flying, rosary beads clicking like an infestation of locusts. Her veil trembled about her face, her fists clenching in fury. "This is none of your affair!" She closed in on Jesse, leaning so close her breath brushed Jesse's hair. "Leave this alone," she growled.

Over Sister's shoulder, Jesse caught a glimpse of a pale sliver of light. As it grew, the room turned icy.

Sister Alphonse rubbed her arms, a puzzled frown on her face. She glanced at the closed window, then scanned the room. Gasping, she jumped back as the entire figure of Sister Rose Marie flickered before them.

"Oh, my God." She made the sign of the cross.

It sounded more like a curse than a prayer.

"This is why I'm here. To help Sister Rose Marie."

Sister Alphonse's eyes flashed with anger. "You work with the devil." She inched toward the door, her eyes bulging with fear. But at the threshold she stopped, reaching out a hand toward the apparition.

"Could it really be you?" Her expression softened. She crossed herself again and fled.

"Sister Alphonse saw Goody Graham with the devil." Jesse whispered. "I think I'm really in trouble now, Sister Rose Marie, but I won't give up on you."

The figure pulsed with a rosy glow.

<hr>

GLAD TO BE HOME, Jesse hugged herself to lessen her trembling. It was enough that Sister Rose Marie had shown up, always unnerving no matter how many times it happened. But then the mouse and Sister Alphonse arrived, one with its skittering feet and one with a flowing black veil. She snuggled into the afghan Susan had crocheted for them as a wedding gift.

Just as she reached for the cup of chamomile tea on the coffee table, a car engine droned down the road. She clicked off the nearby lamp and crept to the window. Drawing the curtain back, she peered into the night.

There it was. The sleek, black Ford Galaxie slowing down as it neared her house, then pulling to the side of the road. The driver extinguished the headlights.

He had never done that before. Come this close to the house. Stopped and killed the engine.

She checked her watch. It was ten thirty. Why did he come so much later than usual?

Her heart kicked against her ribcage. Joe was gone until tomorrow. Marty wouldn't be here for almost another hour.

She ran to the hallway. The deadbolt was secure on the front door. She raced to the kitchen.

Her hands shook as she tested the lock. Locked! But there wasn't a deadbolt, and probably a nailfile could unlock it.

Memories of a man's shadow passing the window of this door as she fled to the basement exploded in her mind. Then his footsteps as he followed her down the steps. The gunshot. The blood.

She grabbed a kitchen chair and braced it against the door. Peeking around the window curtain, she scanned the yard. Nothing moved.

She returned to the front window. The car was still there, but she couldn't see if the driver was still inside. She waited for what seemed like hours.

The headlights flashed on.

She ducked away from the window lest he see her. The engine purred like a stalking leopard as the car eased in front of her house, pulled into the neighbor's driveway, and coasted down the road.

Jesse collapsed on the sofa, panting. Her heart pounded and her body shook. She climbed into the afghan again and lay in the dark.

Whoever he was, he'd probably killed Sister Rose Marie. And now was after her.

Chapter Thirty-Four

Jesse jolted awake. Sitting up, she arched her back and stretched her arms to ease the ache from dozing curled up on the couch. Then a leg cramp took hold, and she stood bolt upright trying to stretch her calf muscle. After a few lurching steps it finally released.

Brushing aside the curtain, she peered out the front window. No sign of a black sedan.

She exhaled, puffing out her lips. *How could I have dozed off?*

"I need coffee."

She staggered to the kitchen, flipping on the small light on the stove. Squinting in the semi-darkness, she fumbled with the coffee pot, spilling some grounds on the counter.

"Crap." She scooped them up and brushed them into the basket.

As the coffee percolated, she stood at the sink staring out into the yard. Who was in that car? Why are they interested in her? Certainly, it must be because of her investigation into Sister Rose Marie's disappearance.

Not just disappearance. Sister Rose Marie had made it abundantly clear she had been murdered. Strangled. And someone—surely the same person—had tried to strangle her. But had they intended to murder her? She had believed not, but maybe they'd been interrupted, perhaps by a noise or a neighbor.

The image of the black car came to mind, and she shuddered. Had that same person been parked outside her home earlier tonight? Had they followed her home from the convent? Then they must have been watching and followed her to the convent, too. She rubbed her arms.

The sound of the coffee bubbling in the pot brought her back to the present. She filled her mug and again scanned her back yard. A shadow moved off to her left. She broke out in a sweat. Frantically searching the kitchen, she grabbed a broom and stationed herself behind the back door.

She watched with a mix of horror and fascination as the door-knob turned.

Where had he parked? She'd checked the street and didn't see it.

The doorknob rattled, and the door pushed inward, bumping against the chair she'd jammed against it earlier.

She raised the broom ready to swing it.

"Hey, *Bella*! Are you in there? Whatsa matter with your door?"

She stopped mid-swing and collapsed against the wall.

Shaking, she pulled the chair away.

He opened the door and glanced at her broom. "A little late to be cleaning, isn't it?"

"I almost cleaned your clock, Marty. You scared me half to death."

He furrowed his brow. "Why? I told you'd I'd be here later."

Still distraught, she sank into her chair. "Help yourself to some coffee. I'll tell you all about it."

"You're as white as a ghost...er, that is..." His face reddened as he filled his mug. "Maybe that wasn't a good comparison." He sat across from her. "Tell me what's up."

Jesse explained her visit to the convent and Sister Alphonse's appearance. "But it was worth her wrath because look what I found." She held up the copy of *Gospel of Mary*."

Marty pursed his lips to the side. "Is this some women's lib thing? I thought it was just Matthew, Mark, Luke, and John. Who's this Mary?"

"Mary Magdalene. Marty, they found this scroll in the desert. It was written before any of the gospels we know about."

Marty gave her a skeptical half-smile.

"Think about the ramifications of this. The Church doesn't give women any leadership roles and now this appears. Marty, this is why Sister Rose Marie was murdered."

He nodded slowly.

"That wasn't all that happened tonight. The black car showed up again."

Marty's face paled. He gripped his coffee cup in both hands. "While I was at the station tonight, I got a call. It took some doing with only a partial license plate number, but with some cross checking and the process of elimination I was able to run the license plate on that car."

Jesse leaned back in her chair. Did she want to hear this? Did she really want to know who was stalking her? And who had killed Sister Rose Marie? She trembled. She had to know. It was the only way to give Sister Rose Marie peace.

The clock ticked by the seconds. Crickets sang their nightly song. A dog barked in the distance. Life went on as if nothing was out of place. As if no ghost was appearing on the third floor of the convent. As if no one was threatening Jesse's life.

She took a deep breath. "Whose car is it?"

"Father Kevin Murphy."

Jesse and Marty sat in silence. Occasionally the coffee pot gurgled, reminding them there was more to savor. But neither savored anything. The taste of fear was in the air.

Finally, Marty got up and refilled their mugs. He plopped in his chair and rubbed his hands across his face. "You could get a personal protection order."

Jesse didn't move.

"You okay, *Bella?*

She met his gaze. "I always suspected him, but I so didn't want it to be true. Maggie adores him."

He leaned forward, elbows on his knees, concentrating on his clasped hands. "I know she does. He's supposed to officiate at our wedding. She asked him right after we told her parents."

Jesse felt hollow as if she was filled with sand and it had all seeped down out of her body. It had been easy to suspect Father Kevin, but the reality shocked her.

How could she file a personal protection order on the priest who was currently meeting with Marty and Maggie for their marriage preparation? The priest who'd be standing at the altar where she would stand beside Maggie while she and Marty said their vows. Can the matron of honor perform her duties from the back of the church? Probably not since at some point she'd have to hold Maggie's bouquet and manage her train.

"Have you told Maggie yet?"

He flipped his spoon over and back, over and back. "No."

She propped her elbows on the table and dropped her head into her hands.

"This is a nightmare."

"Sure is. I mean if he's the one who attacked you..."

She raised her head and flopped back in her chair. "Who else could it be? He's been stalking me for a week." She crossed her arms.

"Do you want me to have the local sheriff contact Joe and have him come home?"

While the idea was tempting, Joe had looked forward to this trip for so long. "No. I'll be fine."

"If you change your mind let me know. I'll be here tonight, all day tomorrow, and overnight."

She smiled at him. "Thank you, Marty. You are so sweet. With you here, I'll be fine."

The knot in her stomach assured her she would probably not be fine.

Chapter Thirty-Five

❧❧❧

"Hi, Honey, I'm home."

Their ritual.

Jesse ran and jumped into Joe's arms.

"Wow! I need to go away more often." Joe laughed, then kissed her.

"How was your conference? How did your presentation go? I am so glad you're home. Mainly because I missed you."

"Mainly?" Still holding her in his arms, he leaned back to face her.

Marty sauntered out from the living room with his overnight bag. "Welcome back. I'd like to say that Jesse behaved herself, but then I'd have to go to confession." He winked. "Just kidding."

Before Joe could respond, Jesse deflected him. "Marty told me that the Ford Galaxie belongs to Father Kevin."

Joe pulled her close and kissed the top of her head. "Oh no."

Marty nodded. "See you. I've got to pick up Maggie and we'll be back later for dinner. *Ciao!*" He waved on his way out the door.

"He suggested I file a personal protection order against Fr. Kevin." She stepped back and took his hand leading him to the sofa.

Joe's flushed face signaled his rage. His jaw twitched and he tightened his fist. "You won't have to. I'll go see him and tell him exactly what will happen to him if he doesn't stop stalking you."

"No, Joe. I don't think that's wise."

Joe stared at nothing; his lips drawn tight. "He can't do this to you and get away with it."

Jesse's head ached. She was torn. Maybe if Joe spoke to him this would end. But if he killed Sister Rose Marie and strangled her, what would he do to Joe?

She studied her husband. Joe had been in the Marines and served two tours in Vietnam. Though he owned his construction company, he was usually out on a job with his crew rather than behind a desk. His arms and legs were muscular, his hands strong.

Maybe she wasn't as worried about what Father Kevin would do to him as she was what he might do to Father Kevin.

"Why don't you get cleaned up and unpack. I'll make dinner and you can tell me about the conference."

His gaze met hers. "I'm not going to let this go."

She nodded. "I know."

THE SETTING SUN streamed through the kitchen window as Jesse set the table for four. How could she stop Joe from confronting Father Kevin? Now she worried more about that confrontation than about being stalked. After all, Joe was a redhead, too. The anger thermometer could rise quickly. Give him a little time to settle down. And talk to Marty. That was her plan.

The phone rang.

"Hey, *Bella*."

"Marty! I was just going to call you. What time are you two coming over? Dinner's almost ready."

"Uh, that's why I'm calling. Maggie has a bad headache."

Jesse heart clutched. "You told her about Father Kevin's car. Try to talk her into coming. We need to talk."

"Yeah, I'll tell her you hope she feels better soon."

Maggie was right there, and Marty couldn't talk.

"I need to talk to you. Joe's furious and I'm afraid he's going to do something stupid."

"Yeah, we'll get together soon. I hear ya'. Gotta go."

The line went dead.

Jesse held the receiver to her ear as if she could continue to transmit the message of her fears. Did Marty hear what she said about Joe? Did he hear how worried she is?

The strident dial tone interrupted her musings. She replaced the receiver in the cradle and headed to the kitchen.

A few minutes later, Joe entered the kitchen smelling of sandalwood, his hair recently tousled by the towel around his neck. He pulled her into a bear hug.

"I love you so much, Jesse."

She snuggled into him. "I love you, too, Joe."

They stood in the embrace for a few silent, wonderful moments.

"I need to do something about this." His breath brushed her hair.

"I worry a confrontation could get ugly. I worry about you."

He released her and ran his fingers along her cheek. "I promise I won't hurt him. Too much." He grinned, then sobered. "He can't get away with this."

"Wouldn't it be better to just get a PPO?"

Joe ran his hands through his already disheveled hair. "I don't know. Would that really keep him away?"

Jesse smoothed his messy red hair down.

"He's a priest, Joe."

His brows angled down. "So what? Is that supposed to protect him? If he's stalking you... if he killed Sister Rose Marie and almost killed you, I don't care if he's the goddamn Pope!"

"But won't you go to hell if you hit a priest?"

His eyes couldn't have gotten any wider. "What?"

Jesse thought about what she said. Her mouth quirked up.

They burst out laughing. But only for a moment. The seriousness of the danger sobered them both.

The timer on the stove dinged, and Jesse pulled the tuna casserole from the oven and set it on the table.

Joe checked the clock above the sink. "What time are the lovebirds arriving for wedding planning?"

Tears stung Jesse's eyes. "They're not coming over. Marty just called. Maggie has a bad headache."

She wiped at a tear.

Joe wrapped her in his arms. "I'm sorry, babe. He must have told her about the car."

"I'm sure, though he spoke in code. She must have been right there."

All the excitement of Marty and Maggie's happy news was overshadowed by the threat of Father Kevin. She disliked him more than ever.

And she had been right about him. She took no comfort in that.

Chapter Thirty-Six

During sixth hour, Jesse yawned in the middle of reading about the *Pequod* in *Moby Dick*. The ship's name became "Pequaaaww."

"Sorry, ladies, I didn't sleep well last night."

"Just read this book. It'll put you right out," came a soft voice from the back of the room.

Voices rose in agreement.

"Why did you change from *The Crucible* to *Moby Dick*?" another girl whined.

"*Moby Dick* is a literary classic. We talked about the different types of conflict, and this is a great example of Man vs. Nature. And we'll explore other themes like Fate and Free Will."

"So, it's our fate to read this rather than have the free will to read *The Crucible*?" the whiner asked.

Oh, she was tempted to agree. And to add the theme of silencing women just as she had been silenced by the bishop. Just like the women and girls in *The Crucible*. Just like Maggie with her father.

Just like Mary Magdalene.

Instead, she forced a laugh. "A valid point." She couldn't stop herself. "But you have the free will to choose whatever book you wish to read on your own."

A flurry of whispers bounced around the room. She felt sorry for the sister who ran the library. How many copies of *The Crucible* did she have in there?

The dismissal bell rang, and the girls hurried out the door. How Jesse wished she could be dismissed, but the Monday staff meeting called. Judging by the agenda, it was going to be a long one. Because of that, Sister Therese had invited lay staff to stay for dinner.

It was going to be a long night.

THE ONLY SAVING grace in the staff meeting was sitting next to Jam passing notes. When she passed the one about Father Kevin stalking her, Jam gasped aloud.

Sister Therese smiled at her in appreciation. "Yes, Sister John Mary, these modifications in curriculum will affect all of us. We must learn to collaborate across disciplines to implement these changes." She turned back to her outline on the blackboard.

Jam passed a note. "What changes is she talking about?"

Jesse wrote, "Pay attention, Sister John Mary."

Jam stifled a laugh, then sobered. She wrote, "We have to talk. What are you going to do about Father K?"

Jesse slipped her note over. "Let's meet in your lab after supper. Are you going to make me wash test tubes because I'm passing notes?"

"No, I'm going to make you serve me beer next time I come over."

Mercifully, the staff meeting ended.

Jam leaned in, eyes wide, as Jesse described Father Kevin's nightly drives past her house.

"You were so smart to copy down part of his license plate so Marty could trace it. But what are you going to do now?"

Jesse shrugged. "Either file a PPO or let Joe throttle him."

"I vote for the latter. How can I help?"

Jesse took a deep breath. "Sister Rose Marie has communicated with me using the scent of roses. A scent that turns increasingly into a stench. I think she's telling me where she's buried."

"Holy shit." Jam leaned in closer. "Where?"

Jesse gazed toward the window. "The grotto where Mary Magdalene's statue is. Father Kevin was chaplain at that time, so he would have had easy access to the grounds. I need to get back there and see if I can find any clue to where she might be. It would have to be an earlier planting—at least ten years old."

When she turned back to Jam, a shadow moved by the door to Sister Vincent's classroom. She put her finger to her lips. St. Bart students were expert eavesdroppers.

Jesse glanced at the wall clock. "I've got to run. Joe knew we had a staff meeting and dinner, but I don't want to be too late and worry him."

"Listen, I'll go poke around back there, you know, meditate. I'll see if I can figure out which area would have been planted first."

Jesse cocked her head. "I could ask Sister Vincent. She's tended these gardens for years. She'd know which ones were the oldest."

"Good idea."

"Yeah. She's helped me a lot with this quest for information about Sister Rose Marie. I'm sure she'd help me again."

Chapter Thirty-Seven

When Jesse opened the car door, she fumbled in her pocket for her keys. Not finding them, she rummaged through her purse.

"Crap, I left them in my classroom. Be right back, Bert." She patted the hood of her car.

Finding her keys on her desk, she quickly locked her classroom door. Sister Vincent called to her from down the hall.

"Jesse, Sister John Mary is looking for you."

"Oh, okay." She headed for toward the stairs.

"She's not in her classroom. She's with Father Murphy. Actually, he's the one looking for you." She laughed. "For some reason, she thought you might be out in the gardens."

"Why is he here? Where is Jam now?" Jesse's heart raced. Why would Father Kevin come to St. Bart's? Maybe she should be relieved. Surely, he wouldn't harm her—kill her—in front of the sisters.

Sister Vincent shrugged. "I guess he wants to see you. Sister John Mary is trying to help him find you. They headed outside."

Jesse wanted to run, but she froze in place. Cold sweat seeped into her clothes.

Move, Graham. He could hurt Jam. Why would she even go with him?

It didn't make sense. Her head buzzed, and she couldn't think. All she knew was she had to act. Now.

She broke into a run, sprinting out the back door of the kitchen.

JESSE STUMBLED ACROSS THE LAWN, the setting sun in her eyes. How could this be? Another death? And it would happen in the grotto where she'd suspected Sister Rose Marie had been murdered. The twilight shrouded her in purple light as she struggled to keep pace.

If it hadn't been for Sister Vincent, she would never know that Jam was in danger.

In the shadowy darkness, a mound of dirt appeared just beyond the grotto. That's where Sister Vincent was creating a new garden. She'd secretly told Jesse that it would be dedicated to the memory of Sister Rose Marie. Knowing that Sister Therese would not approve, she'd asked Jesse not to reveal her plan.

She sprinted through the gardens, calling Jam's name. But no answer.

As she approached the statue of Mary Magdalene, a glimmer of light appeared and gradually grew until the form of Sister Rose Marie took shape.

"Oh no. I can't stop right now, sister. I have to find Jam—Sister John Mary. Can you help me?"

The apparition nodded. Then she stretched out her hand and pointed to the mound of dirt.

"Yes, that will be a rose garden in your honor."

Her form pulsed, seeming to grow and shrink. She'd never done that before.

"I can see that you're pleased."

Sister Rose Marie shook her head and pointed again. Instead of pleased, she stabbed at the mound, agitated.

"Oh, no. You're upset. Of course. Having a small garden in your honor doesn't make up for being murdered."

"It will be small, but the compost will create magnificent flowers."

Jesse jumped at Sister Vincent's voice.

"Oh, you startled me."

The nun smiled. "Did I?"

Jesse glanced from her to Sister Rose Marie. Sister Vincent wasn't afraid of the ghost, in fact, she wasn't even surprised.

As if reading her mind, Sister Vincent pointed at Sister Rose Marie. "Why am I not surprised? Oh, I've seen Rose Marie before. Many times. I was the first she appeared to, I believe."

Sister Rose Marie seemed more agitated than before. Her hands were clasped as if in supplication.

Jesse's gaze returned to Sister Vincent. She noticed the nun carried a spade. Odd time to be working in the garden. "Why...?"

"Why do I have a spade? To destroy any vermin that invade Paradise."

Jesse frowned. What a weird thing to say.

"The Church has rules, order. Traditions lasting almost two thousand years. People who disrupt that order need to be dealt with." Her eyes shifted to Sister Rose Marie. "Placing Mary Magdalene on the same plane as St. Peter? Saying Jesus loved her more? Heresy. Do you know what the Church does to heretics?' Her eyes glinted.

Jesse thought of the Inquisition. Her pulse raced and she wrapped her arms around herself.

Sister Vincent advanced a step. "Rose Marie was so proud of her research. She shared it with me, flaunted it, actually. 'Mary Magdalene this, Mary Magdalene that.' I pretended to be interested, but the more she talked, the more I realized the threat to the Church. She had to be silenced, you see."

Jesse's mouth was dry, Despite the cold evening, her skin was clammy.

This can't be happening. Sister Vincent has been so supportive.

"I couldn't do anything about Father Kevin except ruin his reputation. When she ... disappeared, Bishop Harris didn't know what to do. I went to him for confession, you see. Because of the seal of confession, the bishop could not reveal what I'd done. A scandal would put St. Bartholomew's at risk of losing wealthy parents who are so generous to the diocese, so he planted a story about Rose Marie moving to Selma.

"He didn't approve of Father Kevin's research either, so the priest was accepted into the monastery to continue his blasphemous study of the gnostic gospels and, of course, Mary's gospel. I started a rumor that they had run off together."

Sister Rose Marie had faded into a wisp.

Jesse took a couple steps toward the convent, hoping to escape, but Sister Vincent held the spade across her body like a spear, blocking her way.

"I hadn't planned to plant another rose garden, but I must put you somewhere. Just as I did Rose Marie."

Jesse faked to the right, then jumped to the left to pass Sister Vincent, but the nun swung the spade grazing Jesse's temple.

"Geez!" Jesse tried to run, but she tripped over the rock edge of the grotto. Desperate not to fall to the ground, she twisted and windmilled her arms to catch her balance.

Sister Vincent swung the spade again, striking her across her back.

Jesse cried out in pain and collapsed onto the cool grass.

Sister Vincent raised the spade, but just as she brought it down, Jesse rolled away. The spade hit the ground with a thud.

"Ooof!" Sister Vincent raised the spade again. She brought the spade down, slamming it into the ground beside Jesse's head.

The woman grabbed Jesse's arms and yanked her to standing. She wrenched Jesse's arms around to her back.

Jesse struggled to break free, but Sister Vincent's grip was iron, her large hands a vise. Jesse's legs wobbled. She tripped, almost falling to the ground, but Sister Vincent clutched her arms to keep her upright. She dragged Jesse to the open hole in the ground where new rose bushes lined the edge like bridesmaids. Soon they would be planted to hide her body.

Jesse's mind whirled as she tried to make sense of what was happening. Her heartbeat hammered in her ears, her blood rushing hotly through her body. Except her arms. Her arms prickled with numbness.

"No sense in having to drag your corpse over here when you can still walk. So much for your meddling foolishness." Sister Vincent shoved Jesse into the gaping hole.

Jesse landed on her knees, her useless arms collapsing beneath her so that her face slammed into the dirt. She rolled over on her back, her lungs in agony as she shuddered rasping breaths.

So this is how it would end. No one would find her. And who would ever suspect Sister Vincent? Father Kevin might be arrested in connection with her disappearance since he was involved with Sister Rose Marie and somehow also with her. And that would be her fault since she had pointed a finger at him all this time.

In the darkening sky, Sister Vincent's shadow towered above her. She raised the shovel, preparing to deliver the final blow.

Jesse scooted to sitting and raised her arm to deflect the attack as best she could.

"Stop!" A voice thundered.

Jesse's jaw dropped. "Holy Jesus!"

Sister Alphonse stood with one arm raised, palm outward like a crossing guard.

"Don't do this." Her eyes burned into Sister Vincent. Her voice softened. "Don't do this again, Vincent."

"But the Church..."

"The Church will be fine. Maybe the Church needs to make some changes."

"No! Vatican II was already too much. Too much change." She faced Sister Alphonse and raised the spade.

Sister Alphonse stood taller. "God taught us 'Thou shall not kill.'" She held out her hand. "Sister Vincent, please give me the shovel."

Out of the shadows, Sister Therese and Jam appeared.

Sister Vincent gaped at them. Her gaze shifted left and right like a trapped animal.

Willing her arms to work, Jesse crawled out of the hole and eased up to a crouch.

The three sisters stood side by side. Sister Therese reached out her hand. "Give me the shovel, Vincent."

The moist, thick air deadened the night sounds. The trees and creatures around them held their breath as Sister Vincent's expression played from fear to anger to determination. She swung the spade back and forth toward the sisters. On a swing to the left, Jesse grabbed the handle and pulled with all her might.

They both toppled to the ground. Jesse wrested the tool from Sister Vincent and jumped up and away from her.

Sister Vincent cowered on the ground. "Oh my God I am heartly sorry for having offended thee…" Her words trailed off.

Sister Alphonse bent and helped her up. "Come with me. You need to rest."

The fire in Sister Vincent's eyes had faded. Now she whimpered as she cast her gaze around the garden. "What have I done? My beautiful garden, just like Eden. Only I was the serpent."

Jam helped Jesse to her feet. Taking off her jacket, she wrapped it around Jesse's trembling shoulders.

"Come, Sisters. Let's get them into the warm convent." Sister Therese gasped and halted. Glowing in the path stood Sister Rose Marie. She held an alabaster jar and a red rose. Though ethereal, her smile was peaceful.

"You might want to say goodbye to her, Sister Therese. I doubt you'll see or hear from her again." Jesse pulled the jacket closer.

Sister Therese stared at the ghost. Finally, she raised a hand in silent farewell.

Sister Rose Marie dropped the rose and rested a hand over her heart.

"I think she just said, 'Thank you.'" Jesse grinned.

Jam laughed. "Damn!"

Sister Therese held Jesse's gaze. Her eyes glistened. "Why?"

Jesse wanted to say *Because, despite your resistance every step of the way, you helped her find peace.* Instead, she simply said, "Because you helped her find peace."

Sister Rose Marie faded away. On the ground where she had stood was the red rose.

Sister Therese picked it up and smelled it. "It's real. She was real."

Jesse nodded. "Yes. And now she's at peace."

Chapter Thirty-Eight

Jesse accepted the cup of tea Sister Therese poured for her. They sat in the common room on beige chairs surrounded by beige walls. A nondescript room where, usually, sisters chatted quietly about problem students and the love of Jesus. Such a paradox to the events of the evening.

Sister Vincent sat in an adjacent chair, picking at its fabric. Her fingers in a constant pattern of pick, pick, pick. Her eyes staring vacantly. All fight had left her as she sat compliantly, not touching her tea.

Sister Therese was speaking softly to Sister Vincent as she poured a cup of tea for Sister John Mary. Sitting on the chair beside Jesse, Jam wrapped her hand around her steaming cup and blew on the hot liquid. Sister Alphonse stood off to the side, her hands resting on the back of the chair opposite Sister Vincent's. Nearby, resting against the wall, was the spade. Within Sister Alphonse's reach.

"I thought he would be pleased." Sister Vincent whispered.

"Who would be pleased, Vincent?" Sister Therese touched her shoulder, encouraging her to speak.

Sister Vincent continued to stare at nothing. "Bishop Harris. He hated the research Rose Marie wrote about. He told me how angry it made him. When I confessed how I took care of it, I thought he would be pleased. But he was silent."

Jesse shifted in her chair and pulled her sweater tighter. Her scalp prickled, and she brushed her hair back. They hadn't seen how calm Sister Vincent had been. How conversational, almost pleasant, when she'd first appeared just an hour ago. In a heartbeat, she'd become crazed, and Jesse wasn't sure it wouldn't happen again any minute.

From the corner of her eye, she spotted one of the sisters enter the room and stand beside the fireplace. Sister Therese kept speaking softly of inconsequential things: how many students planned to leave for the holidays, the final score of the volleyball game, what the weather forecast was for tomorrow.

Sister Vincent still stared straight ahead.

Two more sisters entered. One touched Sister Vincent's shoulder, the other patted her hand. Then they stood next to the door to the dining room. Another sister entered, made the sign of the cross on Sister Vincent's forehead and stood by the entrance to the foyer. Two more followed, one pressing a rosary into the nun's lifeless hand.

In twos and threes, they continued until the room was full and all the sisters were present. At an unspoken command, they began the rosary as they crossed themselves. "In the name of the Father, and of the Son, and of the Holy Ghost."

Jesse remembered Maggie at their picnic saying, "Rituals are important, Jess. I've lived a life of daily rituals."

Jesse understood. This was a sign of gentle strength. They were here to pray with and support Sister Vincent but also to make clear that together they would guard Jesse and protect each other. She closed her eyes and smiled as their voices washed over her. These beautiful women, so gentle yet so strong. Her heart warmed at their show of compassion and unity as they recited the rosary.

Rosary.

Where it all began with a visit from Sister Therese who thought she heard "Rosary," but really heard a plea for help.

The doorbell rang, and the sister nearest answered it. She returned followed by Marty and another police officer. Marty's drawn face reflected his sorrow at what he had to do.

"Sister Vincent, you need to come with us, please." His usually boisterous voice was soft.

Sister Vincent sat like a statue, still staring at nothing.

Marty knelt before her, taking her hand. "Sister Vincent. You need to come with us please," he repeated.

She met his gaze and nodded.

Sister Therese touched his shoulder. "Please don't put her in handcuffs."

He smiled at her. "I couldn't if I tried."

Sister Vincent stood, almost as tall as Marty. The sister who'd answered the door wrapped a coat across her shoulders and Marty led her out.

As soon as the door closed, the sisters picked up where they'd left off on the rosary. "Hail Mary, full of grace..."

Sister Alphonse tapped Jesse's shoulder and nodded toward the dining room.

They sat at the far end of the table, Sister Alphonse at the head, Jesse to her right.

"Sister Rose Marie and I were best friends." She traced the wood grain on the oak table with her index finger. "When she left for Selma without saying goodbye, I was really hurt. I received a couple letters from her, typed with her name signed, but they weren't in her voice, do you know what I mean? When I answered them, she never responded. I thought she might be miserable down there."

She clasped her hands on the table.

"I went to Sister Monica, my Mother Superior at the time. She was elderly then and died several years ago. When I told her of my suspicions, she told me to leave it alone and to not share those thoughts with anyone else." She spread her hands out. "I'd taken a vow of obedience, so I complied.

"After Sister Monica died, I was instructed to pack up and send her personal items to her family. I found a letter from Bishop Harris instructing Sister Monica to support the Selma story about Rose Marie. I was too scared to confide in anyone else. If the bishop was involved in this cover-up, I could get in a lot of trouble."

She clasped her hands, her knuckles white. "I changed after my suspicions were confirmed by that letter. I could only imagine what had happened to Rose Marie. I didn't know who to trust, and whatever had happened to Rose Marie could also happen to me. I finally confided in my brother." She shot Jesse a quick glance. "After all, he was the sheriff. But he alluded to the fact that the bishop had him, as he put it, 'by the short hairs." A blush rose in her cheeks. "Looking back, I think maybe the bishop was aware of his...involvement in Helen Cavanaugh's death."

Jesse gasped.

She held Jesse's gaze. "That's why I've been telling you to leave it alone. I didn't want anything bad to happen to you."

Jesse's eyes widened. "You were protecting me?"

She chuckled. "As best I could. You're a hard lady to protect. Stubborn redhead."

Jesse laughed. "Joe would agree."

Sister Alphonse covered Jesse's hand with hers. "I know our relationship has been rocky."

"That's putting it mildly."

"As I said, Rose Marie was my best friend. When that happened, I closed up. I was scared. Being cantankerous kept people at a distance which meant I couldn't be hurt again. And I didn't know who to trust. Even my brother..." She pulled her lips in tight.

The memory of Sister Alphonse's brother trapping her in the basement of the Cavanaugh House to kill her raised goosebumps on Jesse's arms.

"I'm sorry." Sister Alphonse's eyes glistened. "I'm sorry for all of it."

Jesse squeezed her hand. "Thank you for telling me. I'm so

sorry you lost your best friend." Jesse's throat tightened at the thought of losing Maggie to such a terrible fate. It was bad enough that they were barely speaking right now.

Sister Alphonse gazed in the direction of the grotto. "She was here all along."

Jam entered followed by Joe.

He rushed to Jesse's side and held her in his arms.

The two sisters left them.

"I'm okay, Joe."

He inhaled a ragged sigh and held her closer.

"I love you, Just Jesse." His voice was muffled against her neck.

"I love you, too."

He leaned back and studied her, his eyes misty.

"Sister Rose Marie is gone?"

"Yes, she is at peace. And now so am I."

Chapter Thirty-Nine

Jesse removed the corned beef from the pot and added cabbage wedges to the potatoes, onions, and carrots that continued to simmer. As she covered the brisket with aluminum foil, the doorbell rang.

She glanced at the clock. Susan, Jim, and Marty weren't due for another half hour.

Wiping her hands on a dish towel, she hurried to the front door.

Her heart leapt when she opened it.

"Mags!"

"Hey, Jessie." Maggie cuddled a steaming apple pie in the crook of her arm.

"You're here. You're...I'm so glad you're here." She could hardly speak with the lump in her throat. She wanted to throw her arms around her best friend, but wasn't sure Maggie was ready for that. Plus, the pie.

"Are you going to let me in?"

"Yes! Oh, yes, of course." Jesse held the front door wide open.

Maggie headed to the kitchen and placed the pie on the counter.

"I'm inviting myself to dinner."

"Maggie, you're always welcome. I would have invited you but —hell, you don't need an invitation. Of course you're invited…" Jesse's words tumbled out in a rush of fear, joy, and uncertainty. Though the pie gave her hope.

When she stopped, an uncomfortable silence fell between them.

Tears ran down Jesse's face. "Maggie, I am so sorry. I was so wrong to blame Father Kevin."

Maggie's eyes glistened and she blinked back tears.

Jesse sighed. "You were absolutely right, and I was absolutely wrong."

"That's what I wanted to hear." Maggie smirked and opened her arms.

"You goof, Keegan." Jesse laughed and hugged her tight.

"That's what I really wanted to hear." Maggie's voice caught as she spoke.

"Oh, Mags, I've missed you."

"Even though I was really mad at you, I missed you, too."

"We could talk about wedding plans before the others arrive."

"I can't right now, but let's get together this weekend. We could do a campfire at my cottage. Right now, I have an errand to run. I'll be back in a little while."

Jesse didn't want her to leave, afraid she was imagining this. She held Maggie's hand.

"Seriously, Jess. I'll be back before you know it." She gave Jesse a reassuring hug.

Jesse watched her leave, then spotted the pie on the counter.

Yes, Mags was really here.

JESSE TOOK JOE'S HAND. She paused for a moment to enjoy the warmth that always filled her when her family was around her table.

Family means the people you love, and that doesn't always mean blood relation.

She smiled.

"Jesse, that's quite a story." Jim brushed his hand over his face in relief.

Maggie nodded. "I always liked Sister Vincent. I never suspected a dark side to her."

"People who do terrible things usually have a cause that they find worthy." Jim spread his hands out. "Every villain is the hero of his own story."

"Or hers." Jesse added and took a sip of her Genny Cream Ale.

"Correct." Even when relaxing, the literature professor came out.

"How did Sister Alphonse know to come and help you?" Susan leaned forward.

"Sister Rose Marie led her to us. First, she appeared in Sister Alphonse's room, then out on the lawn, and kept appearing like cookie crumbs in Hansel and Gretel. Except she didn't get eaten by birds."

"*Aye yi yi*! I hope not!!" Marty's eyes bulged.

They all laughed. Maggie patted his hand.

"Jesse meant like in the story of Hansel and Gretel. Hansel drops breadcrumbs to find their way home, but the birds eat them."

"Oh." He leaned back and took a deep draught of his beer.

Joe put his arm around Jesse's shoulders. "Jesse made it home just fine." He winked at her.

Jesse continued. "Jam saw me run out the kitchen door and then Sister Vincent follow. She had a bad feeling about me going out there at night again, so she went to Sister Therese. They spotted Sister Alphonse leaving and followed her."

"What's going to happen to Sister Vincent?" Susan asked.

Marty sat forward, resting his hands on the table. "She's been arrested, but we haven't found a body yet, so no proof of a murder. She's being interrogated and held in the jail. Up to now, she's been cooperative, but sometimes criminals can go just so far and then they clam up."

"I hate to hear her called a criminal." Maggie pursed her lips to the side.

Jesse rubbed her forehead. "What I learned through this whole experience is how the Church patriarchy have silenced women. Especially strong women like Mary Magdalene."

"When I teach my class, "The Bible as Literature," we discuss why so few women are represented in the stories." Jim opened his hands as if giving a lecture. "Most scribes were men, but perhaps not all. Men told the stories, and men selected which stories would be in the canon of the Bible."

"But if Jesus treated women as equals, why don't Christians follow his lead?" Jesse sat back and crossed her arms.

Jim chuckled. "Oh, if only we followed his lead, or the Buddha's or any of the great spiritual leaders. In so many ways, this would be a better world."

"So, according to the Bible, women were silenced from the start." She sat up and clasped her hands on the table.

"Actually, no. Women like Phoebe and Prisca were leaders in the early Christian community," Jim said.

"So, what happened?"

Susan shrugged. "Men happened. And women were silenced."

No one argued with her.

"Bishop Harris was not happy about Sister Rose Marie's research, but it was Sister Vincent who ultimately silenced her." Jesse stared at her hands, energy seeping from her. "When a woman silences a woman it's somehow even worse. But, of course, Sister Vincent murdered her because of her twisted belief in the teachings of a patriarchal church."

Joe took her hand. "But they couldn't silence you, though they tried hard."

She smiled.

"And you are a strong woman, Jess. Stubborn, too." Maggie winked at her.

A chorus of agreement rang as they clinked their bottles together.

Marty grabbed another beer holding it up in question. Jim and Joe raised their hands for seconds.

Marty popped off the caps with the churchkey. "If they find a body, she'll be tried for murder. Based on Jesse's statement, we're searching in the grotto area. At this point it will be attempted murder if Jesse presses charges."

They pondered this for a moment until the doorbell rang.

Maggie jumped up. "I'll get it."

Jesse furrowed her brow. "Okay. Thanks, Mags. Probably a Fuller Brush salesman."

Maggie's voice floated to them. "Come in. No, I'm sure it's fine. Follow me."

Maggie returned followed by Father Kevin Murphy.

Jesse's cheeks warmed. She'd made no secret of her mistrust of him. How wrong she'd been.

A chorus of greetings met him.

"Hello, Father Kevin."

"Hi, Father."

Marty stood up and nodded like he was a royal

Jesse didn't know what to say. *Hey, sorry I accused you of murder and didn't like you from the start* seemed so inadequate.

Joe got another chair from the desk in the living room.

Father Kevin waved him off. "No need. I don't want to interrupt."

"Please, join us." Joe indicated the chair. "How about a beer?"

"No thanks. I came to apologize for causing you so much distress, Jesse. Maggie told me of your fear of me." He looked around the table, a sheepish grin on his face. "I was actually trying to protect you."

"What? Protect me from what? Did you know about Sister Vincent?"

"No, I had no idea. I suspected something unusual had happened to Rose Marie, but the bishop confirmed she was in

Selma and was very busy. I pestered him quite often, so I think he was quite relieved when I requested a sabbatical at the monastery."

He glanced at Joe. "I owe you an apology, too."

Joe spread out his hands. "What for?"

Father Kevin took a deep breath. "When I saw the bruises on Jesse's neck, I thought...well, in my business you see a lot of ugly things."

Joe's eyes bugged out. "You thought I did that to her?"

"I wasn't sure, but I wanted to...check things out. That's why I drove by your house every night. I was doing a mission at Our Lady of Peace Church, so when I drove home, I'd swing by your place. I thought...I don't know...if Jesse were in trouble, I might see it. Sense it. One night when your truck wasn't in the driveway," he nodded to Joe, "I parked and wrestled with the idea of coming to talk to Jesse while you were out of the picture."

Marty chuckled. "She would have whacked you with a broom handle."

Jesse winced, grateful that never happened. "That was the night you came by later than usual. Why?"

He turned to Jesse. "It was the last night of the mission, so they had a reception in the parish hall. I'm so sorry to have caused you so much anxiety."

Jesse stared at the label on her bottle that she'd almost peeled off as he spoke. She cleared her voice. "Well, I owe you an apology, too." She met his gaze. "All this time I thought you were the one who, you know, murdered Sister Rose Marie. Maggie insisted that you would never do something like that, but I was convinced..." Her voice trailed off. "I'm sorry."

Father Kevin laughed. "I'll take that beer now."

Marty jumped up before Joe could leave his chair. He grabbed a bottle, popped off the cap and, with one hand on his heart, handed it to Father Kevin like an altar boy handing the priest the cruet of water at Eucharist.

Jesse laughed, then she sobered. "Marty said if they find Sister Rose Marie's body, Sister Vincent will be charged with murder.

She'll get attempted murder for sure if I press charges. I don't want to do that."

"I'm scheduled to visit with her tomorrow. I'll let you know how she's doing. But, Jesse, you must do what is right for you."

Jesse chewed on her lower lip. "What good would it do? She'll be sent to a psychiatric hospital anyway."

Maggie took her hand and smiled.

The telephone rang, and Joe rose to get it. He returned immediately, eyebrows raised.

"It's Sister Therese."

"What trouble am I in now?"

She put the phone to her ear. "Good evening, Sister Therese..."

When she returned to the table she grinned from ear to ear.

"What did she want?" Maggie asked.

"She called to check on me and see if I'm okay. That was sweet. What was even sweeter is that she put *The Crucible* back in my curriculum."

They all laughed.

"You can't silence strong women." Joe raised his glass in a toast.

They all clinked glasses together.

Jesse's heart was full. Sister Rose Marie found peace. Father Kevin wasn't a stalker, and he would continue to research and publish the truth about Mary Magdalene.

And she was finished with ghosts.

Maybe.

Dear Reader,

Thanks for sharing my characters' journey. Curious about the true ghost story that inspired this series? Click here to download the story of "The Ghost of Isabella." This will allow you to sign up for my newsletter so we can keep in touch!

When you sign up for my newsletter, you'll be the first to know about new books, freebies, and giveaways available only on my newsletter. Be privy to deleted scenes and upcoming ideas from my books so you can step into the world of my characters and know them better than any other readers. You may even help me name characters or decide on a plot direction—see your ideas in print!

Want to leave a review? That would be great! Click here or visit my Amazon Author page. Thank you.

Love,
Elizabeth

Visit Elizabeth at:
Amazon Author Page
Website:
www.elizabethmeyette.com.
Facebook:
https://www.facebook.com/elizabethfmeyette/
Instagram:
https://www.instagram.com/efmeyette/
Threads:
https://www.threads.net/@efmeyette

About Mary Magdalene

In this book, I hope you learned the truth about Mary Magdalene. My heart burned to reveal the truth of her story. During Covid quarantine, I "fell in love" with her. I read every book I could find and even took a six-week course with Episcopalian priest Cynthia Bourgeault about Mary Magdalene.

I hope you've enjoyed reading *The Silenced Ones*. A hearty and heartfelt thank you if you choose to leave a review. Please check out my other books and audiobooks on Amazon, Audible, and iTunes.

Acknowledgments

No book is created in a vacuum—it takes a village. My family, friends, and colleagues are the village that gives me support and encouragement and enables me to stay the course in my story. As always, my beloved husband, Rich, has been my main supporter. Thank you, Rich, for your patient listening and sage advice dispensed during our "staff meetings." You always help me clarify plot issues and deal with persnickety characters.

My daughter, Kate Bode, continues to be my biggest cheerleader. Thank you, Kate, for your enthusiasm even when you're wrangling two-year-old twins.

Handing off my book to my first readers is always scary, but I trust my beta readers, H.J. Smith, Luana Russell, and Sarah Yoder. They've walked this journey with me from the beginning. My book is so much better after their insightful feedback—feedback that only great English teachers can give. Thank you, my dear friends Sarah, Luana, and H.J. for your continued willingness to read my stories and guide me to make them the best they can be.

I am fortunate to be surrounded both locally and online by amazing authors who share the blood, sweat, and tears of our crazy profession. To my Grand Rapids Region Writers Group friends and my Michigan Romance Writer chapter mates, I thank you. A special shout-out to my Friday write-in group, Leesa Mason, Patricia Kiyono, and Anne Stone, who traveled the journey of this book with me.

Thanks to Shonda Fischer for suggesting the name Agnes Stern for a character in my book. It was perfect! Thanks to all my newsletter readers who sent in suggestions. So many good names to choose from!

Along the way, I met an extraordinary woman who became a research source and fact-checking guru. Joann Hinz is a former Sister of St. Joseph. Our paths almost crossed when I was a senior at Nazareth Academy in Rochester, NY, but she was assigned to teach there the year after I graduated. Though we never met, in our correspondence we found that she knew all my teachers, including the sister who was my inspiration for Maggie. Joann answered many questions I had about life in the convent which made Jesse's experience more credible.

As always, special thanks to my muse, Boris. Readers ask where I get my ideas from or how I come up with a plot. I am not kidding when I say this: Boris tells me. There are times when I read what I had written the previous day and scratch my head asking, "Did I write that?"

Finally, to all you readers who trust me enough to enter the story that my characters and my muse, Boris, have whispered to me, I thank you.